Aye Do
or Die

A Darcy Cavanaugh Mystery

Aye Do or Die

Candy Calvert

MIDNIGHT INK
WOODBURY, MINNESOTA

FIRST EDITION
First Printing, 2007

Book design by Donna Burch
Cover design by Kevin R. Brown
Cover illustration © 2006 by Kun-Sung Chung / www.kschung.com

Midnight Ink, an imprint of Llewellyn Publications

Library of Congress Cataloging-in-Publication Data
Calvert, Candy, 1950–
    Aye do or die / Candy Calvert.—1st ed.
        p. cm.—(A Darcy Cavanaugh mystery ; 2)
    ISBN-13: 978-0-7387-0904-8
    ISBN-10: 0-7387-0904-2
        1. Cruise ships—Fiction. 2. Nurses—Fiction. 3. Weddings—Fiction. I. Title.

PS3603.A4463A93 2007
813'.6—dc22

                                                    2006051542

Midnight Ink
Llewellyn Publications
2143 Wooddale Drive, Dept. 0-7387-0904-2
Woodbury, MN 55125-2989, U.S.A.
www.midnightinkbooks.com

Printed in the United States of America

ACKNOWLEDGMENTS

My heartfelt thanks to:

Agent Natasha Kern, acquiring editor Barbara Moore, my talented in-house editor Karl Anderson, and the entire team at Midnight Ink. The dynamic duo of cover designer Kevin Brown and illustrator Kun-Sung Chung, whose vision and talent give Darcy Cavanaugh the panache she deserves—and great sparkly shoes!

A special thank-you to: Gifted writer and critique partner Nancy Herriman, who, despite her own deadlines, is always there with a word, an idea, applause, or a well-timed kick in the keister. Independent editor Carol Craig, of The Editing Gallery, for her invaluable advice on how to keep my characters quirky, yet give them heart—and for teaching me, finally, to tackle "theme" without popping antacids.

My grown-up "kids," Bret, Brooklynn, and Wendy, whose encouragement means everything. And, always, a big thank-you to my husband, Andy, for his love and support—and for so many golfing days spent driving me to book signings, toting huge posters, drinking Starbucks, and taste-testing my shortbread anchor cookies.

This book, part mystery and part romance, is dedicated to the memory of two special and supportive people: Randolph Dewante, a wise and loving father with a taste for mysteries, brainteasers, peanut brittle, Scottish shortbread . . . and the occasional fine cigar. And for Dorothy Calvert, a strong woman and devoted mother who loved romance novels, red convertibles, world travel, mini-schnauzers . . . and a good belly laugh, always.

ONE

"So, is there a time limit on boob scratching before I go certifiably nuts?" I asked as I glared into the cabin mirror and daubed calamine lotion around a dozen spot-size Band-Aids above my cleavage.

"You're . . . umm . . . way beyond it, babe."

Marie Whitley's reflection slid into view from behind me, dark brows raised as she mumbled around the slim cheroot pinched between her teeth. "Light years maybe."

"Great." I moaned and inspected the Band-Aids; not the trendiest accessories for cruise wear but maybe—*oh jeez.* A long strand of my coppery hair stuck to the calamine and I picked at it while fighting yet another tidal wave of itching. A rash from "nervous anxiety"? No way. Did that dermatologist forget that I was a trauma nurse? Darcy Cavanaugh, Emergencies "R" Us, that's me. And, bet your sweet ass, we ER nurses wear our nerve like boxing gloves. So it's not like a little . . . *life stress* would give me blotches.

I peered at my pathetic reflection and sighed. Maybe I did have a few things weighing on my mind, but it wasn't anything I couldn't handle. This five-day wedding cruise would give me the time I needed to—I raised my brows at my best friend's deepening smirk. "Well?" I whirled to face her. "C'mon, tell me the truth here. What are you laughing at, the Band-Aids or this pink gunk?"

Marie took a quick drag on her cheroot and exhaled, flicking a spray of ashes from the front of her polka-dot bridesmaid's gown. "Neither. Sorry." Her gray eyes squinted under a curly fringe of bangs while cherry smoke wafted into the air, mingling with the scent of my calamine. "It's these dresses. 'Vintage'? Would you just look at us?"

She wrestled with her matching dotted belt as the ship's whistle began a series of blasts. "You realize that in a couple of hours we're sailing under the Golden Gate Bridge and right into a freaking re-run of *I Love Lucy*?" Marie rolled her eyes. "I'm forty, not vintage. And these dots do scary things to my hips. I feel like Ethel Mertz."

I looked back at our dual reflections and shook my head. Navy polka-dot dresses, shoulder pads, white cuffs, scarlet lipstick, and polish. I glanced at my reddish curls top-knotted with a silk scarf high above my itchy skin and then opened my green eyes wide. Marie had nailed it. We were the wacky duo for a new millennium: Itchy Lucy and Gay Ethel. And we were traveling with a group of practical jokers that made even those endless reruns look tame. Horny firemen and traveling nurses. Not a good combo, trust me.

I glanced toward the cabin window as a roar of laughter preceded the hollow thunder of Conga drums. We'd barely survived squirting cameras and blue-dye chewing gum; could whoopee cushions be far behind? Lord help us. The sail-away party had begun.

"How the hell did I get shanghaied into this clown gig?" Marie grumbled.

"For Patti Ann, of course," I said, tossing lotion-soaked cotton balls toward a wastebasket. One pink blob missed and stuck to a banana in the complimentary fruit basket. "We're her 'dearest and closest gal friends.'"

Marie stared at me. "We've known her for exactly nine months, Darc." She picked the cotton off the banana and wrinkled her nose. "Nine months does not a bridesmaid make. Not with polka dots. You're way too easy."

I shrugged and felt the Band-Aids strain. "Okay, maybe her closest friends geographically."

It was true. Patti Ann Devereaux, cruise ship bride, was from Mobile, Alabama, and had been a traveling nurse in our Morgan Valley Hospital for nine months now. Three tours. Tours? *Like combat?* Maybe so. Working with someone in the trenches of a trauma ward with short staffing, rerouted ambulances, mandatory overtime, and the occasional crackhead armed with a knife did make for wartime camaraderie among nurses brave—or foolish—enough to stay enlisted. Like Marie, and like me, too. Eight years. Couldn't believe I was still there. No, not true. What I still couldn't believe was that I'd almost left it last year to sell orthotics for a podiatrist. Burnout can do that, but the job definitely made for some interesting moments. Like zipping you into a polka-dot, high-seas nightmare.

"And besides," I said, smiling slowly, "she found that great wedding planner with a last-second discount on this cruise . . . San Francisco, Seattle, and Vancouver Island—great places for a few hundred bucks. And you don't even have to work onboard this time. Pure relaxation. Can't complain about that."

"Watch me," Marie said, holding the full skirt out. "At least Carol's not here to witness this humiliation. If she weren't at that Book Expo, she'd have talked me out of cruising with you again." Marie narrowed her eyes. "She still has those issues about my getting too close to cross-dressers and kinky lingerie sculpture and dead bodies. Not to mention the torching of my favorite pair of spotted cow socks."

I crossed my arms. "It was one sock, and the FBI replaced it for you. Six months ago." *FBI.* My stomach did its roller-coaster plunge and I bit my lower lip to fight a sudden fireball of itching. FBI. *Luke.*

Marie nodded. "Only because you were about to hop in the sack with a federal agent." She raised her brows. "Which reminds me, are you still denying that this itch—pardon the word—to sail away into the sunset has nothing to do with running away from Luke Skyler?" She pursed her lips and gave a smug nod as I raised a fingertip to rub at a Band-Aid. "Right. And I'm also supposed to believe you forgot all about that little velvet jewelry box you found hidden under his stack of boxer shorts." She sighed. "So, are you going to tell me what happened with him last ni—"

A knock on the cabin door made us turn, and a chubby brunette bounced inside. Patti Ann Devereaux wore a dotted illusion veil and a tee shirt stretched taut across ample breasts, its hot-pink glitter letters proudly pronouncing, "I AM THE BRIDE."

"Oh my Ga-awd," she gushed, dark lashes fluttering. "Don't y'all look just wooonderful?" She stretched her arms wide and launched herself toward Marie.

I smothered a laugh as Marie squirmed in the bride's arms. But mostly I studied Patti Ann. It had become like some weird hobby for me since she'd begun her wedding plans a few weeks ago. I'd been pretty close to obsessed with it since I'd accidentally found the jewelry box in Luke's dresser. I just didn't understand. How could someone only twenty-two years old be so certain that marriage was the right thing to do? For godsake, I was thirty and it had taken me weeks to commit to keeping my grandma's goldfish. This whole confusing mess had me close to tearing open boxes of macaroni and cheese. You know, that stuff you mix with milk and half a cube of hydrogenated oil and eat right out of the pan ... this was a bad sign.

Patti Ann released Marie and raised her palms like the just-healed in a revival tent. "Oh Lord. Marie Claire, this is sooo beyond perfect. You look exactly like one of our old photos." Her voice choked up and I bit my lip as Marie backed her polka dots into the fruit basket. "In Grandma's wedding picture? You are just the spittin' image of Great Aunt Ethel."

* * *

On deck, I smoothed my coral tee over my striped capris and watched Marie jab a paper umbrella into her drink like some psychotic Mary Poppins. If I called her Ethel again she was going to haul off and slug me. It had been hard enough to get her to agree to be a bridesmaid. Not that I blamed her since, frankly, hopping onboard a "Booze Cruise" with an uprooted Southern belle, her paramedic fiancé, and his half dozen firefighter cohorts wasn't my first choice of a getaway, either. But it was a getaway. And I needed to. *Luke bought an engagement ring?* And there was still that creepy problem with FedEx.

5

I slid my arms along the teak deck rail and nudged an elbow into Marie's L. L. Bean flannel. Beyond us, the San Francisco skyline rose from a scattering of low-lying clouds and stretched upward toward the late afternoon sun, purple, silver, coral pink . . . and heart-rending familiar. I could tell you the exact mileage from my place to Luke's apartment near the Marina. And all the shortcuts I took when lust smothered my fear of speeding tickets. "At least Patti Ann's satisfied now, so we don't have to climb back into polka-dot hell until we walk down that aisle in Victoria Gardens."

I nodded toward Coit Tower, the Transamerica building, and the Bay Bridge in the distance. "And meanwhile, we've got the City by the Bay and—"

Marie poked me with the umbrella stick. "Quit stalling and just tell me. What did you say to Luke last night?"

I took a deep breath of salty air and let my gaze drift away from the hubbub of the Embarcadero Pier and back out across the bay. A fishing boat, its deck stacked high with crab pots, chugged on toward Fisherman's Wharf with a flock of greedy gulls squawking overhead. Farther out, sailboats leaned into the breeze, and I wondered if one of them was Luke's. The *Shamrock Tattoo*. I groaned. It shouldn't have surprised me that a guy who'd name a boat after my left breast was getting way too serious.

"Well?" Marie reached for another drink from a passing deck steward and sailed her paper umbrella overboard. "Did you tell him you'd move back East with him, or did you break the big fed's heart?"

The itching on my chest was giving way to a strange achy feeling and I didn't know which was worse. I stopped watching the sailboat and turned back to Marie.

"The Boston assignment starts in two weeks and I told Luke that I don't see how I can go with him." I glanced down, avoiding Marie's eyes, and cleared my throat. "I mean it's not like I can just pick up and traipse across the country, you know. My grandma's in that legal mess, and how would the ER replace me on such short notice and . . ."

The ship's horn blasted, drowning my pathetic and well-rehearsed litany. The horn repeated three more times and then a deafening chorus of taunting laughter and hoots replaced it decibel for decibel. I turned and shook my head. "Great. Looks like our groomsmen are in fine form."

"Yup." Marie rolled her eyes. "And here comes the reason."

Sure enough, the firefighters' heated response had announced the entrance of Patti Ann's twenty-three-year-old wedding planner, Kirsty Pelham. The tall, leggy blonde in black-framed glasses and crisp green Ann Taylor linen marched along the deck, taking the whole thing in stride just the way she did everything else. Cool as a celery stalk in ice water. Could anyone really be that calm and organized? It was a good guess that "itch" wasn't even in her vocabulary. You could bet that a little thing like a black velvet jewelry box wouldn't send her off the deep end. Maybe studying the bride was the wrong thing to do. I needed to be more like this woman.

"So do you think Dale Worley will make it under that limbo bar while he's ogling our wedding planner?" I asked, nodding toward the groomsmen gathered around the pair of stewards holding a bamboo pole. A forty-something man, with a handlebar mustache, silk shirt, and way-too-tight leather pants, leaned precariously backward. He aimed a toothy grin toward Kirsty.

Marie grimaced. "I think his pelvis is in serious jeopardy—*eew!*" She shielded her eyes as the man managed to spread his legs wider and began bobbing his butt like a bumblebee. "Who the hell is that guy?"

I frowned. "'Worley's Wheels.' You know, that car dealer who has the commercials with the talking animals."

"No way—the llama wearing lip gloss and a bustier?"

"That one. Anyway, Dale's also a volunteer firefighter and pretty damned proud of it. Not that he ever gets near any flames. But he does love to ride the truck and handle the horn."

"Yes." Marie shuddered as we watched Worley stand upright and smooth the front of his leather pants. "I can see that he does. Let's go get something to eat before I'm tempted to push him over the rail."

We maneuvered through the partygoers to the opposite side of the deck, and Marie munched a shrimp-on-sourdough canapé while pointing toward Alcatraz Island and the Golden Gate beyond. The sky was turning a rosy gold as the sun sank toward the sea. My gaze lingered over Sausalito and Tiburon in the distance. I'd just caught a glimpse of a sailboat tacking toward the pier with a blond-ish man at the tiller, when the band suddenly stopped playing and people began to scream. And then a shout erupted behind us.

"Man overboard!"

The ship's horn began an ominous series of blasts.

"What the hell?" Marie stepped forward into the swarm of passengers surging toward the opposite rail, and I followed. It was impossible to see what was causing the commotion. I leaned my head around a deck steward and saw that a line of uniformed crewmen had formed a human barricade, arms extended to keep the crowd back, while a trio of others grasped at a man's hands clinging to the far side of the teak rail. The crowd parted enough so that I could see Patti Ann and her groom, "Cowboy" Kyle, watching in horror.

I inched forward, squeezing between people until I was beside Patti Ann, just as the crewman hauled the victim onto the deck. The crowd gasped in relief and a crescendo of applause began. Dale Worley. Why wasn't I surprised?

"Oh my Lord," the bride whispered, covering her face with her hands. "I knew he was going to fall, the fool. Drinking all that rum and then trying to climb up on the rail like a scene in the Titanic movie." Patti shook her head, short curls bobbing. "King of the World, my Alabama ass! And just look what a jerk he's making of himself now."

I strained to see as the crew attempted to disperse the crowd. I stood on tiptoe, swayed, and then almost bumped into Kirsty Pelham who was entering notes into her ever-present Palm Pilot. Her voice was cool as the glass on a mai tai.

"One hundred and six feet," she murmured, nodding her head with authority. Her pale hair skimmed her shoulders, then swung back into place with military precision.

"What do you mean?" I asked.

"The distance from that rail to the cement pier below," she said like she was figuring the cost of little ribbon-tied sacks of Jordan Almonds. She sighed and pressed the stylus pen to the buttons for another note. "That . . . um . . . ," Kirsty glanced down at her PDA, "that Mr. Worley is going to be a challenge. There's no room for practical jokers in a wedding party." She sighed and tapped her heavy-framed glasses. "Still, he's here as a guest of the groom; what can I do? Make adjustments that's all." Kirsty flashed me a warm smile. "I'm glad I can count on my bridesmaids to behave themselves."

Behave? Oh jeez. I smiled back like an idiot, fighting a stupid memory of plaid skirts and nuns and my dubious distinction of being the only six-year-old ever suspended from Holy Spirit School. But, in my defense, the kid I'd fought with had mooned me and dissed my grandma. I'd kick his butt again.

Marie arrived at my side just as a British voice spoke calmly over the PA system and the band began to play once more.

"This is Captain McNaughton with a reminder that we are to set sail for Seattle at nineteen-hundred, in exactly thirty-five minutes. It is our pleasure to now serve complimentary drinks on the Lido Deck, aft."

"Not to Dale Worley, I hope." Marie smiled. "You know, they really should have just shouted, 'Everyone duck, jackass coming down!'"

I nodded and then peered over the rail at the dizzying distance below; the sheer whitewashed side of the ship and the narrow ribbon of murky seawater alongside the tar-covered cement pier. What would it have been, drowning or bone-shattering death on impact? I shivered. *God.* I'd been a trauma nurse too long.

"Still," I said, feeling goose bumps lift along my forearms, "jerk or not, he could have been killed. Not the best way to start a cruise."

* * *

We'd followed the crowd to the Lido Deck when the PA crackled overhead once more. "Will Passenger Cavanaugh contact the Purser's Office? Darcy Cavanaugh, please."

"What the hell?" It took me a few minutes to locate the courtesy phone; just inside the deck door and alongside yet another huge, surreal color photograph of bare feet. What was with all of those feet, anyway? While the call was being forwarded from the Purser's Office, Marie handed me the complimentary sail-away drink, a Golden Gate Piña Colada. She was obviously hell-bent on getting me wasted, but it did seem to help the itching. Plus, I'd finally stopped thinking that every sailboat in San Francisco Bay was manned by a federal agent coming to propose. I hugged the receiver against my shoulder. What was this about? A mix-up in the preboarding paperwork?

The drink was frosty cool and coconut sweet, and I bit into the pineapple wedge, letting the juice dribble down my chin—a pretty clear indication of my blood alcohol level—as I waited for the call to connect. I licked my lips and then raised my eyebrows at Marie, pointing my glass toward the huge photograph on the wall behind us. "What's with all these stupid bare feet—" A voice came on the line before I could finish.

"Miss Cavanaugh? Cabin eighteen eighty-two?" The Purser questioned.

"That's me."

I dropped the pineapple back into my glass and glanced at Marie again. She was looking as curious as I felt. What the hell was this? The British voice sounded hesitant, then apologetic, and all of a sudden its tone made my skin start to itch.

"I hope there's no problem, Miss Cavanaugh. But I must advise you that there is a federal agent waiting in your cabin."

TWO

I OPENED THE CABIN door a crack and my breath caught, my face warming. Luke was gazing toward the window, holding a single red rose. He'd obviously flashed his badge in order to board the ship so close to departure. And was cocky enough to think that, because he wasn't too much of a tough guy to carry a rose and because half the women—and a hefty percentage of the men—in San Francisco thought that he could double for Matthew McConaughey, I'd fall right into his arms.

I pushed the door open wide and nearly gasped again, for an entirely different reason. *Oh crap.* In Luke's other hand, tapping as steadily as a metronome against his thigh, was a FedEx envelope. Another one. From my poet stalker. My stomach lurched and my mind whirled.

How . . . ? Wait. Luke must have picked up my mail, no biggie. That didn't mean he knew what was going on, that I'd been on the receiving end of a dozen of these. Ugh. The whole thing was so humiliating and creepy. My chest started to itch way beyond what calamine lotion was guaranteed to handle. And then Luke turned toward me and smiled that lazy, sexy smile.

"Surprised?" His voice was husky and tentative, the hint of Virginia drawl stretching the word like soft molasses taffy. I tried not to think of all the times, and all the wild things, that this same voice had whispered in my ears over the past six months. He was wearing the old leather flight jacket over a thermal shirt and faded jeans, his cheeks ruddy and dark blonde hair tousled . . . from his Jeep, or a sail across the Bay? The FBI shield was clipped to his belt. His blue eyes watched my face as he lifted the rose and stepped closer. "Not mad at me for showin' up?"

I forced myself not to look down at the FedEx envelope still in his hand. But was it there, the little winged emblem like on all the others? *Who the hell is sending these?* No, I'd look at it and think about it later. The last thing I wanted now was to involve Luke in this weirdness. The man all but showered with his 9 mm Glock. And ever since I was nearly squashed by a lifeboat on my last cruise, he had this thing about keeping me safe. It was just poetry after all, and a pretty feeble attempt at that. No need for overkill.

I reached for the stem and smiled my answer, hearing Luke's soft chuckle and sigh as I moved into his arms. Hell, the guy was holding a rose, right? The Cavanaughs' Irish blood made us suckers for all that sappy stuff. I was even pretty sure that a dozen roses figured somewhere in my mom's defection from St. Ann's convent. And, besides all that, right now there was no black velvet box in sight.

"Well hello there, Skyler," I murmured with my lips against his chest.

It was a conspiracy that this man smelled so good. Leather, warm skin, a trace of that ginger soap I'd left in his shower and . . . sea brine? Yes, he'd sailed. And there was no way I could deny that Luke Skyler still made my knees weak. Just like when we met aboard that New England cruise last fall—undercover Special Agent meets immune-to-love trauma nurse amidst murder and mayhem. I'd fought him like a wildcat, of course, convinced that he was a dance host gigolo fleecing old widows. But the sparks were undeniable even then. *Still are.*

I snuggled closer, stretching my arms around Luke and letting one palm rest over a back pocket of his jeans. Worn denim, frayed threads, and . . . I grinned against his chest and sighed. A rose and a butt like an Abercrombie and Fitch ad.

"So," I said, leaning away and looking up into his face. "Are you going to kiss me . . . or what?"

Silence.

"Well?" I prodded, watching that rascal gleam crinkle the edges of his gold-flecked blue eyes.

"'*Or what*,'" he whispered. "Definitely."

Luke dropped the Express envelope onto the dresser and hoisted me into his arms just long enough to pivot toward the bed and plunk me on top. He grinned down at me as he slowly shed the flight jacket, belt, and badge, and then draped his shoulder holster across a chair. I knew he was teasing me and . . . damn. My eyes widened. This FBI man could be a Chippendale. The bed springs creaked as Luke lowered himself over me. I was toast.

His kiss left absolutely no doubt about his reason for showing up. I wound my arms around Luke's neck and buried my fingers in his hair, kissing him back. I shouldn't have worried about the poem. This visit had nothing to do with FedEx; just pure and simple U.S. Male. Mouth and lips, tongue, and . . . *oh boy.* His fingers traced along the inside of my thigh, then marched due north.

"Hey, wait," I said, laughing against his mouth when I could catch a breath. "Really, I think—"

"Don't think," he murmured.

I lost my voice again as Luke's other hand moved under my shirt, fingertips lifting the lower edge of my bra. *Wait.* Oh jeez . . . too late. His search ended in a spastic clutch over a dozen spot-size Band-Aids. He uttered a small incoherent noise and I choked on a laugh.

So much for glamour.

"What in holy hell?" Luke leaned back on one elbow, lifted my shirt and shook his head in disbelief at the adhesive collage. "Cut yourself shaving?"

My laugh dissolved into a groan. "The bridesmaid dress has a low neckline. You know, that stupid rash."

Luke grinned, the teasing back in his eyes. "Oh, yeah, the Muppet Disease."

I narrowed my eyes. "Ooh. Not funny. I told you the dermatologist called it Grover's Disease or maybe prickly heat, or . . ." *Or maybe just jewelry-box-under-a-stack-of-boxers panic disorder?*

"Jeez." My eyes filled with tears before I could stop them. Where was that coming from? "Sorry, the itch pills make me squirrelly."

Luke smiled gently, touched a fingertip to my nose and then folded me to his chest with a sigh. His voice was suddenly different, quiet, and his breath warm against my hair. I could hear his heartbeat. "Or maybe it's that you're suddenly allergic to me?"

I drew back, wanting to say something and afraid to say anything, but he pressed a finger against my lips and spoke before I could try.

15

"No, wait. I've been thinking about last night." Luke shook his head. "I feel awful about it. Pressuring you like that about moving to Boston. Everything you said about your work, your family problems, your . . . goldfish is valid." He ran his hand through his hair, brows furrowed, the blue of his eyes gone stony gray.

I hated seeing him like this. What could I say? "No, Luke, I—"

"Wait. Please, Darcy," he interrupted, smiling suddenly and shaking his head again. "What I'm trying to say is that I figured it out. We've known each other for almost six months, right? You're thinking maybe that's not long enough to know someone before packing up and following him three thousand miles. Not without some sort of security, not without . . . a promise."

Oh no. My stomach lurched and my skin screamed beneath the Band-Aids. I had to stop this whole deal right now. No way was I shopping for a tacky "I AM THE BRIDE" glitter shirt. "No, Luke, I—"

The ship's whistle blasted overhead, stopping me. The PA crackled and reverberated, then echoed with Captain McNaughton's voice. "Last call for visitors going ashore. Please be prepared to present your pass at the gangway, B-Deck, midship. I repeat: all visitors must now disembark."

My breath escaped in a whoosh.

Luke glared up at the overhead speaker, then pointed to his holster and badge slung over the chair. "Then maybe I need to officially handcuff you. Do a body search. A federal investigation supersedes maritime law."

"You wouldn't."

Luke touched a fingertip to my left breast. "Can't leave until I'm at least sure you didn't rub the tattoo off with that stupid lotion."

He peeled away a couple of Band-Aids and grinned down at my shamrock. "Good. Hated to have to change the name of my boat."

He kissed me and the whistle blasted again. "Damn. Oh, wait. I brought you something. I was saving it, but . . ."

Luke stood and turned away, reaching for his jacket. My gaze dropped to its slash pocket, soft leather gaping open to expose the black velvet jewelry box. My hands flew to my mouth and I pulled them away, fighting to compose myself before he noticed. I had to do something, but—

There was a knock on the cabin door and Marie stepped inside. She shook her head and pointed her little cigar at Luke. "Hey, you want to get arrested, fed? They're calling 'All ashore.'" She glanced down at me, shaking her head as I struggled to pull my shirt down. Then she turned back to Luke. "Trust me, anything you have going with this woman is not worth having to sail with that jerk Worley. Better jump ship."

I stood up and watched as Luke slid into his shoulder holster and lifted the leather jacket from the back of the chair. Prayers answered, the jewelry box stayed put in the pocket. The cabin floor rolled gently beneath us as the ship's engines began to thrum.

Luke gave Marie a soft cuff on the shoulder and then reached for my hand as he crossed to the door. His lips brushed my fingers before he whispered. "I'll see you in a few days then? We'll figure something out?"

I nodded, and tried to swallow the lump in my throat that was a crazy mix of relief and . . . regret? Man, I was a squirrel.

"Oh," Luke turned and pointed toward the dresser. "Forgot about the FedEx. I found it on your porch this morning, on my way back from Monterey. Were you expecting something?"

I pretended not to see the look on Marie's face. Then I smiled sweetly and shrugged my shoulders, despite an inferno of itching. "Haven't a clue."

*   *   *

"It wasn't a lie. I didn't have a clue," I told Marie twenty minutes later, tapping my fingernail against the envelope. No little winged emblem. No revolting poem. Just an answer to yet another inquiry I'd made to the attorney at Grandma Rosaleen's retirement home. And now we were at sea—no mail arrived out here, thank God. One less thing to worry about. I lay back on the bed and used the edge of the cardboard mailer to scratch my Band-Aids as I glanced over at Marie. "Don't look at me like that," I moaned. "You're causing a Catholic school flashback. What are you gonna do, suspend me for godsake? I didn't lie to Luke. It was simply a sin of omission."

Marie was maddeningly silent. Suspension was easier.

I took a deep breath and turned toward the window. Outside, raucous explosions of laughter accompanied Cajun music. I figured we'd been sailing maybe twenty minutes and I'd bet the bar stewards had served . . . I did the math . . . two thousand passengers multiplied by a drink and a half per . . . maybe three thousand cocktails. Easily.

"You're a jumper, too," Marie said as I turned back toward her. She was nodding her head and rubbing her chin like Sigmund Freud. Always a bad sign. "You're just as dangerous as Worley and his near miss over that rail."

I stared at her. "What the hell?"

"Only you jump to conclusions." Marie shook her head. "About this FedEx just now, about Luke being a gigolo on that last cruise, and now you think he's chasing you with an engagement ring?"

"Luke had the jewelry box with him here tonight."

Marie shook her head and fumbled in her fanny pack for a cheroot. "Uh, huh. And do we know what's in that box, for sure?" She produced her pink VW Bug–shaped lighter and flicked the wheels until the hood sparked, then flamed. Cherry smoke wafted around her head like a halo as she took a drag and exhaled.

My plaid skirt training told me a sermon was coming.

"Look, all I'm saying is that you take too much on sometimes," Marie said, studying the end of her cigar. "Borrow trouble. You get all overly responsible like you're . . . tilting at damned windmills."

I raised my brows and Marie smiled sheepishly.

"Sorry, that last thing was one of Carol's favorite lines. Don Quixote. You try living with a writer." She took another drag on the cigar. "But would it be so hard to tell Luke the truth? That you think some fruitcake poet is stalking you? That your work is a war zone and his job scares the piss out of you? And now you're preparing to do battle so your grandma won't be evicted from her retirement home?"

I opened my mouth and closed it again. There was no use arguing; the woman was tap dancing on a soapbox now. Marie had minored in animal behavior in college, and for some reason that gave her license to counsel. Especially after more than two drinks topped with paper umbrellas.

Her voice softened. "And maybe, just maybe, you could ask Luke what he's hiding under that stack of boxers. If it's an engagement ring then fine, you'll know. Tell him that the sparkle's way cool, but the timing's not right." She watched my face and smiled knowingly. "That you love him like crazy, but right now white satin and rice make you itch."

Love? I felt my heart thud and I wanted to protest, but decided not to say anything at all. Partly because I knew Marie was under the influence of paper umbrellas, but mostly because right this minute things didn't seem so bad. We were sailing away from the jewelry box, and the FedEx had been detonated. Just for that fleeting sense of peace, I was willing to zip myself into polka dots and walk down a garden aisle pretending that marriage—I turned my head toward a sound at the door. What now?

The cabin door burst inward and a purple-feathered mask intruded, followed by a high-pitched Alabama shriek. "Moon Pie, Moon Pie!"

I yelped and then ducked as something round and plastic-wrapped and chocolate brown whizzed by my head. Another one hurtled, like a flying saucer, toward Marie.

Patti Ann lifted her mask and giggled, sputtering as a wisp of feather stuck to her lower lip. She was wearing a too-short purple suede skirt and her neck was draped in yards of multi-colored plastic beads. The bride swayed and then grabbed the doorway to steady herself. She held out another plastic-wrapped disc and giggled as I flinched.

"Lord, steady there galfriend, haven't ya ever seen a Moon Pie? Chocolate and marsh-sh-sh"—she slurred the word and giggled again—"marshmallow? Good Ga-awd, what are y'all still doin' inside your cabin? You're missing my Mardi Gras!"

I fought to stay upright as Patti Ann lurched forward and flung an arm around my neck, then pulled Marie close into a three-way hug.

"My bridesmaids," she choked, "Have I told y'all how wooonder-ful I think you are?"

Marie shot a withering look over the top of Patti Ann's head and I squinted against the bride's breath, doing a quick mental re-calculation: four thousand cocktails. I could only imagine how to-tally wasted Dale Worley, the car dealer, must be by now.

Patti Ann finally let go and rubbed a fingertip across her brim-ming eyes, her smile white-tulle dreamy. "It just couldn't be more perfect. Kirsty's thought of everything. When I told her how sad I was not bein' home for Mobile's Mardi Gras this year, she said she'd make me one right here."

Her lower lip quivered. "Is that the sweetest thing you ever heard? And she's havin' the Cowboy Night for Kyle. Karaoke, too." She smacked the Moon Pie against her thigh and shook her head again. "She's even got that dickhead Worley staplin' up crepe paper with Ed and Ryan. You won't believe this, but Kirsty's got herself a little tool belt with pink-handled tools. Kind of sexy in a strange way, I guess . . . a hammer and pliers and the biggest damned sta-pler I've ever seen. All I know is that when she straps those tools on you'd think it was a garter belt . . . swear, those firemen are like little rats following the Pied Piper." Patti Ann nodded her head and sighed. "Of course, would you just look at the woman? Stick-thin, hair the color of moonlight on corn silk . . ." She made two attempts before standing, and Marie gave her a discreet nudge to-ward the door. "I probably should hate Kirsty, just on principle," Patti Ann added, "but she's so *nice*, you know?"

21

I nodded and nodded again, then bit my lip to keep from laughing as we ushered the bride to the door. We agreed to anything and everything just to get her purple skirt gone. Yes, we'd join everyone in ten minutes up on the Lido Deck, aft. Of course, we'd love to try the catfish and fried pickles. Fried pickles, for godsake? And wow, we thought it was just great that Kirsty had gotten the Personal Training Team to do foot rubs for the bridesmaids. Yes, everything was just perfectly perfect. Buh-bye.

The door closed behind the bride and Marie had barely let out a moan of relief when the door pushed inward again.

Patti Ann handed me a large manila envelope.

"Oh look, darlin', I just found this taped to your door. It's got your name on it."

She pointed to the little winged emblem affixed to the lower corner. "Now isn't that just cute as a bug's ear?"

THREE

I watched as Marie grabbed the deck rail and snorted through her nose, battling another spasm of laughter. Great. I was in no mood for Mardi Gras, let alone the groomsmens' stupid-ass pranks. There'd been a poem taped to my door.

"But, Darc', you've gotta respect someone who actually owns a remote control fart machine . . . *Oh God.*" Marie crumpled again then swiped at her tears, nearly poking herself in the eye with half a fried pickle. "Besides, it would do you good to lighten up a little, babe."

"Lighten up?" I uncrossed my arms and bounced my Pinocchio mask against its narrow elastic strap like a paddleball. "He had someone tape that poem to my door—*my door!*" I shuddered. "Might as well have been fondled, for godsake." I moaned and turned away, staring out over the ship's rail. Why had I thought that miles of ocean would put any real distance between me and the three-ring circus of my life?

Over the deck rail, the white-light constellation of San Francisco Bay receded into the inky distance, pushed back by the impressive wake of our seventy-thousand-ton pleasure boat. Cruising at . . . what had Kirsty Pelham quoted from her little PDA? Twenty-four knots? I thought of Luke's sailboat sliding almost soundlessly through the currents of this same bay. So different. Crisp flap-flutter of the sail, soft bowstring hum as rigging lines bounced against the mast . . . late afternoon sun, lazy silence, then Luke's soft chuckle as he watched me dangle my bare leg over the side. I swallowed, hard. What would Luke do with the boat? Move it to Boston? Sell it? We hadn't talked about any of that.

I looked back down at the cruise ship's boiling wake, maybe seven stories below. No dangling your foot there. You fall overboard and that's it. Sucked under in darkness. It wasn't like they could just stop an eight-hundred-foot ship; whip it around like a Chris-Craft after a downed skier. Dangerous. And that was a fact. Like the manila envelope.

In the last several weeks I'd driven myself close to crazy trying to figure out who could be sending them; psychiatric patient, some jokester on the ER staff, that too-friendly handyman at Grandma's retirement home? Nothing seemed to fit. And, no matter how many times Marie had suggested it, it couldn't be Sam. Firefighter Sam. No way. He'd finally accepted the fact that our relationship was over and moved to Portland nearly a year ago. And back with the wife he'd never bothered to mention, probably. Sam Jamieson and poetry? I shook my head. Sure, if you considered reciting the Forty-Niners' offensive and defensive stats somehow lyrical. Definitely not Firefighter Sam. But still, someone had managed to have that envelope sent to—*oh Lord*. Goose bumps rose as the full realization hit me.

"Marie?" I watched as she popped the fried pickle into her mouth. "Maybe that guy's here somewhere. On the ship."

"You mean the Lord Byron of FedEx-th?" she lisped over the crumbs.

"Yes." I scanned the crowd milling around the lighted pool, couples dancing to the Louisiana zydeco music. Accordions, fiddles, and rub boards. Shoulders, elbows, and hips swayed, feet stomped, and there was the occasional I'm-a-wild-thing yelp. But no more than a dozen of them wore the Mardi Gras getups. I didn't think Patti Ann and Kyle had more than maybe thirty friends aboard, including the wedding party of seven. They'd simply posted a flyer in the ER lounge and firehouse, "*Last Minute Cruise, Great Deal, Drink up and Kiss the Bride*." Anyone could come. It was a Booze Cruise, plain and simple, and even the immediate families were wise enough to travel directly to the ceremony site on Vancouver Island.

My eyes drifted up to the Sports Deck above and to the little lighted eighteen-hole miniature golf course out on the fantail. People everywhere, two thousand of them. Ten decks with lots of places to hide. And write poems. Where was he for godsake? I nudged Marie. "Well? He could be onboard, right?"

"Or he could have asked to have it delivered to you from shore, or maybe . . ."

Suddenly Marie wasn't smiling anymore, and I didn't like it.

I groaned. "What can I do? I mean I'm pretty sure that security wouldn't think that poetry was on the same scale as terrorism or killer icebergs."

"I've told you a million times what I thought you should do."
Marie reached over and flicked Pinocchio's long nose with her fingers. "But no, you wouldn't tell Luke the truth."

"He's got so much on his mind with closing up the case in Monterey, and I . . ." Even I could hear the fakey whine in my voice.

"Hold on." Marie squeezed my arm. "I was just going to say that even if you won't take advantage of an honest-to-God federal agent, then you're damned lucky that I happen to have the next best thing."

"Huh?"

"Lesbians."

I opened and closed my mouth mutely.

"Carol and her writers' group, of course." Marie grinned.

"So . . . ?" I wrinkled my brows. Obviously, I would have to limit this woman's paper umbrellas.

Marie sighed. "I'm saying that I showed her some of the stuff this guy's been sending you."

"And?" I wished to hell I knew what Marie was getting at. But—
ugh—she showed it to Carol?

"And she sent it off to some of her online groups."

"Online?" My eyes widened. "You're flashing my body parts around on the Internet?" I clasped my hand over my mouth. "Oh my God."

"Darcy! Stop jumping to conclusions." Marie reached out and pulled my hand down. "Listen, no names were mentioned. They simply did an analysis; you know, about style, tone, time period of the quotes. Themes? Other writers' shit like that. I mean let's face it, this group is educated, talented, and has a wealth . . . of . . . well, collective experience with describing women's bodies." Marie's voice faded into a mumble and she cleared her throat. "Anyway, she's working on it, okay?"

I smiled. "You're blushing."

"Am not." Marie fumbled in her fanny pack for a cheroot and grumbled. "Just trying to help you." She found her Volkswagen lighter and flicked the wheels like a driver laying rubber.

"Oh Lord, you're beet red." I bit my lip, knowing I was pushing it, but—"Wait. Carol writes poems about you?"

Marie took a drag of her cigar, blew a perfect smoke ring, and then smiled slowly in the darkness. "Let's just say she doesn't have to tape 'em to my door."

*   *   *

A half-hour later we managed to find the ship's Business Berth Computer Room, tucked off the library and adjacent to the card room on Promenade Deck. I pulled my grandmother's legal papers out of the FedEx envelope to check the signatures again before placing it on the fax machine. Signed, dated, and ready to sail.

"Man, do you see all the stuff they've got in this place, Darc'?" Marie whistled and turned in a slow circle on the blue carpet, arms outstretched. "No such thing as carefree vacations anymore, I guess. Fax, Internet, laser printers, photo copiers, and conference phone." She peeked into a little refrigerator. "Fresh fruit, bottles of spring water . . . what else, antacid by the quart?"

I shrugged, trying to read the directions on the fax machine. "Got to cater to businesspeople, I guess." I looked over my shoulder and wrinkled my nose. "Not everyone has the luxury of leaving their 'clients' hooked to an IV and straddling a bedpan."

Marie's eyes widened. "Do you see that?" She pointed to a waist-high machine, stainless steel and bolted to the floor. All the machines were bolted. In the event of rough seas, I guessed.

"Swear that's the biggest shredder I've ever seen. Industrial size." Marie peered down into the feeder slot at the top. "Bet it does double duty in the galley." She peered up through her bangs. "You know, like maybe coleslaw for two thousand." She leaned down to retrieve a slip of paper poking out from under the machine. "Looks like someone dropped something; let's see how this shredder-on-steroids handles." She raised the sheet of paper over the huge slot then yanked it back, gray eyes wide. "Holy shit."

"What?" I set the fax down and reached for the paper in Marie's hands.

There were handwritten lines, awkward attempts at calligraphy, uneven and edited. The ink was smudged like a sweaty palm had moved across it. It was clearly a rough draft. Of a poem. With a familiar winged emblem sketched at the bottom.

*　*　*

An hour later, the midship glass elevator hummed to a stop in front of us and I took one last look around the atrium. There were full-size palm trees, trailing orchids, a waterfall, and a marble staircase, all under a ceiling shimmering with Venetian glass. Incredible. And not exactly a sinister setting. For godsake, it was a poem. Words. What was that thing Grandma used to say about sticks and stones? I needed to remind myself of that before I turned into a complete nutcase.

I smoothed the waistline of my scarf-hem dress, antique yellow silk with a few outrageous touches that some might say were a tad Gypsy Tart. Especially with the beaded slide heels. I'd drooled over the dress at a fashion event in San Francisco, but even when I figured up night-shift overtime, it was still way out of a nurse's budget. And then a certain federal agent showed up with a beautiful ribbon-tied box and a bottle of wine. Seems the man has a thing for gypsies.

I glanced over at Marie in her tailored pinstripes, Birkenstocks and, of course, her evening's choice of socks: orange and aqua elephants.

"So do you know where we're supposed to be going?" I asked as the passengers unloaded and I followed Marie in. I squeezed beside her and glanced at the faces around me, fighting a sudden and irrational urge to frisk every person in there. Yeah. Shout, "*Spread 'em, everyone,*" and just pat their sorry asses down for calligraphy pens. I needed a drink.

"Back to the Promenade Deck," Marie answered, adjusting her fanny pack. "So, down a deck and then forward, to the bow. Kirsty's got something going for the bridal party in the Schooner Bar. Can't remember what." She lowered her voice to a whisper and nudged her elbow into my ribs. "And stop eyeballing these people. I told you that Carol thinks this whole poetry thing's basically harmless."

The passengers surged forward as the doors opened, and Marie and I stepped out onto the plush diamond-patterned carpet of the Promenade Deck. The bass guitar of a jazz combo thrummed along to a blend of keyboard, tinkling cocktail glasses, foreign languages—a sort of international fusion of conversation and laughter. Man, I love cruise ships.

"This way?" I asked, pointing toward a corridor of sparkling glass and tiny white lights—the Galleria Boutiques. Shopping surrounded by water. Doesn't get better.

Marie nodded and followed.

"So what did Carol say that the little winged thingy on the envelope meant?" I asked.

"It's the symbol of some Roman God. Hermes. But then she said it could be Mercury, too. Kind of interchangeable, I guess. And the thing's a foot. With wings."

"Right," I said, turning a little sideways to accommodate a group of fur-draped elderly women who'd made a sudden stop in front of the jewelry store. "I remember the first time I got one of those damned cardboard mailers, maybe a couple of months ago at the hospital. I thought the little symbol was a shoe. A stylized running shoe. Like from my marathon group."

I shook my head, remembering. "There I am reading aloud what I think is an artsy newsletter about the upcoming cross-country routes, and then all of a sudden I hear my lips saying, '. . . *the grass is worn with the feet of shameless lovers . . .*'" I grimaced. "Eew."

Marie nodded. "Aiken."

"Huh?"

"Conrad Aiken. The poet who wrote it. That's what Carol said, anyway."

"Terrific. And then all those other ones came, ranting on about little dimples on elbows, the apple of a cheek, and the cherry curve of a smile. Fruit? And so blasted many ankles." I shuddered and scratched at a Band-Aid. "Like that one last week." I closed my eyes, remembering. "*He followed—close behind—his silver heel upon my ankle, my shoes . . . overflowed . . .*"

I stopped and grabbed Marie's arm. "See? Basically harmless? Scared enough to pee in your shoes doesn't sound harmless to me."

"Emily Dickinson," Marie said, prying my fingers away. "And calm down, for crissake. She was a very respectable lady, and the poem was about walking on the seashore or something. Seriously, Carol says this is old-fashioned flattery, probably from someone very shy. Nothing dangerous."

We passed the casino, and I saw the door of the Schooner Bar just steps ahead. I sighed, still not convinced. "So now I know what Carol thinks, but how about you? Do you think all this body part stuff is nothing?"

"Sure, babe." Marie reached for the brass door handle and waved me inside. "Unless, of course, it's a *Silence of the Lambs* deal."

* * *

The Schooner Bar was shiny with brass and lacquered teak, each table topped with a flickering mariner's lantern and a full crew of elbows. Above the heads of the patrons, framed lithographs of sailing vessels hung stem to stern along paneled walls. At the center of the room a piano rose from a reconstructed ship's bow and a tuxedoed musician grinned beneath a rainbow of maritime flags. His fingers moved across the keys to release vintage Billy Joel— my blackjack-dealing mom's favorite, "Piano Man"—as the floor swayed gently beneath us.

I had risen on tiptoe to peer over the heads of the crowd when a cool hand caught my elbow. I turned to see Kirsty Pelham's dark lashes and huge blue eyes, magnified behind the dark-framed glasses. She smiled and I found myself wondering which was brighter, the wedding planner's teeth or the whites of her eyes. Medically, I mean, weren't eyeballs supposed to be whiter? I was sure this woman was close to dental bleach overdose. I smiled back, feeling my tongue press against the tiny space between my less-than-perfect front teeth. My neck started to itch.

"Darcy, Marie, I've been looking for you." Kirsty smiled again and gestured, using her Palm Pilot an airport ground controller, directing us toward a doorway at the far end of the bar. "We've got the whole wedding party just about assembled now, and I've tried to piece together a few special surprises for everyone." Kirsty shook her head, corn silk hair swirling across very expensive silk. Her perfect shoulders shrugged. "I want to jump-start our cruise experience."

Marie cleared her throat as she began to walk. "I think that's what Dale Worley tried to do, wasn't it?"

Kirsty raised her brows. "Oh, you mean his stunt on the deck rail?" Her fingers tightened on her Palm Pilot. "Yes, I've talked to Mr. Worley and he's agreed to tone down that playful stuff. Besides, a business problem's come up that's going to take his time." Her eyes looked puzzled behind the very trendy lenses. "About how to get a pair of armadillos to pose quietly on the hood of a Humvee." She stopped for a moment and glanced back across the bar. "He's gone to the ship's Business Berth Computer Room to send a fax, I think."

Kirsty smiled again, a hundred watts bright, as she began to walk on. "I think we can agree that all the surprises now should be in the spirit of the occasion and well deserved. Like how our little Southern belle deserves a wonderful wedding."

The snarky part of me wanted to gag at this wedding planner's perkiness, but it would be hard to argue her point. Patti Ann did deserve all the happiness she could get, and that was no joke.

We stepped across the threshold into the private party room and were greeted by a yelp of delight from the bride, timed to perfection with a raucous eruption from the nowhere-to-be-seen fart machine. Kirsty's face flamed and she strode away like a bloodhound on a godawful scent.

"Oh my goodness," Patti Ann giggled as she trotted toward us, breasts bouncing beneath a sheer, floral tunic. "Can y'all believe these guys with the stunts? I think they're giving Kirsty heartburn; the poor thing's been popping antacids non-stop. But would you just look at what she's done for a surprise?" She took my hand and gestured to Marie, leading us through the wedding guests and past waiters carrying trays of beer and plates mounded with Buffalo wings and mini-pizzas. It was obvious that the firefighters had planned the menu.

Patti Ann stopped in front of a wall covered edge-to-edge with photo posters under a rainbow of twisted and stapled crepe paper. She glanced down at the floor for an instant and shook her head, stooping to retrieve an enormous pink stapler and a roll of duct tape. "Men," she sighed, sliding them onto an adjacent table.

She tapped her fingernail against a grainy photo of a chubby toddler in pigtails and a hoop skirt, then at one of a towheaded tyke in cowboy boots. Her eyes filled with tears and she clasped her hands over her heart. "Kyle, and me! Can you believe it? Grew up two thousand miles apart and here we are, side by side." She looked back at the endless collage of photos. "Can you believe Kirsty went to all this trouble?"

"Whoa, yeah," Marie agreed, biting at her lower lip and scanning the cluttered wall. "I can hardly believe that she was able to find that great one of you sitting on the potty chair naked and eating an ice-cream cone." She coughed as I poked her with my elbow. "Lots of great stuff. What's that one, though, over there? Looks more like an ad."

I looked to where Marie was pointing. Sure enough, a huge poster with sharp, stylized graphics, its vivid color in direct contrast to the fuzzy photo collage. Legs, bare feet. Same as the others we'd seen practically everywhere on the ship.

"Yes, it is," Patti Ann confirmed. "The Personal Training Team ad. Kirsty's worked out a deal; another little surprise for us girls: foot rubs and acupressure treatment. At our Spa Day, remember?" She turned her head as the music paused in the distance, then someone keyed a microphone and laughed, sending a screech of painful reverb across the room.

"Sorry," the man with the microphone said and laughed again, sputtering and wiping at his mouth. "Excuse me . . . what the hell?"

I watched as the silver-haired man, a little familiar, reached for a napkin, coughed, and then spit something into it before lifting the microphone again. His voice was thick with alcohol.

"Kirsty, babe—and isn't she a babe, folks?" He beckoned with his beefy hands until a round of applause and several hoots responded. He pointed to the discarded napkin. "Honey Buns, tell the cook he got a damned piece of metal in my Buffalo wing. Tell him not to let it happen again, or I'll own this little boat."

Patti Ann excused herself, and I turned back toward the man with the microphone, finally recognizing him as Paul Putnam, retired from Kyle's firehouse. Sure, I remembered him now. He had multiple commendations for bravery, but a raunchy sense of humor. Even Sam had cringed at some of old Paul's antics. I watched his face, puffy eyelids and ruddy complexion, as he prompted the crowd to share embarrassing stories about the bride and groom.

I squirmed and rubbed the neckline of my dress where a Band-Aid pulled against my skin under the gypsy dress. No. Paul Putnam was a dirty joke by e-mail kind of man, not a poet. But I found myself scanning the faces of the guests at the tables: a few hospital technicians, a couple of single nurses, firehouse personnel, and more than a few people I didn't recognize. Ryan and Ed, the groomsmen. Blonde-headed Kyle, with his arm protectively around Patti Ann. Kirsty Pelham, barely picking at her piece of pizza. I tried to picture one of them holding a fancy pen, copying verses. *Who the hell is it?* I jumped as Marie touched my arm.

"Hey, Darcy. Did you see this shot? Remember who that was?"

I glanced one last time at Paul, whose face had grown redder and even puffier if possible. He was glistening with sweat and looked awful. I turned back as Marie said my name again.

She was pointing at a photo in a more current section of the collage, just below the toes of the Personal Training ad. It was a firehouse picture of Paul Putnam, Dale Worley, Sam, and a vaguely familiar young paramedic. Who was he? Maybe I'd tried too hard to forget firemen after I broke things off with Sam. Beside them in the photo was a heavy-set young woman peering from beneath thick, dark bangs. She was wearing a firefighter's turnout coat, sleeves too long, and holding a dalmatian puppy. I'd started to look closer, to remember who that paramedic was, when an adjacent photo caught my eye and my stomach plunged like a runaway elevator. *Couldn't be.*

I stepped closer to where a spotlight illuminated an enlarged photo of a man balancing a young woman on his incredibly wide shoulders, the kind of shoulders it took to wield a fire ax, force open a barricaded door, and carry a terrified child from a burning building. He was tall, muscular, and bare-chested, with curly dark hair and a wide grin. His hands were holding the ankles of a young woman who had her hands buried in his hair. Her head was thrown back, laughing, and the top of her strapless bathing suit dipped low enough to worry an Irish grandmother. A dark spot was just visible over her left breast.

In the overhead light the dark spot looked like a smudge or a flaw in the photo finish, like you could rub it off with a dab of spit on a fingertip. But I knew better—can't rub off a tattoo. A green shamrock. I was that woman in the photo, and the man was . . . *damn*. I couldn't stop the God-knows-why enticing memory of musky cologne and smoke that still came when I thought of him. The man responsible for a macaroni and cheese binge that had put four scary pounds on my ass. And then a familiar voice spoke behind me. *Oh my God.*

"Good picture of us, don't you think?" Sam Jamieson's voice asked softly.

Before I could react, a shout erupted in the distance, followed by a series of screams. There was the metallic scrape-thunk of a table overturning and then the unmistakable sound of shattering glass. Sam whirled and ran toward the crowd and Marie yanked at my arm.

"Shit. Let's go. Paul Putnam's down."

FOUR

HE LAY ON THE floor between the overturned table and a life-sized cardboard cutout of Worley's dealership llama dressed as a bride. Paul Putnam struggled to raise his head and his breath escaped in a prolonged wheeze, sucking inward again with a thin screech like he'd swallowed a Mardi Gras whistle. His tongue protruded between swollen lips and his eyes, their whites blistering like a fried egg, were wild with terror. "Ca-an't . . ." the whistle ended in a gag, "bre-eathe . . ."

"Hang in there, Paul." I stopped wrestling with his greasy shirt buttons—barbecue sauce for godsake—and ripped open the front of his shirt. Buttons and the contents of his breast pocket scattered across the floor plinking against pieces of a broken plate. Beneath a mat of gray hairs, the man's chest fought for air, flesh retracting around his ribs and his breastbone hollowing inward with the struggle. Hives had risen, blanched against the redness of his skin. I pivoted on my knees and shouted into the gathered crowd.

"Where's the doctor? We need to give him some adrenaline here!" Dammit, we were running out of time.

Marie slid to her knees beside me as a series of bursts from the ship's PA system blasted overhead. "That's the official call, but Kirsty says she got through on her cell phone first, at least five minutes ago. Kyle's watching for the doctor and Sam's doing crowd control; keeping people from getting in here through the bar." She glanced back down at Paul Putnam. "You're thinking allergic reaction?"

I nodded, watching Paul's face. His eyes were beginning to swim, the struggle to breathe ebbing along with his ability to remain conscious. If we didn't get some equipment here soon, this man was going to die. Trying to carry him to the infirmary would take just as long. *Please, God.* "Paul, stay with us. Are you allergic to anything?" I pressed my fingers into the side of his neck and searched for his carotid pulse. It was rapid and thready but present. "Paul?"

His eyes focused through lids swollen to mere slits and his voice was barely audible. Paul reached down to scratch at his belly, then his hand settled over his crotch. "Pee-n-n—thsss."

Patti Ann inched forward on her knees and grasped his chin. Her face was flushed, eyes riveted on his. "No, Paul, darlin'. We're asking if y'all are allergic to anything."

"Pee-ee—nsss." Drool leaked from the corner of Putnam's swollen lips as he scratched at the fly of his slacks.

"Penis?" Marie scrunched her brows at me. "Is that what he's saying?"

"Shit, Putnam." Dale Worley's voice rose to a falsetto above us as he stepped forward out of the gathered crowd. His face was pale, eyes wide and scared-stiff sober. "This is no time to be thinking about your dick for crissake. Quit screwin' around and tell 'em what they need to—" His voice cut off and he lurched sideways as a huge hand shoved him aside.

Sam Jamieson looked down at me, his dark eyes serious as backdraft. "Kyle's here. Ran ahead with the emergency kit, and the nurse is just a few minutes behind. He told her that you think it's an allergic reaction. The doctor's tied up with a heart patient down in the infirmary." He stepped aside to let Kyle pass through, and in less than a minute we had the portable oxygen cranked up to full flow. It wasn't helping.

I looked down at Putnam's face, blue-gray now with eyes rolled back and mouth slack, and then at his chest and its gills-out-of-water breathing. No time to wait for the doctor. Or the nurse. I squeezed my eyes shut for an instant. Shit, could I do this here— legally? If I stopped to think about that, Paul would die. I reached into the opened emergency kit and pulled out a tourniquet, pausing for a split second to scan the faces of the people kneeling beside me; Marie, Patti Ann, Kyle, and now Sam. *My team. Just like home. Picture it that way and get on with it.* I stretched the noodle-thin latex strip around Paul's arm, secured it, flicked my fingernail against the flattened vein at his inner elbow, and then took one last look up at my friends.

Marie nodded. "We wait and we'll be doing CPR. I've got the adrenaline here. One to ten-thousand."

I squirted air from the syringe and slid the needle, bevel up, into the vein just as the infirmary nurse arrived—and Paul's breathing ended in a ragged gasp. Blood backed up in the syringe and I saw Marie check for a pulse then shake her head as Patti Ann prepared to start mouth-to-mouth. The infirmary nurse put her hand on my shoulder and nodded furiously. I pressed the plunger and prayed, holding my breath. Until Paul's began again.

* * *

I lowered my wineglass, rolling the chardonnay over my tongue before I swallowed. It was the second sip of a second glass and already the seeping warmth had my teeth feeling kind of fuzzy. I looked out over the deck rail at the sea and smiled as the ship swayed beneath me. *Mmm, way better.* And, thank God, the drama was over.

I'd showered and changed; had to after scrambling around on the floor in all those spills—beer, barbecue sauce, and broken glass bits. Barely avoiding the "mystery puddle," of course. I shook my head. It was like one of those bad jokes: how many nurses and firemen does it take to translate that a man was struggling to say, "Pee"?

I'd passed on Marie's itch to hit the casino card tables, choosing my own little solitaire time instead. So I changed into a mint green halter dress, pulled my hair up with a glittery clip, dabbed on a little ginger scent, and felt way better. Combine that with two glasses of wine, the cool prickle of Pacific fog across my bare shoulders, and the unparalleled rush that comes after saving someone's life . . . and yep, things were looking good. I glanced sideways out of the corner of my eye. Now if I could just figure out what to do about the big fireman who'd parked himself at the deck rail beside me.

Sam Jamieson smiled. "So what I'm saying," he explained, "is that if you save someone's life, then you're responsible for them from that moment on and forever. Swear. It's that Asian thing, Feng Shui." His cognac brown eyes caught mine, pushing the smile one tentative step farther. The night breeze blew across the shoulders of his corduroy sport coat, riffling the edge of his tie and Sam smoothed it back against his denim shirt. He raised his brows and the smile blossomed.

"Feng Shui?" I held onto my glass with both hands to keep from slopping it over as laughter bubbled into my throat. "Feng Shui for Petesake?" I met his gaze and shook my head. *Sam.* What was it about that smile of his that always made me think of my brothers, Grandpa Charlie, and, who else . . . Clark Kent? Maybe it had something to do with his sort of homespun sincerity, comfortable as a pair of old Levis. Kind of puppy-ish, cowlicked, and honest . . . no, not always honest. Not about his marriage. Face it; he wasn't ever going to be Superman after that massacre of truth, justice, and the American way.

I narrowed my eyes, but a laugh escaped anyway. "Feng Shui is about design. Decorating. Jamieson, you are such a liar . . ." My voice trailed away and I felt the crimson rise in my face. Crap, that was a dumb thing to say. I turned my head toward the dance music in the distance, and then looked back and did my best to return his faltering smile. There was no sense in thinking about that other stuff. That's why they called it the "past," right? And I'd had more than enough drama for the evening.

Sam shrugged his big shoulders and took a step closer. "So then maybe Old Man Putnam could be a patio decoration. You know, like one of those garden trolls?" He sighed and took hold of the deck rail for a moment, his big hands flexing and releasing on the polished teak, then looked back at me. "I guess I'm working up to saying that it's good to see you again, Darcy. In action like you were back there, I mean."

God, it looked like he was holding his breath.

41

"It's what I do," I said, shrugging.

Sam exhaled and laughed, running his fingers through his dark curls. "Yeah, but I heard you were bailing out of the ER."

I watched his face for a moment. *Keeping tabs on me? How— why?*

"True?" Sam asked softly.

I shook my head. "Well, almost. Last year. But Marie would tell you that I was crazy at the time." I tapped a fingertip to the side of my head. "Maybe I was. I almost accepted a cushy job as a sales rep for a podiatrist. You might know him—Dr. Phillip Foote?"

Sam blinked quickly, then stared. "That guy who drives a Range Rover with the huge shoe horn bolted to the top?"

"It's an arch support," I said quickly, surprised to find myself defending the mousy little man. But then maybe I still felt guilty about leaving him in the lurch. "A mock-up of his best seller. Custom, every one. Doctor Foote is almost like an artist." *Oh jeez.* I deserved the expression I was seeing on Sam's face. "Anyway, I was going to be a rep for orthotics. You know, use my medical background to—"

"To sell corn plasters?" Sam choked on a laugh. "Sorry, I just can't picture that."

"I know, I know," I said. "And it does seem stupid now, but the way the ER's been lately, with this nursing shortage . . . It's like dancing in a frying pan, Sam, every day." I squeezed my eyes shut for a moment, and then took a sip of my wine. "You have to see it from a nurse's perspective I guess. Sometimes it feels like you don't ever get a chance to do what you're trained to do—connect with people, make a difference in their lives. Not to mention the increased liability in all that chaos, and how your license is always on the line." I caught my breath and then groaned. I hadn't meant to climb on one of Marie's soapboxes.

"Okay," I said, just wanting Sam to understand, "try being in charge of a place full of temporary staff who come and go too fast to develop a real sense of teamwork. I spend my whole day just puttin' out fires."

I stopped when I realized why he'd just chuckled. Then I laughed myself, my tension diffusing. "Oh yeah. Fires, that's your job." I swirled my wine and smiled.

Sam's face grew serious and his voice softened. "So, you turned down the podiatrist. His loss." He took a slow breath inward, and his voice quieted to a husky whisper. "But what about the lawyer? Say 'no' to him, too?"

Lawyer? I'd opened my mouth to ask what he meant, when it dawned on me. Heat rushed to my face. Luke's cover story for his FBI identity. *"Just say I'm a lawyer, Darcy."* Obviously it worked. I rubbed at an itchy spot on my collarbone and tried to think of how to answer Sam's question. Had I said "no" to Luke?

Sam bowed his head to look me full in the face. "So . . . the lawyer?"

A door opened behind us and pure jazz saxophone flooded out. Another one of Mom's old favorites, "Girl From Ipanema." Kirsty Pelham stepped onto the deck and I watched Sam's eyes move over her body, head-to-toe. The lyrics floated out behind, *"Tall and tan and young and lovely . . ."* Could Kirsty have planned that entrance better? The woman was batting a thousand. Maybe more.

"Darcy, and . . . Sam, is that right?" Kirsty smiled and Sam nodded.

"Sorry to interrupt," she explained, "but I'm trying to catch everyone for a little update on how our patient is doing."

She stepped toward the rail as the deck shifted under us, her long legs covering the distance gracefully even with the ship's movement. Her icy blue dress was nearly knee length, slim without hugging her body; modest really, since it was topped by a matching shrug jacket that covered her breasts. And expensive, I'd bet. I thought of Patti Ann and her too-tight tee shirts, glitter, and purple suede skirt. This wedding planner had ten times the figure the bride did and had never flaunted it once.

The breeze blew a strand of hair across Kirsty's face. She swept it back into place and then adjusted the strap of her small beaded purse. Behind the glasses, her blue eyes shone in the deck lights.

"We're all so grateful for your quick action, Darcy. That infirmary nurse seemed so slow, even though I," she patted the cell phone sticking out from the opening of her purse, "called for help right away." She put her hand on my arm. "Really, th-thank you." Her hand was clammy, cool, and her words softly slurred. Been drinking probably. Hadn't we all?

"Do they know yet what caused the allergic reaction?" I asked.

"No." Kirsty hugged her little jacket closer and shivered. Her face paled in the deck lights. "I think . . ." her chin quivered like her teeth would chatter and she pressed her lips together for a moment, "that he's too sleepy now. The doctor said they'd have to wait until the antihistamines wear off before they can ask him all that." Kirsty reached up and removed her glasses, tucking them into her purse. She rubbed her fingers across her forehead and scrunched her brows, then yawned and shivered again.

"Are you all right?" I asked, noticing that Kirsty was the only one of us who seemed to be swaying. The deck was motionless now.

"Yes, of course." Kirsty smiled. Her voice sounded hollow, like it was coming up from fathoms below. "Just a little c-cold." She started to giggle. "Cold. Not to be confused with old or bold." She giggled again and raised her hand to her lips. Her fingers were shaking. "What's that saying? There are no old, bold wedding planners?" She reached out and caught hold of the deck rail after two attempts, dropping her little purse and scattering its contents. She stared at it like she wasn't certain what it was.

"I'll get it, no problem." I shook my head and knelt down to pick things up before the deck rolled again and sent it all sailing. Blast, had I been right about this marriage stuff or what? If the ceremony itself was so stressful that a wedding planner had to get drunk, then how did that bode for the future of Patti Ann and Kyle? Sam and his mystery wife? *Or Luke and his hidden engagement ring?* Marriage. I was right to run the other way. Too much risk.

"Shit, she's wasted," Sam whispered over to me. "Let's get her inside." He slipped his sport coat off and draped it around Kirsty's shoulders, smiling down at her like he'd just rescued her kitten from a tree. "Better? Now let's all go find some hot coffee."

"Ooh," Kirsty's eyes filled with tears as she tucked her chin down into the enormous coat, inhaling deeply. She gave a small moan. Her eyes were huge and her face dotted with perspiration. "Your coat. No s-smoke?"

"Nope. I don't smoke. And you shouldn't drink so much, you know?" Sam began to guide her gently toward the door of the ship, his arm around her to steady the staggering.

God, I felt bad for the woman. She'd seemed so together. I looked back down and grabbed her cell phone. I scooped up Kirsty's glasses, not broken thank goodness, her lipstick, roll of antacids, and . . . what was that? I tilted the small prescription bottle and vial toward the light and squinted to read the labels, just as I heard the soft groan behind me.

"Darcy, quick," Sam shouted, "I think she's passing out!"

I snatched the purse and dashed to where he held Kirsty in his arms. "Hurry," I said, holding the door for him. "We need to give her some sugar. She's having a diabetic reaction."

* * *

Half an hour later, I took one last peek over my shoulder at Kirsty and then turned back to Marie with a sigh. "Stubborn woman. She let me give her a dose of her injectable glucose, but she won't go to the infirmary, won't lie down. I give up."

It was nearing midnight and the Schooner Bar was sit-on-a-lap full and still luring them in with Karaoke Madness and free hors d'oeuvres. I raised my voice as Dale Worley began another chorus of "Drive My Car" and the crowd roared back in unison: "*Beep beep—mm—beep beep. Yeah!*" I shook my head. "But at least she's finally eating something over there."

Marie rolled her eyes. "Right. What'd they do, hang a hummingbird feeder from a light fixture? Have you seen the production that woman makes of not eating?" She shook her head. "Swear she was counting the olives on that little pizza earlier, then probably spit the whole damned thing in her purse. Gracefully, of course." Marie closed her lips over a second drippy wedge of Brie and moaned with pleasure. "Anorexic's my guess."

I handed her a cocktail napkin printed with Kyle and Patti's names. "I hope not. No pizza in her purse, but it was definitely the diabetes pills that dropped her blood sugar like a rock. Probably needs the dose adjusted. Strange to be a type 2 diabetic at her age. But I'm glad she carries oral and injectable sugar. She really bottoms out fast."

I glanced back over and saw that one of the security men who'd helped out earlier with Paul had joined Kirsty at her table. He looked protective and a little nervous, shifting in his chair to accommodate the bulky equipment on his belt, a radio, small baton, mace, and holster. I watched him watch Kirsty for a moment and shook my head. The poor guy had it bad. But then, amazingly, the wedding planner seemed to be encouraging him. I should warn her that dating a lawman could make her break out in a rash.

I turned back to Marie. "She seems like she knows her stuff about diabetes, but I'd feel better if she just checked in with the doctor, you know?" I reached over to beat Marie to a stuffed shrimp. "She totally refused. You'd think I'd asked her to dance on the bar naked for godsake. Embarrassed, I guess." I rolled my eyes. "At least she didn't pee all over herself like old Paul did." I popped the shrimp into my mouth. *Mmm.* Blue cheese and shallots. Marie was wrong, no one could stay anorexic on a cruise. "But at least Paul tried to warn us."

"Well, actually no." Marie fiddled with the zipper on her fanny pack. "Thanks for reminding me. I wanted to show you something."

"No?" I glanced toward the bar and then back quickly when I saw Sam holding a beer and watching me. "What are you talking about? I just meant that poor Paul was trying to tell us that he had to go to the bathroom."

"But he wasn't." Marie fished out a few cheroots, then held up a wadded greasy napkin. "I was wrong. He didn't say, 'Penis.' But you were wrong, too." She waggled the napkin in front of me. "He wasn't saying, 'Pee,' either."

Lord, what was this, a kindergarten show-me-yours conversation? I scrunched my brows and struggled to hear over Patti Ann and Kyle's off-key duet of "I Got You Babe." I was getting a headache. "And your point?"

Marie grinned. "After I lost my money in the casino, I stopped by the infirmary to see how Paul was doing. Fine by the way. And back to normal if you'd call comparing adrenaline to Viagra normal."

She waited as I mimed gagging, and then continued. "Anyway, while he and Dale were having the I-wonder-what-else-Darcy-could-bring-back-to-life discussion, I was talking to the nurse." Marie took a breath and smiled. "Paul's allergic to peanuts. He was saying, 'peanuts.' Apparently not easy when your tongue is swollen like a toad and you can't breathe."

"And what's that?" I pointed to the napkin, and watched as Marie opened it carefully and presented a disgusting brown glob like it was a gold nugget.

"Peanuts." Marie wrinkled her nose. "Sort of chewed up. The nurse must have accidentally picked them up off the floor when she was gathering up the emergency kit."

"Paul was stupid enough to eat peanuts when he knows he's allergic?"

"No." Marie smiled cryptically. "He didn't know he was eating them. I found something else when I was helping the nurse clean up her equipment." She opened the napkin again and lifted something alarmingly finger-sized, and oozing with red onto the table.

"Oh for godsake, what's that?" I grimaced, afraid to know.

"A chewed up Buffalo wing." Marie raised her brows. "Remember when we were looking at the photo wall and Putnam was at the microphone mouthing off about suing the chef because there was metal in his food?"

"Sort of." I leaned forward and squinted down at the Buffalo wing remains as Marie prodded it with a toothpick. I felt like part of a CSI team.

"See that?" Marie pointed to what looked like a short row of mangled . . .

"Staples?"

"Yeah, to hold these babies inside." Marie poked the meat like a coroner with a scalpel, and a couple of tiny peanuts slid out.

My mouth gaped and I almost knocked over my wine. "Oh my God. How . . . ?"

I whirled around and stared at the group of wedding guests clapping and hooting for the bride and groom. "Bunch of sickos. Can you believe it? Who in the hell? I mean blue-dye chewing gum and squirting cameras are one thing, but to take a chance on something like this? What did they think, he'd just break out in hives and scratch and look stupid, or—"

"Or die?"

Behind us, Dale Worley keyed the mike and introduced his next song as the fart machine blasted like a shotgun.

Marie's voice lowered. "I hate to seem like I'm the one jumping to conclusions here this time, Darc', but . . ."

"No. No." I buried my face in my hands. My head throbbed like murder. "I came on this cruise to get a little break." I peeked between my fingers at Marie's face. "And we've been on board for maybe seven hours and already I've had Luke and the ring, a FedEx from Grandma's lawyer, Sam Jamieson rising up like Lazarus, two people to resuscitate, and . . ." I watched Marie dig around in her fanny pack again. "What now?"

Marie tried to smile and I started to itch. "I'm sorry," she said, "but there was one other thing I found. At the cabin."

"No."

Marie set the envelope on the table beside the Buffalo wing. The foot of Hermes sealed its flap.

FIVE

SUNLIGHT FILTERED THROUGH THE gym's window as I slammed my leather glove against the punching bag with a hook that sent it sailing sideways. I righted it with a second hook and a stiff jab. Sweat splashed onto my lips and I sputtered, forcing myself to concentrate on the boxing combinations, mouthing the familiar litany: *"Muscle" it, punch "through" it, control it, feel "bigger than the bag." Concentrate. Got it. Here we go.*

One-two jab, straight right, left hook, right hook. I shifted my weight and delivered a vertical uppercut, feeling the immediate pull in my hamstrings and belly. My dripping ponytail whipped against my neck. Take that, you perverted poet! Petticoats and shoestrings this time. Shoestrings? Who would write a poem about something as stupid as that? But at least it wasn't body parts. I had to believe this was all a stupid joke. Like the fart machine and Paul Putnam's stapled snack. I wasn't going to let any of it rattle me. I jabbed the bag again, then jumped as someone tapped my shoulder from behind. I turned, glove raised.

"Whoa there, easy Rocky. I'm not the enemy." Marie raised her hands in surrender, gray eyes squinting above a sleeveless logo tee shirt, *ER—Where everything is STAT.* "Really. Couldn't give a rat's ass about proposing to you and can't rhyme to save my soul. Innocent. Swear." She pressed her fingers against her eyes and groaned as a breathy chorus rose from the step-aerobics class. "Do they really have to do that?"

I raised my brows and smirked as I struggled to loosen a glove lace with my teeth, tasting salty leather against my lips. "Someone have a little hangover?" I scowled at the stubborn glove, then shook it like a cartoon character stuck to flypaper. I gave up and smacked both gloves together in a thunderclap. "Damn."

"Shit, why don't you just set off a bomb? Here, gimmee." Marie grabbed one of my gloves and went to work at the laces. "And I'm not the only one feeling a little sick this morning." She pulled one glove off and tugged at the laces of the other, pausing to nod toward the gym's far doorway. "Did you see that sorry-ass lineup in the Sports Bar?"

I nodded. I had for sure, at six-thirty, while taming my mermaid-wild hair after a foggy jog on the Promenade Deck. It was ridiculously early, I knew that, but I figured the more I sweated the more macaroni and cheese I could eat. And then move right on to sloppy joes. It was a fair trade. But the groomsmen weren't up at that hour for health reasons, obviously. Marie was right; they'd looked like hell.

I'd taken a short cut through the Sports Bar on the way to the gym, yanking my long curls back into a stretch band as I walked, and was startled to see so many people up that early. Overhead, on a collage of TV screens, soccer and CNN competed with Easy Eggs

Benedict, Composting to Save the Earth, and a regrettable rerun of Katie Couric's Virtual Colonoscopy. But I took a second look around the Sports Bar and realized these folks had simply been there the whole damned night. Didn't take a triage nurse to assess that one.

Tousle-headed firefighters were huddled on barstools beneath a banner-draped replica of a football goalpost, their faces greener than the wall-to-wall AstroTurf. Dale Worley, groomsmen Ed and Ryan, and the legendary Sam Jamieson were all well past shit-faced and way into selling their souls for a cure. Sam had raised his head from the bar, his dark eyes heavy-lidded, and attempted to smile while raking his fingers through his hair. A spiral of hot-pink confetti dropped to his shoulder. I recognized the look, his I've-been-a-naughty-boy smile.

"Yeah," I answered, dropping the boxing gloves and reaching for a towel. "I saw them all right. Pathetic. Offering up all the old cures for a hangover like they were candidates for the Nobel Prize." I rubbed the towel over my neck, taking a few extra swipes over the prickly rash on my chest. "Bloody Marys, aspirin, Alka Seltzer. And Maalox poured into coffee." I grimaced. "But at least Worley was inventive." I sighed. "Of course, first we had to listen to him brag about sedating those armadillos for his car commercial. Then he conjured up a Puerto Rican cure for a hangover."

I rolled my eyes and then lifted one arm like I was applying deodorant. "Half a lemon. Rubbed under your drinking arm." I started to laugh and stumbled over one of my boxing gloves. "Swear. I'm not lying." My voice choked off and I snorted through my nose, my words escaping again in a howl. "Wait, this is a very important part of the tip: rub it clockwise in the Northern Hemisphere. Counterclockwise in the Southern!" I clutched my stomach and howled again.

Marie covered her ears, then smiled weakly and cleared her throat. "Yeah, well, lemon cures weren't all they were discussing."

I glanced away for a second and caught a glimpse of Kirsty Pelham across the room, long legs folded in a Yoga pose. She wore a loose-fitting lilac tunic and leggings, her pale hair swept back with a matching clip, glasses perched on top of her head. Her eyes were closed, inky lashes against fair skin, her face beautifully serene and posture impeccably controlled. I stretched tall and a rivulet of sweat trickled between my breasts, itching like the devil. Maybe the wedding planner had the right idea; boxing could be depolarizing my Karma. I sighed and looked back at Marie, raising my brows. "So? What else were our hungover firemen talking about?"

Marie rubbed her hand across her brows. "Wait a second. Man, I need a cup of coffee. Let's go to the brunch buffet. I'll give you the scoop when my head stops pounding." She reached her arm overhead and tapped her knuckles against the punching bag. "Damn, you need a quieter sport."

I draped the towel over my neck and started to reach for my gloves, then stopped and stared at Marie, my mouth gaping. "What the . . . oh, you *didn't*." My voice rose and I choked on a laugh. I swiped at Marie's armpit and squealed. "Lemon pulp?"

*　*　*

The Lido Deck buffet line was elbow to tray with a crowd of seniors who seemed way more focused on stewed prunes than hangover remedies. The clatter of silverware competed with the swish of zippered rayon loungewear and a waft of Ben Gay followed in

54

its wake. I jockeyed for position and scanned the steaming mile of chafing dishes ahead: link sausage, huevos rancheros omelets, smoked salmon, a pyramid of berries and melons, prime rib, bow-tie pasta with fire-roasted vegetables, and cheeses fanned out like playing cards. Ooh, below a crystal tier of éclairs. I glanced back over my shoulder at Marie. "Hey, did you see that ice sculpture in the middle of the butter pats and yogurt? I think it's supposed to be the Seattle Space Needle."

Marie groaned. "Well hold it against my forehead, would ya?" She paused, raising her coffee to her lips, then frowned as a woman nudged her from behind. "No, really, I'm feeling a little better now." She grinned sheepishly. "Lemon probably kicked in. And by the way, another important tip? Don't try that one right after shaving." Marie stepped to the side and let the impatient woman pass. "Darc', grab me some juice and I'll go find us a table."

I filled a second glass with orange juice and wove my way past potted palms and a gigantic acrylic sculpture toward the glass doors leading to the deck. I took a deep breath and willed my boxing-tight shoulders to relax; this was a cruise, fabulous setting with world-class food and I'd be plain stupid to let a bunch of practical jokers ruin it for me.

I squinted as the automatic doors opened onto the sunny deck and then spotted Marie at a table near the rail. She was wearing her dark glasses and pointing across the deck and one level above. I scanned the ocean, scattered white caps in a gray-green expanse, knowing that we were somewhere off the coast of southern Oregon and another day's sail from Seattle. What the hell was Marie pointing at?

"No, Darc', up there on Promenade Deck. Yeah there, isn't that . . . what's his name?" She scrunched up her brows as I seated myself, now clearly pointing toward a deck chair and its occupant, motionless under a pile of plaid blankets.

I nodded my head. "Right. Gordy something. I finally remembered his name. It was bugging me ever since I saw him on Patti Ann's picture wall—remember, the paramedic beside Worley and the fat girl with the puppy? Long-time friend of Kyle's." I bit into a piece of smoky salmon and moaned. "Mmm. Anyway, I saw him up there this morning when I was jogging. Scared me for a minute. Thought he was dead."

Marie raised her dark glasses and narrowed her eyes at me.

"Okay, fine. Maybe I was jumping to conclusions, but hell, it was barely daylight and foggy, and there he was all sprawled out on the deck chair, wearing shorts for godsake. Can you believe these guys? Lucky he didn't freeze to death." I poked my fork into the yolk of my Eggs Benedict and watched it run like molten gold over the edge of the muffin. "I gave him a nudge and heard him say he was fine. Good God, talk about alcohol breath. Anyway I figured old Gordy was only going to wish he were dead." I shrugged and raised my fork. "So I covered him up with a ton of blankets and left him there."

"He was out there all night?"

"Who knows? But we saw the condition of the rest of the wedding party, right?" I smiled. "Present company excluded of course. But wait, you were going to tell me about the guys in the Sports Bar. Something they were talking about?" I closed my lips over a forkful of lemon-sauced eggs.

Marie slid her glasses down her nose and peered over. "Peanuts."

"What?" I swallowed quickly. "Are you saying someone admitted to feeding Putnam the peanuts?"

"Well, no. Actually the bar steward started it. Saying he'd heard from the medical staff about Paul's allergy. And that they'd been questioning the galley crew about using peanut oil when the Buffalo wings were prepared. They all denied it." Marie smiled. "Worley was keen on that idea apparently. Offered to check with his attorney to see if Paul could sue somebody."

"So you're saying no one knows about the actual peanuts?"

"Only us." Marie pushed her glasses back up her nose. "And the person who put them in there, of course."

"You mean stapled them in there." I poked at a caper with my fingertip and watched it disappear under a slice of salmon. "I've been thinking about that. The staples. No one's admitting anything, but it still had to be some sort of practical joke, right? Staples aren't exactly subtle. If someone wanted to kill Paul Putnam they wouldn't do something so obvious. So, it had to be a dumbass prank. To be sure and get noticed."

"No one's admitting it."

I smiled and picked up my orange juice glass. "Would you? After it ended so scary? And remember, no one admits to owning that fart machine, either." I rolled my eyes. "So I've decided we won't allow these idiots to ruin our trip." I'd started to take a sip of the juice when a hand patted my shoulder from behind.

"There y'all are." Patti Ann drawled, smiling and holding onto Kyle's hand. She tugged at my ponytail before plunking into a chair beside Marie and peering into her face. "Well, my Ga-awd, you don't look half bad, Whitley. From what I heard just now I thought you'd be 'bout as useless as tits on a boar."

I stifled a laugh as Marie swore under her breath.

"Oh, never mind, girls," Patti Ann cooed, waving her hands and then moving her chair so that Kyle could squeeze in. "It was just one of Worley's tall tales, right darlin'?" She leaned toward Kyle and rested her hand on his arm, her diamond solitaire sparkling in the sunlight.

I rubbed at my collarbone and tried not to think of an antique dresser in an apartment in San Francisco. With a velvet jewelry box under a stack of boxers. I watched Kyle's big hand cover Patti Ann's gently, his hazel eyes softening. Did Luke look at me that way?

"Worley said something about Marie and a lemon," he said quietly, after clearing his throat. His forehead flushed pink beneath a thatch of sun-streaked hair and he fidgeted, rearranging his long legs under the table, like he'd be far more comfortable straddling one of those bulls he'd ridden at the Salinas Rodeo. Was that just last July? Yes, that was when Patti Ann had first met him; in the back of an ambulance, his own fractured wrist tied up with a dusty bandanna so he could tend a youngster trampled in a trailer accident.

Patti Ann had been the first one to sign Kyle's cast, with a little smiley face beside her name and a telephone number lettered boldly beneath. Permanent marker. Open invitation to pecan pie and much, much more. I smiled, remembering how Patti Ann loved to brag that Kyle still had that cast, hanging on the wall over his bed, right next to his spurs. And now, less than a year later, they were getting married. Married. What made her able to take a risk like that?

Patti Ann grabbed my hand. "You're scratchin' like crazy, sweetie, and I know just the cure." She pointed toward the glass doors of the dining area. Beside them, inside a Plexiglas frame, was one of the huge, stylized ads for the Personal Training Team. Bare legs and feet against a backdrop of crimson, shining with the reflection of the morning sun. "That's why I came to find you two, to remind you of our spa date, and the acupressure treatment from the Personal Training Team." She squeezed my fingers. "Sauna, massage, aromatherapy, pedicure, and mimosas. Now doesn't that sound like just what every nurse needs, a little personal TLC for a change?"

Patti Ann glanced around for a moment. "Kirsty's around here somewhere, carryin' that Palm Pilot like it was the Holy Bible and trying to round everyone up. Not easy. With Paul checkin' out too early from the infirmary and you jogging around the decks in the fog." She shook her head. "The 'boys' are flopped all over the Sports Bar and we still haven't found Gordy Simons—" She stopped as Marie raised her arm and pointed. "What?"

"Up there." Marie pointed toward the plaid lump in the deck chair above us.

"Oh my Lord." Patti Ann sighed. "Well, I feel sorry for Kirsty, really. She's used to society parties; doubt she's ever planned an event for such a rowdy group." She shook her head. "She's probably thinkin' we should have just hired some damned rodeo clown." Her dimples deepened and she smiled back at Kyle, cheeks rosy pink. "Sorry, darlin', I didn't mean anything against rodeos."

"So how'd you find Kirsty anyway?" I asked.

Patti Ann beamed. "Well that's the miracle part, really, she found us and—"

A wail like the howl of a wounded animal split the air overhead and the passengers at the tables around us leaped to their feet, scattering silverware and overturning a chair. The wailing continued and people began to point to the Promenade Deck above. I wedged myself between the bride and groom and stared upward.

Gordy Simons was stooped over, screaming like he was gutshot. We headed for the stairs at a run.

He was wearing neon-pink skater shorts, and stood hunched beside the deck chair with both hands buried in his crotch and one skinny leg hiked up like a flamingo. He flinched as I knelt and stretched my arm toward him.

"Hey, Gordy, let go so I can have a look at you." I reached toward his clenched fingers and then glanced back up at his face. His skin was fish-belly white against his red hair, upper lip dotted with perspiration. He choked back a gag and moaned again, pupils enormous with pain and fear. I softened my voice to pediatric-ward gentle. What was going on with this guy? "It's okay, Gordy. I'm a nurse, remember? Marie and Patti Ann are here, too. Can you give us a clue?"

He moaned again and then wobbled sideways, still flexing one leg high. Patti Ann reached out to steady him. "Bellyache, hon'? Ate a bad clam maybe?" She turned to me and whispered. "Let's get him to lie back down until they get the stretcher here. I'm afraid he'll faint."

Marie stepped forward and Gordy shrieked, throwing himself off balance again. "Nooo!" His eyes were wide with terror. "Don't move me—God, *don't*!"

"What the . . . ?" Marie raised her brows at me. "Kidney stone?"

I bit my lower lip. "Doubt it. Those usually make people pace around. He won't budge an inch. I'm thinking maybe a hot appendix?"

Marie shook her head. "He's holding his crotch, not his belly." She bent down and peered into Gordy's face. "What hurts when you move?"

Gordy swallowed hard and his eyes darted toward the small group of assembled passengers, then back at Marie. "It's my . . . it's stuck." He whispered, eyes rolling upward and suddenly showing way too much white.

"He's gonna faint, I told y'all. Grab on!" Patti Ann thrust her arm around Gordy's waist while Marie and I reached for his arms.

"Here, try this." Kirsty Pelham sliced through the crowd and lifted something from her tote bag. She paused to brush her hair back, then held a tiny white object outstretched like it was a remote control. "Might help." She pressed her thumb down and there was a gritty pop. Tears sprang to my eyes, burning as the acrid scent of ammonia rose like a mushroom cloud.

"Smelling salts," Kirsty said, her tone matter of fact. "Never know when you'll need them at a wedding."

"Oh for crissake!" Marie waved her away, coughing.

I moved aside and Kyle stepped forward. He knelt down, his face inches from Gordy's. "I'm here, Bud, what's going on?"

Gordy moaned, eyeing Kyle like he'd found someone speaking his language at last. "Oh God. You gotta help me, Kyle." He shook his head. "I think maybe it's Super Glue or something. Damn. Can't scrape it off, can't move."

I saw him grab a fistful of Kyle's shirt, his voice lowering to a tortured whisper. "Someone glued my dick to my leg."

SIX

THE DEAFENING THWOOP-THWOOP OF the Med-Evac helicopter faded to a soft flutter and I squinted at the sky, watching Gordy Simons disappear. Along with Ed, the groomsman, who—pale-faced with worry, and maybe guilt—had ducked low under the rotor blades to crawl aboard with him. All the guys had looked that way, standing like defrocked court jesters outside the infirmary, hungover, queasy and squeezing their eyes shut against Gordy's terrified screams. The male component of the wedding guests were going down like bowling pins. I shook my head. But, on a positive note, I seriously doubted there would be further problems with staples and peanuts or wayward glue. Men took crotch trauma very seriously. And who knew, maybe even a poet could be subject to a reality check of that magnitude.

I pinched a strand of my shower-damp hair through my fingers and glanced over at Marie. "Let's hope they have a good urologist on call in Portland. And maybe a plastic surgeon, too. Gordy did some serious damage trying to unstick himself." I groaned under my breath. "How could one of these guys possibly think that squirting Super Glue in someone's shorts would be harmless? How?"

Marie set her gym bag down on the deck and fished around in her fanny pack. The ship swayed beneath her and she widened her stance, quickly retrieving a cigar. "Because they were drunk and Gordy was too wasted to care." She shook her head and flicked her Volkswagen lighter, sparks flying. "The irony is that Gordy's famous for stupid stunts himself."

Marie touched the flame to her cheroot and took a drag. She exhaled and rolled her eyes. "At least that's what I heard. That Gordy was the one who rigged the squirting toilet at the firehouse. The time we ended up treating one of the guys for Tidy Bowl Eye?"

I smiled, remembering. "Sam."

"Sam rigged it?"

"No. It was Sam's eye." And that was how we'd met.

It had been one of those awful days in the ER; a family of seven barfing venison stew into sixties-era Tupperware; the new trauma surgeon throwing a temper tantrum and a Number Eleven scalpel; plus one more "Code Brown" than the backordered adult diapers could mercifully handle. Volunteering for the "quickie eye case in Treatment Room Three," had sounded like the best bet to me, something little and easy that would give me a moment to catch my breath. Fat chance. Firefighter Sam hadn't been little or easy, and he'd taken my breath away the instant I opened the door.

At six-foot four, some two hundred forty plus pounds, Sam Jamieson had been almost too big to fit on the treatment room gurney. He'd straddled it instead, curly headed and bare-chested, one huge paw holding a dripping compress to his face. His uncovered eye was as dark and mournful as a St. Bernard puppy's when he greeted me with an embarrassed grin. He'd staunchly defended Gordy, insisting that his co-worker only meant it to be a harmless prank. And then I'd had to bite my lip hard to keep from laughing as Sam described the attack by the toilet, stooping and miming and making a red-faced fool of himself. In the end, we'd both crumpled side-by-side on the gurney and simply howled. I'd needed the laugh more than I knew and my tension drained away for the first time in hours. Sam talked about being new to the area, how he was filling in for a firefighter out on medical leave . . . and then when I finally leaned over to put the anesthetic drops into his eye I was caught completely off guard. My skin flushed and, for the first time in my career, I was suddenly and unprofessionally way too aware of my patient's face—lashes, nose, warm breath, and lips just inches from mine. And how Sam's skin smelled like an intriguing blend of musk and smoke and—I turned as Marie nudged my arm. "Oh, sorry, what?"

"I said that now I remember the Tidy Bowl Eye thing was Sam." Marie lifted her gym bag and tilted her head, peering up at me. "Hey, Jamieson popping up on this cruise isn't a problem for you is it?"

I pried my fingers from the rail. "God, no."

Marie watched my face for a moment and sighed. "Good. Just didn't want to find you somewhere with your head in a bowl of macaroni and cheese. Anyway, let's head on to the spa. You brought those forms you need, right?"

I lifted my tote and followed Marie down the deck. "Forms?"

"The release forms, the ones the Personal Training Team wanted."

"Oh, yeah. I thought you meant the fax for Grandma's attorney; still have to send that. Remind me, okay?" I raised my brows. "So why do these guys need release forms anyway? Last time I checked, foot rubs weren't in the same class as neurosurgery."

Marie paused and pointed to a poster beside the spa door ahead of us. A man and woman's legs, calves-to-toes in an almost airborne jog along the sand, tan and muscled and the epitome of health. "They've got a big promo going and our," Marie wrinkled her nose, "ever-re-sourceful wedding planner got the freebie only if we all agreed to publicity photos. You remember her spiel, a couple of weeks ago?"

"Oh, yeah." I frowned as Marie reached for the door handle. "Great. We're foot models. But what can you do?"

"Not shave my legs."

"What?" I saw a smile spread across Marie's face and watched as she stubbed her little cheroot into the ashtray outside the spa door.

"For two weeks." Marie's gray eyes danced. "Isn't that what everyone wants in an eight by ten glossy, a forty-year-old lesbian with legs like a woolly mammoth?"

*　*　*

The pool area of the Sea Spray Spa was awash with sunlight through a canopy of glass. A dozen leafy ficus trees, their braided trunks in shell-encrusted urns, rose skyward casting shadows across those of us stretched out on green-and-white striped lounges below. We were clustered in small groups, the areas divided for privacy by marble sculptures of sea nymphs and mossy planters filled with red, pink, and white cyclamens. Steam rose from the crystal blue water, a skin-quenching humidity that made the panes overhead cloudy as old sea glass. *Unbelievable.* I leaned back on my chaise, still wanting to pinch myself. Kirsty was right: nurses definitely need this kind of R and R. I was going to speak to our hospital recruiter. She'd get a lot more bites if cruises were part of the hire-on package. This was definitely making me forget my troubles.

Classical music drifted from hidden speakers as I reached for a second mimosa. I thanked the spa steward before turning back to tug at the hem of Marie's shorts. I wrinkled my nose. "I still can't believe your legs. You looked like a damned porcupine."

"Better than looking like a foot model." Marie squinted as I shook the contents of a tiny zip-lock bag into my palm. "What's that, your itch pills?"

I took a swig of the orangey-sweet champagne and shook my head after I swallowed. "No. Gingko biloba." I popped a slippery capsule onto my tongue then took another sip. "And vitamin E." I frowned. "Damn, forgot the folic acid. I'm trying to take one of those every day, too."

Marie raised her brows. "So what's with this medicine chest all of a sudden?"

I sighed. "Grandma. They're not sure if Alzheimer's is hereditary, or . . ." The familiar ache rose in my throat and I cleared it away with a laugh. "What's that joke, anyway? 'I forgot when the Alzheimer's group meets'?"

"Right. How's that stuff with Rosaleen's retirement home going, anyway?"

"Going?" My fingers tightened on the champagne stem, my lips tensed and my voice rose way louder than I'd intended. So much for being relaxed. "Well it's not Grandma that's *going* anywhere. Not if I can help it!"

Heads turned my way and I saw, through a row of cyclamens, that Kirsty Pelham occupied one of the chaises adjacent to ours. Great, now I'd have the perfect wedding planner lecturing me on spa decorum. I lowered my voice and turned back to Marie. "Sorry."

"Nothing to be sorry about. So what's new there?"

I glanced through the cyclamens. Kirsty had donned sunglasses and pulled a straw hat low over her forehead, suddenly absorbed with breaking a piece of dry toast into microscopic fragments. I bet she thought a Sloppy Joe was just some guy who left the toilet seat up.

"Aw, hell," I said with a sigh, "the pathetic part is that Grandma never wanted to go there in the first place." I remembered the way I'd kept talking up the idea about the care home and she looked at me like I'd just run over her cat. "But now it's been what . . . six months? Six months and she's wild about that place, loves the people, the activities—she's painting, Marie! Kittens and sort of . . . petunias, I think." I shook my head.

"But . . ."

"But what?"

"But it's assisted living, not full-care. They've got these rules about being responsible with your belongings, medication, and stuff." I rolled my eyes and sighed. "Can't exactly be passing things out to the other residents."

"Passing things out?" Marie raised her brows.

I sighed again, and then lay back on the lounge with a moan. I'd only found this whole thing out last week. "Grandma was a nurse like forever, right?"

"So?"

"So she loves these other residents. Wants to help them. And nurses are pretty free with medical advice."

"Right, and . . . ?"

I groaned again and squeezed my eyes shut. "And at work, nurses pass out medications."

Marie's brows headed north. "Oh God. Medications? Wait, I thought your Dad was taking her meds to her. So she didn't have bottles lying around."

I pressed my fingers to my eyes. "She doesn't have any med bottles. But you remember Goldie, that huge goldfish she has? The fish that Grandpa Charlie won at the Fire Hall fair when I was ten?"

Marie's expression was skewed with confusion. "Yeah, that grew into an ugly fifteen inches—bloated, scruffy scales and one cloudy eye. Your grandma feeds it scrambled eggs sometimes. Where are you going with this, Darc'?"

I downed the last of my mimosa in a single gulp, welcoming the sudden surge of wooziness. I stared into Marie's eyes. "A big fish that eats big pellets. Koi pellets?" I moaned again. "That might look sort of like . . . pills."

"Holy shit!" Marie bolted upright on her chaise. "You're not saying—"

"Yep, my grandma's been making daily medication rounds at the care home. Dispensing medical advice and fish food."

I stood as the speaker overhead crooned my name for the second time. "And now it looks like it's my turn for a foot rub, thank God."

*　*　*

Forty-five minutes later, I drained a fourth mimosa and stretched my bare foot into the reflexologist's palm with a soft moan. I wondered if the monklike Chinese man had any clue that my big toe was orgasmic. *Aaah.* It felt so great. A brilliant de-stresser. I had to hand it to our wedding planner; this Spa Day was perfect.

After a sauna, massage, facial, and pedicure, my life was sliding magically back into perspective. Poetry, fish food, Super Glue, stapled Buffalo wings, Sam Jamieson's puppy dog eyes, and the whole freaking boxer-shorted FBI—who gave a rip? Right now there were just palm fronds, ginger incense, mandolin music in my earphones, and a combination of ten fingers on ten toes that was better than sex. Okay, almost. But only if Luke played the mandolin.

Goose bumps rose as the monk pressed an oily thumb into my arch and slid it gently downward. Oh yes. Signing the release for the photos had been so worth it. I glanced down at the array of cameras mounted on foot-tall tripods at my feet. Silly, really. Photos of feet for godsake. Even the stupid snake was no big deal.

"So it's a magnet, right?" I pulled the earphone away and raised my left foot, eyeing the metallic serpent twined around my ankle. Its enameled body gleamed in the candlelight, crimson tongue licking my skin like Cleopatra's asp.

The reflexologist raised his head and peered through thick, oil-smudged glasses. "Miss?"

I pointed toward a poster on the wall, next to a maplike foot diagram, and then back at the snake on my leg. "It says that therapeutic mud and magnet therapy are part of the treatment."

"No, miss." The reflexologist pressed a fingertip into the flesh of my foot and began his whispered inventory of corresponding organ sites. "Gallbladder, liver, solar plexus, and this is your kidney, miss."

I fought a shudder. I hated that Hannibal Lecter thing. But what did this man mean about the snake? I sat upright in the recliner and my head floated for a moment. Whoa. Champagne.

"It's not a magnet? Then why did you put that snake thing on my leg?" I raised my fingers to my collarbone and scratched. I was getting another funny feeling, too.

"Sorry, miss, it was for the photographers." The Chinese man held my foot gently by the heel and gestured across the floor with his free hand. "The same as the other things. Props, they said. From a list. You remember, miss, the fur skin, teddy bear . . ." the little man hesitated, clucking his tongue like he was a teacher erasing chalkboard obscenities. "The pudding."

Pudding? My face flamed and I sat up, sliding my foot from the little man's hand. The snake pinched like a Boa. Inside my headset, the mandolin music had evolved into soft drumming, then a voice reciting . . . *poetry?* Was that poetry?

I yanked the earphones away and stared down at the forest of tripods next to a hill of faux fur, stuffed animals, the bowl of congealed brown slop. And a can of whipped cream? Where the hell did the whipped cream come from? What was going on here?

My voice raised an octave. "Pudding? Not therapeutic mud? I had my feet in pudding?"

The Chinese man rocked back on his haunches and sighed. "Chocolate, miss."

*   *   *

Dale Worley stepped out of the Business Berth Computer Room as Marie and I entered. He shifted an armful of glossy brochures and leaned against the door, licking his lips. "Looking good there, Cavanaugh. I told Jamieson that he's one lucky bugger."

"Excuse me?" I attempted to move backward and only succeeded in stepping on Marie's foot. I apologized, then turned back to Dale. "Just what are you trying to say, Dale?" Hell, this was the last thing I needed; one more run in with one more pervert. I just wanted to fax the papers off to my grandmother's lawyer.

70

"You mean about how hot you look?" Dale fingered a tip of his handlebar moustache. "Or you mean about your old boyfriend?" His breath was pungent with a combination of stale alcohol and breath mints, and a single droplet of spit glistened on his lower lip. He grinned down at me.

I narrowed my eyes and Marie squeezed between us like a referee.

"Don't you have some animals to go torture, Worley?" She tapped a fingertip against the photos in his arms. "Oh, sorry, I meant cars to sell, of course. Honest mistake."

Dale laughed and pulled a photo from the stack. "I wanted a rhino. Now that's an animal with balls. But they're expensive, and with the economy the way it is . . ." He shook his head and pointed to the photo. "Damned thing about armadillos—don't really roll up in a ball like a sow bug. Won't try to bite, no matter how many times you pry their stupid mouths open." He shook his head again. "Shit, but the claws . . . they're sonofabitch diggers." He frowned down at the photo. "Scratched the hell out of the hoods of two Hummers."

He held the picture up in front of my face. Two armored creatures teetering on the hood of the vehicle, one wearing a tiny pith helmet and the other—a baby I guessed—turning its little head to the side and in obvious distress. Its eyes were closed and it had a huge stogy wedged between its lips.

"But we got the goods." Dale rolled his eyes and laughed. "Oh, 'and absolutely no animals were injured in the making of this ad.' Says so right there in tiny print, see?" He laughed again. "Except for the little one that couldn't hold his sedatives, of course. Pissant wimp. He's going to make a great ashtray for my desk."

"You, you—" I growled and balled my hands into fists as my mind raced with images from every PETA rally Mom had ever dragged me to. She was going to be so damned proud of me. But before I could blast him, Dale's cell phone rang and he turned away, answering it.

I tossed Marie a look that said it all. *We're gonna kill him, right?*

"Well," Dale closed the little phone and tucked the stack of photos under his arm. "Need to go get my tux fitted, ladies. Formal night tonight." He smiled down at me. "Still think it's the shits that Kyle picked Jamieson as a replacement for Ed after that whole thing with Gordy's pecker getting pasted. Hell, I thought I'd look pretty good walking you down the aisle." He leaned forward and ran his tongue up over his mustache, inhaling deeply. "But anyway, save a dance for me tonight, honey. I never could resist a woman who smells like chocolate." He winked, then turned and stepped through the doorway, calling back over his shoulder. "Good enough to eat."

I stared at the closed door, first sputtering and then completely speechless. My hands were trembling and my stomach roiled against one too many mimosas. I opened my mouth, then closed it again and turned back to Marie. "I swear I'll kill him."

Marie leaned her elbow against the oversize shredder and shook her head, smiling slowly. "He's right, you know."

"What?"

"You smell like a Moon Pie."

I ran my hand across my eyes and sighed. "Jeez, that spa deal was so humiliating. Are you sure they didn't photograph anyone else's feet?"

Marie shook her head. "Nope. I asked. Not even the bride. No one else had their foot on a teddy bear's tummy, dug their toes into mink, wore a snake—"

"Don't." I raised my hand. "Please. If I think about snakes again, I'll puke. Let's just fax these things off to the lawyer." I sorted through

72

the folder and pulled out a sheet of paper, then tapped my fingers against it. "See this? Brilliant if I do say so myself. Got the data off the Internet; the complete nutritional analysis of koi food. Do you know how much crude protein is in plankton?" I smiled at Marie. "Grandma Rosaleen was doing those old folks a favor. She should charge them."

I placed the paper down on the machine, punched in the number and then glanced back at Marie. Her brows were furrowed like she was thinking about something and then she shook her head. She looked up at me with a half smile. "Your foot photo mystery was second on the list today."

"What do you mean?"

"Guess we had one more unexplained bit of weirdness. This morning, or maybe last night to be more accurate . . ." She paused.

"Hey, just tell me," I grumbled, battling mimosa queasiness. "What else could go wrong anyway? I've been humiliated by snakes and pudding, sexually harassed by a car dealer, and now I find out I'm being paired up with Sam—"

"Staples," Marie said simply.

"Huh?"

"I was talking to Patti Ann and Kyle while you were getting chocolate coated and . . ."

"And what?"

"There were staples stuck in Gordy Simon's thigh."

SEVEN

MARIE POKED A FINGERTIP into the back of my mango satin gown and I turned, causing my stick-on bra to bite into my tattoo. "What?"

She frowned. "I'm wondering why we're down here looking at Patti Ann's baby pictures while everyone else is heading for lobster thermidor." Marie tugged at her glitter-edged bow tie. "Not that I'll be able to swallow in this getup, anyway." She bit her lip and then grinned, eyes blinking back laughter. "The cummerbund's squeezin' me like a damned *python*."

I socked the shoulder of her tuxedo pantsuit and narrowed my eyes. "No more snake jokes, dammit. And if you order chocolate pudding for dessert, I swear I'll—"

"You'll what, staple me?" Marie shook her head and I heard her stomach growl.

I sighed and turned back to the party room photo wall, my fingers following the stiff fin of twisted crepe paper. I tapped my fingernail against the metal bits that held it in place. Staples. Hundreds of them, really. I scanned the wall: staples clumped together in the river of crepe like silvery logjams. More staples than were necessary for the job, that was for sure. Hadn't Kirsty recruited a bunch of the guys to do this photo wall for her? Probably even loaned them the equipment out of her sexy pink tool belt.

I glanced over at Marie. "Guess it does sound stupid, but I keep thinking something's weird about all this. Remember how Patti Ann almost tripped over that big pink stapler on the floor?" I touched the edge of a photo. "And it looks like someone had way more fun than he should've doing this. Kind of overkill."

Marie lifted her padded shoulders in a shrug. "And your point?" She shook her head. "They're men, Darc'. The whole 'more power' chromosome thing. How many power tool disasters have we stitched up in the ER?"

"So you think Gordy accidentally stapled himself?"

"Hey, the poor kid was too juiced to feel someone gluing the family jewels."

I nodded and tugged at a wavy tendril of my upswept hair, letting my eyes travel over the patchwork of photographs. It was a nice idea, really, Kirsty's collage of friends, histories, and families. Blended families. A big part of marriage, no getting around that. I bit my lip and tried to imagine a picture quilt of the Cavanaughs and the Skylers. My family and Luke's. Three generations of Skyler men; same name, same law school, same intense blue eyes, and identical all-consuming ambitions. The kind of drive that made Luke want to run for Virginia State Senate a few years down the road. *Good God.* And then there were the Skyler women—hoop-skirted and magnolia-bred—their perfectly matched smiles like strands of antebellum pearls; gracious and strong and so amazingly sure of themselves. How did someone get that way?

I glanced up at the bridal side of the photo wall. And my family? I scraped my teeth across my lower lip again and tried to smile. Didn't work. My side would be a crazy quilt all right. Starting right from the top. Dad. Bill "the Bug Man" Cavanaugh, in his rubber boots, goggles, and coveralls, brandishing an organic pesticide sprayer as if it were a submachine gun. And Mom, a novice nun-turned-blackjack-dealer. And then my brothers, paleontologist Chance Cavanaugh—if you could track him down in a dusty hole in some third-world country; and the baby, Will, who'd finally completed his bachelor's degree. Although I didn't want to be the one to tell Judge Skyler II that it was from Disneyland University— and that now Will's decided his true calling lies somewhere inside an enormous Goofy costume. And then there's Grandma Rosaleen, of course. Fish Food Entrepreneur. I groaned under my breath. My family and Luke's. West Coast and East. Liberal and Conservative. Oil and water. No, worse than oil and water—Jamba Juice and juleps. That about said it all. It could never work and I couldn't risk trying. I pressed my fingertips to my eyes and then looked back at the bride's photo wall. Sweet idea, though. For someone else.

I pointed at a firehouse photo and tapped my finger against Paul Putnam's grinning face. "So you think our staple-happy Gordy might have cooked up the peanut thing, too?"

Marie reached into her pocket, pulled out a cheroot and stepped closer. "Maybe." She touched the tip of the unlit cigar to the photo. "But then again, look at this group. Like a police lineup: Putnam, Gordy, Dale Worley, Sam . . . the whole group, nothing but trouble." She tapped the dalmatian puppy in the photo. "Except for the dog." Marie paused and furrowed her brows. "Who's the girl? She looks kind of familiar, but . . ." she frowned. "My memory's going. Maybe I need some of that gingko, too."

I leaned forward to study the photo. I recognized the setting, of course; the fire house engine room, used brick, heavy beams, pairs of boots lined up on a waxed cement floor below pegs holding hats and jackets. Yes. I could even remember the smell, like soot and diesel fuel and day-old chili beans.

I took another look at the heavyset young woman's face. Frizzy dark hair, double chin, and thick bangs. "Yeah, wait." I squeezed my eyes shut for a moment, then looked back at her oversized firefighter's turnout coat and arms full of squirming puppy. Blue eyes. "I've seen her, too." I glanced at Paul Putnam's arm around her shoulders and compared their features. Not quite, but maybe. "Paul's daughter, I think."

"Wearing firefighting gear?"

"Probably 'Take Your Daughter to Work Day.'" I rolled my eyes. "Don't even get me started on how it feels to crawl under a house to set Have-a-Heart Rat Traps."

"Paul's daughter?" Marie shook her head. "Don't know why I'd ever have met her. Are you sure we didn't know her from the hospital or—"

I tapped my watch and yelped. "Oh blast!"

"What?"

"We're supposed to make the first dinner seating so we can be out in time to change our clothes for the wedding photos." I groaned. "Where I'll be standing next to Sam. Anyway, c'mon."

I lifted the hem of my dress, started off and then stopped to glance back at the photo wall one more time. Even from a distance the silvery lines of staples were obvious. And, come to think of it, there'd been a lot more added *after* Gordy Simons was helicopter-ed off the ship. The single spotlight shining on the engagement photo caught my eye: Kyle with a Western dress shirt and carefully combed hair, stooping down to rest his cheek against a smiling Patti Ann's. Hopeful, committed, and so certain. Both of them. I squinted my eyes and let my gaze go a little blurry, just for the hell of it, to imagine my face smiling there in an engagement photo next to Luke's.

"Hey! I thought we were in a hurry here." Marie tugged at my elbow. "What are you staring at?"

"Nothing." My vision snapped back to twenty-twenty. Maybe clearer. Me, engaged? No way.

I followed Marie toward the elevator, thinking about Patti Ann and Kyle and how they were so much braver than I was. And the more I thought about them, the more convinced I became about something. I walked on for a minute, and then called out to the back of Marie's hustling tuxedo. "Hey, I was just thinking that Patti Ann and Kyle have something pretty rare, you know?"

She nodded and beckoned to me without turning, and I hur-ried to catch up with her, thinking about Patti and Kyle and Kirsty and all the crap they'd been going through. By the time Marie stopped at the elevator, my rash was itching and I was pissed about the whole thing. There was something I couldn't figure out yet about the pranks and the staples and . . . maybe those photos we'd just seen. But I was going to, dammit. Marie took one look at my face and moaned.

"What?" She asked, flinching. "Not that I really want to know. The last time I saw that look, you had me setting fire to my cow socks—right before I got hauled away by the FBI."

"Dammit, Marie," I said, reaching up to scratch my collarbone. "We're not going to let some office supply kamikaze make any more waves on Patti Ann's wedding cruise!"

*　*　*

The Treasure Trove Dining Room was on Promenade Deck and when we stepped from the glass elevator into the foyer, my ankle strap heels sank like the Titanic in the thick carpeting. I followed Marie down the hallway toward the double doors of the dining room under an archway encrusted with gold coins and faux jewels. A suit of armor, complete with bronze helmet, stood guard at the entrance as stiff as rigor mortis. The doors were open and I heard the familiar clatter of silverware and tinkle of crystal blending with—*jeez, what was this?* Marie stopped in front of me, seeing it at the same instant that I did: Kirsty Pelham standing in the doorway, face strangely stony, staring at us. It was uncharacteristic and weird.

She was wearing a pewter gray gown of moiré silk, its rippled sheen silvery as an icicle. A semi-sheer jacket in the same shade topped the dress, the whole effect elegant, controlled, and icy-cool. She'd pulled her pale hair back from her face, making her look like some gaunt, untouchable Norse queen. And so totally pissed.

Marie cleared her throat and walked faster. I smiled and waved, watching the wedding planner's face for a response. Nothing. Why wasn't she smiling for godsake? I waggled my fingers again as we approached and elbowed Marie to do the same. Kirsty responded by crossing her arms, her posture stiffer than the suit of armor in the doorway beside her. She touched the frame of her dark-rimmed glasses, then glared through them. Her voice hissed between too-white teeth, the effort making a vein rise on her forehead.

"Do you have any idea," she said, poking her wristwatch with a pale finger. "How very humiliating it is to arrange toasts to the bride and groom and then be missing something as important as my bridesmaids?" The corner of her mouth twitched as her eyes riveted to mine.

"I, um . . ." My voice was lost in a swallow and I glanced sideways at Marie. *Help.*

"We're sorry. We . . ." Marie shrugged like a kid unsure of the rules.

"Stop, stop!" Kirsty raised her hand to her forehead, fingers trembling very slightly. "You don't understand. It's just that I thought . . . no, I *planned* it all out very carefully, every minute. So you'd have plenty of time to do everything you wanted to today." She paused and bit her lower lip, her eyes glistening behind the heavy lenses and suddenly filling with tears. "The pressure to get it all right, timed just right, and keep on a schedule to do what I have to do . . ." She looked down at her wristwatch again, her face blanching. Sweat glistened on her upper lip. "Now dinner is late, late, late."

Dinner? Food. Oh Lord, the diabetes!

I raised my eyebrows at Marie and she nodded, then we both reached for Kirsty's elbows and hustled her into the dining room. The woman needed food fast, or in a few minutes I'd be digging that sugar injection kit out of her purse.

"You're doing a wonderful job, Kirsty," I said, hoping like crazy she didn't pass out. "Totally the best. And we're really sorry we're late. So sorry." I glanced up at the wedding planner's pale face and scooted faster toward the table. "And eating is a wonderful idea too, for you, for us, for everyone."

Marie nodded. "Right away, STAT."

* * *

Within thirty minutes the first course plates had been whisked away and the wine steward was filling the glasses for a second time. I stole a quick sideways glance at Kirsty and breathed a sigh of relief as she slid the familiar PDA from her beaded bag. A soft blush of color had spread across the wedding planner's beautiful cheeks and her expression was once again confident, controlled. I smiled. She was back on schedule. And I was twice as determined that there weren't going to be any more screw-ups to rattle this poor woman, including my own. Kirsty Pelham worked damned hard at what she did and I had to admire that. I felt exactly the same way about my career.

I bit my lower lip. Thankfully, no one else had noticed the earlier problem with her low blood sugar. This woman's need for dignity and control was as obvious as her black-framed eyeglasses. I fought a sudden image of my grandma being evicted from her retirement home. Dignity. Everyone deserved at least that much. *Your secret's safe with me, wedding planner.*

I turned my head back as an explosion of laughter erupted across the table. Not that anyone else had any dignity. Whatsoever. But at least I had my staple suspects all lined up. I leaned forward to scan the table.

Patti Ann and Kyle were seated at the end, cheek to cheek, reading over their personalized wedding vows; Marie was next to her partnered groomsman, slightly built and soft-spoken firefighter

Ryan Galloway. Their tuxedoes were almost comically similar. And, across the table, silver-haired Paul Putnam, none the worse for his deadly peanut encounter, was crumpled, red-faced with laughter next to that disgusting—

Sam nudged my arm. "So do you think Worley has any idea that the end of his tie is dangling in his Scotch?" He shook his head. "Shit, do you see that jerk?"

I had been trying very hard not to. From the moment I sat down opposite Dale, I'd avoided his eyes and the blinding sheen off his disco blue tuxedo. What was with the tie, anyway—country-western bolo? The slide on the string tie was hammered silver in an unusual shape and studded with tiny stones. What was it supposed to be? *No.* I wasn't going to look and certainly wasn't going to give him the satisfaction of asking, either. I'd ignore it, just the way I ignored the way he'd sucked the appetizer oysters from their shells and let the juice dribble down his chin while leering at every woman within pawing range. Disgusting pig. And Sam was right; the silver-tipped ends of the mystery tie were definitely hanging down into Dale's tumbler of Scotch. Just how many of those had he drunk anyway?

"I'm trying not to," I said with a sigh, leaning back so that the waiter could set my entrée down. Fresh bay scallops in a creamy sauce with wine and mushrooms, inside a sort of golden puff pastry shaped like a little crab with claws. Sloppy joes could wait.

"You're trying not to what?" The sleeve of Sam's tuxedo jacket brushed across my bare arm.

"Trying not to notice Dale's stupid tie, or the fake Super Bowl rings, or . . ." I shook my head and raised my eyes to meet Sam's, hating it that my face flushed. *Or you, Jamieson. I'm trying not to notice you, either.*

I raised my glass of chardonnay and took a sip, watching him over the rim. Sam in a tux? Amazing. How had the ship's valet service managed to find a jacket to stretch over those shoulders? Must have been like squeezing a linebacker into Marie's vintage VW bug. I glanced away from his eyes, set my glass down and lowered my voice. "Don't know why Dale's even here at all. It's not like he's one of Kyle's real friends."

"No." Sam rubbed his fingertips together and winked. "But his dealership makes donations to Community Services. Big donations. Doubt they'd taken Worley on as a volunteer firefighter otherwise."

"And the wedding invitation was posted, of course." I inhaled softly and ignored my body's response to the soap and warm musk scent of Sam's skin. I'd been down that road and I wasn't going back. "By the way, is that why you're here? You saw the flyer on a visit to the station, or did they send you an invitation?" I watched his hand as he reached for his napkin. Left hand. No wedding ring. *And was your little wife invited, too?*

"Neither." Sam's brows drew together. His expression was a mix of confusion and . . . I watched the color of his face deepen. He was blushing. What was the matter with him?

"Then how?" I raised my brows. "Why are you here, Sam?"

He shook his head and looked at me like I'd lost my mind. "You're kidding me, right?" He sighed, raised his hands in mock surrender and then lowered his voice to a whisper. "Oh, I get it. Guess I do deserve a few jabs, but that's not the only reason you wrote and asked me to come on this cruise, is it?"

"What the—" The air left my lungs like I'd traded places with a punching bag. "You think I a-asked you here?" I stuttered, but before I could catch my breath Dale Worley began to wave his napkin furiously. I could smell his breath across the table as he half-shouted, half-lisped Kirsty Pelham's name.

"Kirs-sthy! Hey, for criss-sake, missy!" He bellowed. "Can you stop reciting the Seattle itinerary like a damned school nun? Just for a minute?"

The table fell silent and I watched out of the corner of my eye as Kirsty straightened in the chair beside me and started to tuck her Palm Pilot back into her beaded bag.

"No," Dale said, leaning forward across the table. "You'll need that little gizmo, honey." He turned his head to leer at me openly. "I think we can all agree that this trip's already been wilder than one of Kyle's rodeos." He grinned and pointed at Kirsty's Palm Pilot again. "So here's the deal. I'm giving you a backup plan. Make a note that if Jamieson gets hives or," he winked, "gets his sorry-ass dick glued, that Worley's Wheels are lubed and ready to roll Miss Darcy Cavanaugh down that garden aisle!"

Ugh. I half-rose from my chair and Kirsty reached a hand out to stop me, shaking her head. "Wait," she whispered like her life was on the line. "Please, Darcy."

Damn him. I squirmed under the cool grip of the wedding planner's hand. How could Kirsty be so controlled with this idiot? I was sick of this crap, the jokes and the dangerous near misses. Someone had to set it straight.

Worley laughed and shook his head, the movement sending his string tie swinging like a hangman's noose. I forced myself to study it, avoiding the leer in his eyes and forbidding myself to make a scene. What was that thing? A Western bolo tie with a little silver creature for a slide. Hunched back, slender snout, tiny ears, rhinestone eyes . . . oh God, a little armadillo. Bastard! *Let me at him.*

I felt the wedding planner's grip lessen and noticed that a man dressed in black, head to toe, had arrived beside her. Who was that?

Dale raised his Scotch to his mouth without looking up and then poked his elbow into Paul Putnam's shoulder. The drink dribbled down his chin, his shiny blue lapels, and onto the grotesque armadillo tie. "And Darcy better buckle her seat belt, 'cause you can bet I'll give her one hell of a ride."

That's it!

I leapt to my feet, Sam stood up beside me and Marie shoved her chair back. But before anyone could speak Kirsty rose calmly, smoothed the silk skirt then raised her wineglass, tapping the handle of her knife against its crystal rim. The sound was ludicrous in the wake of Dale's drunken bluster, tinkling like well-bred applause against the Flamenco guitar in the background. But the look on her face was pure, cool, control. Impressive, actually. I shook my head with flat-ass envy.

Standing next to her, I realized now, was a tall, uniformed security officer. He was the man who'd been with her in the Schooner Bar last night; the one with the military haircut and hands-free radio fastened to his lapel. Around his hips was the heavy leather utility belt I'd noticed before, with nightstick, mace canister, handcuffs, and service revolver. One of his hands rested lightly and protectively against the small of Kirsty's back.

The wedding planner lifted her chin and narrowed her icy blue eyes. Then she spoke in a tone that no one in his right mind would ignore. Like a woman with a secret weapon. "Every single one of you—listen up."

EIGHT

I was right. Kirsty did have a secret weapon. With a square head, G.I. Joe jaw, a tight butt, and shoulders like a linebacker. And from where I sat—close enough to get maced—it was pretty clear that this man intended to scare the wedding party straight, far beyond any plaid skirt and nuns deal.

"And so," the wedding planner continued after introducing her security officer, "We'd appreciate everyone's attention for a few minutes and . . . oh, goodness, thank you, Mitchell."

I watched a rare blush infuse Kirsty Pelham's cheeks as the big man helped her with her chair. Hmmm. My Irish blood sensed red roses and . . . maybe a whole lot more. Good. I couldn't think of a better prescription for this stressed-out woman.

The security guy tucked his hands behind his butt and stood with legs spread military fashion, scrutinizing our little group for a moment before he spoke. I'm sure I didn't imagine that his eyes rested the longest on a jerk with a handlebar moustache and an armadillo bolo. Then he narrowed his dark-lashed eyes for a second and spoke.

"As Miss Pelham said, I'm Mitch De Palma from ship security." He flexed his knees and exhaled softly, summoning the beginnings of a smile. "And look, I'm not making this official yet and I'm not here to wreck anyone's good time." His smile surfaced finally and his dark brows rose. "Cruise ships are all about good times, but . . ." Mitch leaned forward and rested his palms on the linen-topped table and I saw Dale Worley take a quick swig of his scotch. He knew as well as I did that the meat was coming and it wouldn't be on a silver platter.

"I'm here to make it clear that there's a line that I won't allow you to cross," Mitch said.

Patti Ann's dark curls were bobbing as she nodded in agreement and Kyle placed his hand over hers on the table. I wasn't sure, but I thought I heard Sam grumble softly beside me, and a quick survey of the rest of the men at the table confirmed what I suspected. The male component of the wedding party didn't like this lecture at all. Marie glanced across at me as De Palma continued.

"There will be no more of the stunts that Miss Pelham has described to me. Nothing that causes public disorder on this ship or requires a helicopter to be landed on the deck of it."

Out of the corner of my eye, I saw Kirsty's blue eyes drop to her lap and I felt for her. Not easy to narc on a group who could fart by remote control. I hoped she got two dozen roses.

Mitch nodded and stood upright again. "I understand that tonight is the bachelor party." He nodded toward Kyle and Patti Ann. "Congratulations, by the way." His gaze shifted toward Dale's end of the table. "Our steward staff is setting up for that, and I'm sure you'll have a great time. Just be aware, however, that my fellow security officers will be around as well." He rested his hands on his hips, the fingers of his right hand grazing his firearm. "For your protection, as always, but also for . . ." his voice trailed off and his eyes traveled the table again. There was no need to finish the sentence. I saw Worley glance sideways at Paul Putnam.

"That's about it, then," the security guy said, glancing down at his pager. "Enjoy your meals, and if I can help you with anything please ask. Questions?"

He scanned the silent table once again and I bit my lip to keep from asking if he could just shoot Worley and get it over with.

"Oh," Mitch said, after glancing down at Kirsty. "I forgot. I told you folks that I wasn't making an official report of anything yet, but I'll be forced to do that if there is any question of criminal activity. Like theft. Even if it was considered part of a practical joke." His brows furrowed and he looked down at the wedding planner. "What was missing again?"

Kirsty's face flamed and I could feel her embarrassment clear down to my toes.

"No, really it's not a big deal, Mitchell." Kirsty twisted her napkin. "I didn't mean that you should say anything." She sighed and then spoke almost apologetically to all of us. "My big pink stapler is missing. I'd really like it back."

* * *

Patti Ann looked absolutely—*perrrfectly*—beautiful in her wedding gown and maybe I was being hopelessly old fashioned, but I wished we weren't seeing her in it before she walked down that aisle in Victoria Gardens. I kept getting this uncomfortable feeling about bad luck and about something happening.

"Oh don't be so damn superstitious, Darcy," the bride said, rolling her eyes and waiting for the ship's photographer. She reached over and fiddled with the buckle on my polka-dot belt. "This way I get nicer formal photos for a better price. We'll take plenty of candid shots at the wedding. And besides, Kyle's already seen my dress." She looked at my face again and nodded, her dark eyes full of reassurance. "Everyone does it this way now, darlin'."

I smiled and then whispered out of the side of my mouth to Marie. "Yeah, but most newlyweds get pelted with rice, not staples."

Marie smoothed her polka dots over her hips and grumbled. "I'd rather wear staples than a dress that makes me look like someone's great aunt."

"Really, though," I said, "wasn't that weird about Kirsty's stapler? When the security guy—"

"Rent-a-cop, you mean," Dale Worley said, slithering in beside me. "And a fag, too, if you ask me."

Marie and I crossed our arms at the same instant in a dizzying rush of polka dots. I stepped toward him, jutting out my chin.

"No one *did* ask you, Worley," I said, squinting against the impact of his eighty-proof breath and the glare off his shiny tuxedo. "What are you doing here, anyway?" The guy wasn't a wedding attendant and if I had to look at his armadillo tie one second longer, I'd figure out a way to choke him with it.

"Waitin' for the boys," he said, nodding to the far side of the wood-paneled gallery room. Kirsty was lining up the groomsmen for a portrait; Kyle, Ryan, and Sam—replacing Ed—were all wearing cowboy hats with their tuxedoes. Sam easily towered over the group. "We're not going to let some pansy-ass security guard keep us from having ourselves one hell of a blowout tonight. Putnam and I have a bunch of great stuff lined up. And it's got nothing to do with goddamned office supplies."

Office supplies? Did he mean—I gritted my teeth and smiled at Dale. If I could get him to admit to taking the stapler, I'd bet Mitch would see to it that all the practical jokes stopped. Before Patti Ann had any more bad luck. It was worth a try.

"Really?" I asked as sweetly as I could. "What do you mean? C'mon, Dale, tell me." I was making myself gag and I didn't dare make eye contact with Marie. I sucked it up and kept going. "I mean, everyone knows you're a genius at stunts. Your TV commercials prove that."

Dale narrowed his eyes and looked suspicious and I knew I'd laid it on a little thick. I smiled innocently, feeling Marie's eyes playing lethal dot to dot on the back of my dress. "Just a hint, Dale," I said, "what have you bad boys got planned?"

Dale's tongue made a swipe at the tip of his handlebar, and then his eyes dropped to the dipping neckline of my bridesmaid gown. I could feel my skin flush beneath the spot-size Band Aids.

He smiled slowly. "Got your little pasties in the wrong place, don't you, honey?"

I felt my mouth drop open, but he turned away before I could form words.

"Oh," he said, looking back at me over his shiny blue shoulder. "If you want to go out for drinks again when we get back home, just give me a jingle. I'll fit you in."

The photographer called to us and I followed Marie, still speechless. The ass, the complete and total *ass!* I sputtered as the photographer's assistant handed me a silk-flower bouquet. "Damn that jerk," I hissed to Marie, trying to fix the petals of a tulip I'd just mutilated. "I'm going to nail his ass for these pranks. Worley's going to wish he never boarded this ship. Do you believe the way he talked to me just now?"

Marie shook her head, and I caught a glimpse of a smile tugging at her lips. In just seconds her polka-dotted shoulder pads were trembling with laughter.

"What I can't believe," she choked out, finally, "is that you . . . had drinks with him? You dated Worley?" Marie's eyes were huge. "Why didn't you tell me this, Darc'?"

I groaned as we took our places beside the bride and the photographer told Marie to remove her fanny pack. The lights were blinding—like a police interrogation.

"It wasn't a date," I whispered through my posed smile. "It was a sort of . . . payback, that's all." The shutter clicked a dozen times and stopped.

"Payback?"

"For a van." I groaned again as I saw the groomsmen approaching. Great, now I'd get to pose with Sam.

"A van?" Marie's brows wrinkled with confusion.

I sighed and picked another petal. "Okay, I admit it. I went out for a drink—one drink—with Dale so he'd give my dad a good deal on a work van."

"Wait. The Chevy with the rats and the termites stenciled on the side?"

"Yes. And it's fully loaded."

"God. Did you kiss him or—?"

I hit her with the tulips. "Did you see a friggin' Humvee in my dad's garage?"

* * *

I knew that pairing me up with Sam was going to be a problem and not just because they made me stand on a box to look tall enough beside him in the wedding photos. He'd loved that of course, just like he'd gotten a kick out of carrying me around on his shoulders. The problem now was that I was off that box and back into my evening gown, but still staring way up into puppy dog eyes that wouldn't go away. I glanced around the Crow's Nest Bar; kind of hoping someone would pull a fire alarm.

"You're going to stick to your story then, about those e-mails?" Sam asked, his dark eyes lingering on mine. A candle from the table's little hurricane lantern cast flickering light across his face. Damn, he was gorgeous. Good thing I was smarter than I was tall.

"Its not a story. I didn't send them," I answered, taking a sip of my drink and lifting my chin just a little for emphasis. "I'm sorry if that loosens any of your chest hairs or—" my face flushed furiously at a rush of memories, and I knew he could sense it. Okay, I wasn't so smart.

Sam tapped the pleated front of his tux shirt and smiled slowly. "Not worried. You might remember that I have plenty. But . . ." his brows scrunched for a moment, "I swear, I did get an e-mail just last week with your name signed to it, Darcy. Asking me to come on this cruise."

I stopped fanning myself with my cocktail napkin and laughed. "You're surprised to get crank e-mails? When you hang out with guys who carry blue-dye chewing gum and steal staplers?" I watched his face carefully to see if I could tell if he knew anything. No clue. Of course, I was the woman who couldn't tell that he had a wife.

Sam sighed and lifted his beer. "Good point. But I don't know anything about office supplies. I only know that the guys aren't very happy about the wedding planner sic-ing that security guy on us." He took a swallow of the beer. "Never seen Galloway so pissed."

"Ryan?" I raised my brows, thinking of the shy firefighter who was set to accompany Marie down the aisle. The poor guy had gotten sick in a wastebasket after the incident with Gordy Simons. Ryan, pissed? Hard to imagine. "I didn't think he'd—"

"Say shit if he had a mouthful?" Sam offered with a soft laugh. "Me either. Maybe his chest hair felt threatened." He smiled and his eyes took their best shot at me again.

I ducked it. "So what's Ryan saying?"

"Only that he couldn't wait until Kyle's party tonight; that they all need to let off a little steam. And that Worley and Putnam were right about Kirsty all along."

I widened my eyes.

"That she's the wrong person to be putting on this party," Sam explained, shrugging. "Too uptight, too snooty. And because she and Patti Ann keep making Kyle look like an ass. Like with all the 'cowboy' stuff tonight."

"Kyle *is* a cowboy. So?"

Sam frowned. "But having the waiters dressed in paper Stetsons and bandanas? Saddle-blankets for tablecloths? Shit, all that's missing is 'Pin the Tail on the Donkey.'" He grimaced like a man with glue in his boxers. "I got a look at the room they're setting up. Believe me, it won't stay that way long with what Paul's got planned. But you'd have to see it to believe it."

93

See it? For some reason my skin prickled and it had nothing to do with the rash. I glanced casually down at my watch, and then back up at Sam. "What time's this rodeo start?"

"Eleven," he said, his hand reaching out to gently grasp my wrist. "But, easy girl, it's a bachelor party. No women allowed."

"Uh huh. Except for the cowgirl who's invited to dance naked on the bar?"

"You bet." Sam grinned and his fingers moved against my forearm with familiar warmth.

A small jazz combo had begun to play in the corner of the room—plaintive sax, the reverberating thrum of bass strings. Sam took a breath and his eyes grew serious in the candlelight. Way too serious.

"Darcy, you never said anything about my being here. Aboard the ship, I mean." Sam's voice was husky-soft and tentative.

"I told you I didn't write that e-mail," I answered, knowing he didn't mean that, but not sure what else to say. *Don't look at me like that, Sam.*

"No," he said, catching my gaze. He reached for my hand and it somehow disappeared inside his. "I mean, are you glad? Are you glad to see me again?"

"Sam, I—" I turned as someone called our names behind us.

"Sam? Darcy?"

Kirsty Pelham stopped a few feet away, blue eyes wide in the candlelight.

I slid my hand from Sam's and my breath escaped in a whoosh. *Damn.* Talk about perfect timing. Where was the florist shop? I wanted to send this woman flowers myself.

"I'm sorry . . ." Kirsty's voice was swallowed by the wail of the saxophone, but I could guess that she was apologizing for interrupting by the look of discomfort in her eyes.

"No problem, not interrupting," I quickly chimed in, hearing Sam's long sigh.

Kirsty cleared her throat. "Its just that I saw you two and then I remembered that Ryan is looking for Sam." Her eyes relaxed a little behind her lenses and she smiled at Sam. "Something about the bachelor party. I think he needs your help with a surprise for Kyle."

Kirsty and I watched Sam walk away and I insisted that she sit for a minute and have a drink. Besides, there was something I'd forgotten to ask her at the photo shoot.

"I know it sounds weird," I said after the waiter brought her diet cola, "but I need to know for sure if I'm the only feet that got photographed today." I tried to ignore the queasy memory of chocolate pudding drying between my toes.

Kirsty hesitated for a moment with her gaze somewhere far away, and then shook head. "Everyone signed the waivers, I'm sure of it," she said like she was reciting from a notation on her PDA. "Otherwise I couldn't have gotten the whole day free for all of us."

"I know we all signed," I said, suddenly feeling guilty for asking. She obviously had other things on her mind. "But the massage therapist seemed to imply that the props," I grimaced remembering the snake, "used for my photos were by some special request." I was feeling more like an ass each minute. Did I think she was going to say she was in cahoots with a foot fetishist for godsake? I'd save the bit about hearing poetry in the spa earphones for another time.

Kirsty fiddled with the lime in her glass and I noticed that her usually perfect nails looked . . . chewed? She reached for her bag, frowning a little. "I know I have some notes on the Spa Day. I could check. Or I could ask the Personal Training Team for you. They're putting together those wellness lectures."

"Never mind," I said. "I was only curious." I smiled at Kirsty with sincerity. "It was good of you to get all that arranged for Patti Ann, and for all of us."

"I saw you there today," Kirsty said softly. "And I overheard you talking about your grandmother."

Jeez. "I'm sorry," I said, remembering my rant about the retirement home and the damned fish food. Can't take me anywhere with free mimosas, obviously. "I guess I'm too protective of her."

"No," the wedding planner said quickly. "Don't apologize."

The candlelight reflected off her glasses and Kirsty's eyes blinked behind them. "I admire you for it. And know exactly how you feel. I'd do anything to keep my mother safe . . . and to make her proud." She looked down at her fingernails like she'd just noticed how raggedy they were. "I guess that's the reason I'm working so hard to make this cruise event successful." She looked up, her beautiful brows scrunching. "But there have been so many problems, Darcy, and I'm worried."

"Wait, Kirsty," I said, hating to see this look in her eyes. "You're doing a great job. Ask Patti Ann. She's thrilled with everything you've done. And it's not your fault that some of these adolescent jerks keep—" a burst of remote control flatulence from the doorway of the bar finished my thought.

And underscored what I had to do.

"This moustache keeps falling off," Marie said, groaning into the mirror. "And there's no way we'll get away with sneaking into the bachelor party. I knew I should have stayed in the casino."

"That thing is upside down, for godsake. You look like Worley. Here, hold still." I lifted the faux fur from her upper lip and repositioned it. "There. You're fine."

"Fine?" Marie looked down at her steward's suit and struggled with the red bandana knotted around her neck. "I don't know how you talked me into this or how you convinced that waitress to give us all this stuff."

I pushed a stubborn strand of hair up into my huge paper Stetson and grinned. My own moustache, crusty with old stage makeup, stretched taut over my lips. "Don't you remember her? She's the one who got so pissed at Worley last night at karaoke." I wrinkled my nose, recalling how he'd pulled the poor waitress into his lap and made her spill a tray of drinks. "Anyway, she's working the party room tonight, and when I told her we were planning some practical jokes on the groomsmen she begged to help and, well . . . voila!"

I pointed to the mound of costume accessories and articles of ship uniforms on my bed. "I did have to promise we'd do something heinous to a certain car dealer."

"Not a problem," Marie said, starting to smile enough that I knew she was climbing onboard. Good, because I had to help put Patti's wedding back on track. And after hearing Kirsty worry about making her mother proud and knowing that even the meek Ryan Galloway was gunning for her . . . well, I couldn't let that happen, either. Any more than I could turn away from Grandma's dilemma.

"We'll stay out of sight, mostly, in the pantry," I explained. "But if we can find out what the guys are cooking up next or hear someone admit to stapling Paul and Gordy, then we can take the information to that security guy." I watched as Marie crossed to the bed to pull on her paper cowboy hat. Not bad actually. She made a much better gaucho than the Holstein cow she'd been last cruise. I was about to risk telling her that when she reached into the mound of costumes and picked up a six-inch strip of purple sequins.

"What's this?" She asked, dangling it.

"Thong. To match the tasseled pasties."

"What—*why*?" She peered at me under the brim of her Stetson.

"Because, I sort of told that waitress that . . ." I shrugged.

"What?"

"That you were going to dance naked on the bar?"

Marie was quiet. Too quiet. Too long. I took a step backward, calculating the distance she could cover with her infamous fastball pitch.

She raised her brows instead, a slow grin teasing her mustachioed lips. "I'll need a drink with a paper umbrella. And a few minutes to shave my legs."

NINE

"Your elbow's in the guacamole again," I said, trying to peek past Marie and through the swinging door into the party room. The stupid pantry was way too small for a tostada assembly line. Marie was caving under the pressure and her pockets—not to mention her cheeks—were bulging with broken tortilla shells.

"Shit, would you just *look* at that?" Marie grumbled, her face shiny with perspiration. She swallowed a piece of tortilla and glared.

"Oh, just wipe your sleeve off. No one will know."

"No," Marie growled, nodding across the pantry. "I mean look at your little waitress friend. Sitting over there doing her nails."

I looked and, sure enough, our girl had her feet propped on a salsa carton and an iPod headset in place. She winked and waved her polish brush in greeting. Great.

Marie scowled beneath the brim of her paper Stetson. "No wonder she was so hot to help you infiltrate this party. We're doing all her work."

Marie was right. For forty minutes we'd been wedged between six other cowboy stewards in the tiny pantry off the party room, a posse of red bandanas and pasted facial hair bent over enough shredded cheddar and guacamole to fill the Rio Grande. We'd made sixty mini-tostadas, topped a dozen bowls of bean dip with carved zucchini cacti but hadn't gathered a single clue about the identity of the staple thief. Or even the owner of the fart machine, not that there hadn't been a dozen incriminating blasts. Beyond a belching contest and roars of drunken laughter, I could hear almost nothing through the door. I wasn't helping Patti Ann or Kirsty by ladling refried beans. I needed to do what any respectable cowpoke would do, mosey on in to Dodge City.

"I'm goin' out there," I said, grabbing a piled-high tray, then tugging the brim of my Stetson low on my forehead. "How's my hat?"

Marie's brows rose. "But I thought we were staying in here, Darc'. Worley will smell you a mile away." She smiled wickedly, "And think you came to play with his armadillo."

I grimaced. "He's too drunk to recognize his own mother. Sam's more of a problem, but I can avoid him. I'll set this tray down and then maybe hang out behind those rows of bottles at the bar and—oh jeez." I stared at Marie's face.

"What?" She rubbed at her face with her bandana. "Guacamole?"

"No," I said, inspecting the tostadas on my tray. "Your moustache."

"It's crooked?"

"Nope." I shrugged, and then smiled as the fart machine echoed beyond the door. "It's missing."

*　*　*

Sam had been right about Kirsty's decorations—way too much, even for a grade-school party. Sort of John Wayne Meets Taco Bell, with piñatas dangling overhead, a lighted neon cactus, a Texas flag, and even Dale Worley's cardboard llama dressed up like a cowgirl. The worst part had nothing to do with Kirsty's design: Worley himself—bare-chested under a fringed vest and in flowered swim shorts—wore double holsters, low on his hips, filled with whiskey flasks. And—*oh shit*—he was heading toward me. I avoided his eyes and set my tostada tray down on the table, not easy to do when the carpeted floor beneath my feet dipped with wave action. I grabbed a zucchini cactus just before it toppled off the bean dip.

"Hey, easy there, pard-nuh," Worley said with a bleary smirk as he snagged a tostada. He landed his knuckles hard on the shoulder of my steward's jacket. "You have to earn those tips, you know."

I bobbed my head, bit my tongue and prayed he'd swallow a lost moustache. Then I scooted off toward the safety of the bar. I was glad to see that the bar steward had things easily under control for the small party of about a dozen guys, so I could just hang out and spy. Were my suspects all here? Better question: was anybody packing staples?

I patted my moustache, reminded myself to slouch enough to conceal my breasts, and then surveyed the room. Dale was talking with Putnam, who was fiddling with a DVD player; Kyle, our groom, lounged at the far end of the food table talking with one of the engine company volunteers; and Ryan Galloway was sitting by himself, hefting a mug of beer. I frowned, remembering what Sam had said about him and—wait, where was Sam?

I peered around the tequila bottles and then spotted him at the photo wall, alone, looking at the older section of pictures. The look on his face was soft, almost reflective, and I had a strange feeling that I knew which picture he was looking at. A certain broad-shouldered firefighter carrying a tattooed nurse and—I jumped as a microphone screeched. The lights flickered and then the room went inky dark. Someone pushed a button on the wall and a projection screen magically appeared from behind wood paneling.

"Okay, guys," Paul Putnam's voice said in a booming slur. "Are you shit-faced enough to take a little stroll down memory lane?"

"Right, Putnam," some guy called out across the room. "Like someone as old as you could even remember where his pecker was!"

The darkness filled with beery hoots, the fart machine exploded, and I began to seriously doubt the wisdom of what I was doing. Marie was right; we'd only known Patti Ann Devereaux for nine months and Kirsty Pelham was almost a stranger, so who said I had to protect them? I had enough problems with my rash and Grandma. Then my eyes widened. *Oh Lord.*

The screen was filled with an enormous image of Sam Jamieson buck naked in the firehouse shower. A rear shot, with a muscled butt and huge shoulders topped by a pissed-off look of surprise aimed back at the cameraman. My face flooded with heat and I glanced to check that the bar steward wasn't looking, before grabbing a shot glass of tequila. The room filled with groans and Worley's voice rose above it.

"Hell, Putnam, we always thought you were queer. But where's Cavanaugh? Was she soapin' up in there, too? Now there's a bare ass I'd like to have on the hood of my Hummer."

I drained the shot glass and tried to figure out how I could crawl under the tables and out the door. Good God, *could* there be a photo? Surely I hadn't been stupid enough to shower at the firehouse? Why couldn't I remember? My memory was going; good thing I was taking those vitamins and gingko.

Mercifully the photo show moved on and my tattooed body appeared nowhere. And when the lights came up the picture that remained onscreen was the same one I'd seen on the photo wall: Putnam, Gordy, Dale, Sam, and that chubby girl with the dalmatian puppy. Yeah, Putnam's daughter, Marie and I had half-decided. That still didn't sound quite right, but I knew that I remembered those big eyes from somewhere.

"You know," Worley said, lifting the flask from his holster. "We should've invited our wedding planner tonight; or do you think she might be offended?"

"Hey," Putnam said, wagging his finger, "careful, she's going to accuse you of stealing a stapler or maybe one of those little rubber finger tips they use for filing papers—should just about fit on the end of your dwarf-size dick. Right, boys? And maybe she'd slide it on there, herself."

The room was filled with hoots again and I watched as Worley scooped up a chipful of bean dip. "Hell, I'd let her try," he said after wiping his mouth on the back of his hand. "As long as she doesn't have any Super Glue." He shook his head and wobbled a little, then grabbed the microphone from Paul. "Confession time, gentlemen—who the hell did that anyway? Not that Gordy didn't deserve it, but . . ." Dale's bleary gaze swept the table, "c'mon, spill it. I think we have a prize for this, don't we Paul?"

I moved from behind the tequila bottles, holding my breath, and tried to see the look on everyone's face. Ryan Galloway was grimacing like the memory of Gordy's pathetic crotch was going to make him hurl again.

Kyle stood suddenly, his face very serious. "Look, I'm not saying that I agree with Kirsty calling security on us, but we've got to put a stop to this shit." He scrunched his brows and widened his stance, looking a lot like some of the bow-legged bull-riding photos we'd just seen on the screen. "Jokes are fine, but Patti Ann's family is paying a lot of money for all this and—"

Ryan Galloway rose from his chair, his mild features pinched with anger. "Dammit, Kyle, what gives you the right to accuse us of screwing things up? Especially after you—"

"Shut the hell up, Galloway!" Kyle shouted, his eyes narrowing.

"Hey," Sam stepped forward spreading his arms out like one of those phony wrestling referees. "Nobody's accusing anybody here. But maybe Kyle's making a good point. Maybe we should back off a little with the jokes."

Worley laughed sharply and pointed toward the photo still projected above the party table. "Yeah, sure, Jamieson. You should talk about jokes. What about that stunt you pulled on the fat chick?"

I raised my brows and glanced from the dark-haired girl holding the puppy back to Sam's face. Well, she obviously wasn't Paul's daughter then. But what was the Worley talking about? There was a murmur throughout the room, a few uneasy chuckles and a cough.

Sam's eyes narrowed and I saw the muscles in his jaw bunch up. "I *didn't* do that."

"Right. The same way you didn't con her into cleaning toilets and covering for you when you were out screwin' Cavanaugh. Tell us the truth—did you blindfold yourself and boink Fatty, too?"

Kyle grabbed Sam's arm, and I wasn't sure what I wanted more, to see Sam smash in Dale Worley's face or to hear the rest of the story. What had happened with Puppy Girl? But before anybody could hit anybody, the lights dimmed again and music began to filter overhead. A door at the back of the room opened and three costumed showgirls, wearing chaps and rhinestone boots, paraded in. They were just sexy enough to keep the guys interested and just modestly dressed enough that I was sure that our wedding planner had arranged this little show; especially when I saw a glimpse of Mitch De Palma and one of his security cohorts outside the door.

The trio began dancing and I took the opportunity to sneak behind the table and head back toward the pantry. Marie was probably going to claim workmen's comp for "tostada elbow," or—I gasped as a hand closed around my elbow. Sam.

I was busted.

* * *

"So you're not going to tell the guys I was there?" I dragged the toe of my plaid espadrille across the AstroTurf, waiting in foggy darkness for Sam to putt. In the deck lights I could see a smile, smug as hell, flicker across his lips. I'd been the target of that same attitude for over an hour now. It was nearly one AM, everyone else had gone and I was getting cranky. "Well?"

Sam sank the orange striped ball deftly into the hole in the center of a giant, lighted clamshell and then blinked up at me.

"Not sure," he said. "Your putt."

I scowled and fiddled with the front zipper of my raspberry stretch hoodie. This hulking firefighter was blackmailing me, obviously. And I wasn't sure that agreeing to a miniature golf game was going to get me off the hook or help me get any more information about the stapler theft, either. Marie had the right idea about going back to our cabin—after peeling her lost moustache off the bottom of her shoe—and Ryan Galloway had finally headed off somewhere, too. I was on a golf course in the middle of the ocean with my ex. My life was a circus.

"Aren't you even going to ask why I went to the bachelor party?" I asked, pushing my ball into the hole with the toe of my shoe. I wasn't going to play Sam's games anymore.

He glanced around the course and then widened his stance as the ship's bow dipped beneath the fairway. The sea-scented breeze lifted his dark curls and I saw him smile again, the smugness replaced by something entirely different. And maybe far worse. Great. He stepped close enough that I could smell his cologne and feel the warmth of his skin.

"I was kind of hoping it was because you couldn't stay away from me," he said softly. His fingers traced across my sleeve.

My eyes widened and I felt the heat rise to my face in strange contrast to the cold prickle of the foggy air. He was wrong of course, and no matter how sizzling our past relationship had been or how great he smelled right now, the fact was that I'd been at the bachelor party to—*jeez*. My stomach fluttered and I wasn't sure if it was from the rolling of the sea beneath us, or the fact that Sam had just taken hold of my hand.

"Let's sit down," he said, leading me to a bench beside an eight-foot fiberglass dolphin. Lit in the distance was the climbing wall, and I could hear faraway dance music mingled with the soft slap of Pacific waves against the side of the ship. We were somewhere off the coast of northern Oregon and heading toward Seattle, and right now I wanted to be anywhere else. A tostada assembly line was sounding surprisingly good.

"Sam, this is not a good idea."

"Hold on." Sam shook his head and the twinkle from the lights on an adjacent palm tree played across his dark hair. "I need to talk to you about Chloe. Finally explain all that."

His wife? No way. I'd heard all I wanted to about that more than a year ago. It was pointless to rehash any of it now or dredge up the way I'd felt about all the lies and—*wait.* That story Worley was trying to tell at the bachelor party about . . .

"That reminds me," I said, wanting to sidetrack Sam, but also feeling my curiosity rise, especially as I recalled the uncomfortable look on several of the firefighters' faces at the mention of that girl. The dark haired girl holding the engine company puppy, the one Worley called "Fatty." "What was Dale Worley trying to tease you about?" I asked, wriggling on the sea-damp bench to put a few more inches between us. "That you'd asked some girl at the firehouse to lie to Chloe about me?" I started to cross my arms and thought better of it; I was far past punishing Sam. But I was interested. There was something so damn familiar about that girl.

"Dale's a prick," Sam said, after uttering a curse. His brows scrunched and I saw a muscle tense along his jaw. "I'd like to get my hands around his throat."

"What was he talking about?" I asked, more than a little surprised at Sam's reaction. Most things rolled off his back like off a big ol' duck. "Some practical joke you played on that girl?"

"*Not me,* dammit," he said sharply, and then forced an apologetic smile. "Sorry, but I'm not going to take the fall for all of that."

Take the fall? Now I definitely needed to know.

"What happened?" I asked as gently as I could.

Sam sighed. "Shit," he said. "It was stupid. But I guess I should have seen it coming." He shook his head. "Karen was sort of a firehouse . . . groupie, I guess you'd call it." He shrugged his big shoulders. "You know, kept hanging around asking questions, bringing brownies, and wanting to help out with stuff."

"Like cleaning the stationhouse toilets?"

Sam's blush showed even in the palm tree lighting. "I didn't ask her to do that for me. I just told her that I didn't like doing it."

"And she volunteered to do those chores because she had the hots for you," I said, knowing without a doubt that it was true. Not that I would have wielded a bowl brush, mind you. Okay, fine, I did take a scrubbie to the firehouse kitchen grout one rainy day, but I didn't have anything better to do and Sam kept kissing the back of my neck and . . .

"Maybe that was true," Sam said, "and maybe I took advantage of that. But I would have never set up a cruel joke."

"What joke?" I asked, already feeling apprehensive for that smitten chubby-faced girl.

"Fake date," Sam said, letting out a long sigh. "With me. At midnight, in that education office we have behind the station house. I'm pretty sure Putnam set it up; maybe with Gordy or Ed. Hell, I wasn't even there, Darcy. But they sent her a note, and signed my name." He groaned. "They even had the place set up with candles and flowers and music." He squeezed his eyes shut and my stomach started to feel funny.

"Damn," I said, picturing the girl's face and fully understanding how she must have felt about a secret date with sexy Sam Jamieson. "What did they do?" A niggling fear crept up my spine and my eyes widened. "They didn't do anything to hurt—"

"*No*. God, no," Sam said quickly. "They just did everything they could to embarrass her. Rigged it up so everyone could hear her calling my name in that dark office, flipped on the floodlights so they could have a laugh and take pictures of her all dressed up with makeup and her hair all fancy. I guess she started to cry and . . ." Sam's voice faded into a sincere moan.

I was silent for a moment, hating every single one of them. "And then what, Sam?"

His shoulders raised and lowered as he exhaled. "And then she was saved by the bell I guess."

"Huh?"

"They got a call. A fire. Rolled the ambulance, too, Code Three. Everyone was out of there in seconds."

"And Karen?"

"She never came back," Sam said softly, and I knew from the pained look on his face that he was telling the truth about the incident. He wouldn't have done that.

"What was her last name?" I asked.

"Pinkley," Sam said. "Or something like that."

I bit at my lower lip for a moment, remembering something. "Pinkel? Could it have been Pinkel?"

"Maybe. Why?" Sam asked, and I noticed that somehow he'd slid back closer to me. I could smell the warm skin that had helped to make a shy, awkward girl agree to a midnight rendezvous.

"I think I remember her from the hospital. As a patient, or a visitor maybe."

Sam nodded. "Yeah, she talked about a sick relative sometimes and—" He tipped his head sideways suddenly, then stood and walked over to the outer shell of the ship. To where a spotlight shone on another one of those huge color posters advertising the Personal Training Team.

I followed him, wondering what in the hell he was doing. What was suddenly so interesting about the same boring posters we'd been seeing plastered all over the ship since the minute we walked on board?

"What are you doing?" I asked, peering first at Sam and then at the pair of glossy feet towering above us.

"I just figured it out," Sam said, shaking his head and looking like he was going to laugh.

"What, for godsake? What's so funny?"

Sam turned to me and raised his brows. "Don't you recognize yourself?"

I stared at him like he was crazy. The man must have guacamole poisoning.

"It's you," he said, pointing at the gargantuan pair of female feet. "It's been bugging me, but now I'm sure. See that?"

He pointed to an ankle bracelet, a little blurred, but visible if you looked closely. Silver. With the Irish design: clasped hands, a heart, and a crown etched with the little "C" for Cavanaugh. Grandma's bracelet that I'd had remade. *Oh my God.*

It was true. They were my feet. But how did they end up on all these posters and . . .

Before I could even go further with the weird thought, I noticed something else. Glinting in the reflected spotlights that shone down from the rock-climbing wall. There, on my huge, glossy, full-color great toe. I reached up to be sure, running my fingers over the long railroad track of metal bits.

I'd been stapled.

TEN

"That's a serious toe job," Marie said pointing her cheroot at my mega-pixel humiliation.

"Yeah," I agreed, as I watched the pale Seattle sun glint off the poster's chunk of neatly placed staples, "this stapling fiend is a sicko."

"No," Marie said, tapping the cigar tip against a poster toe and then glancing down at my pedicure. "I meant the photographer, babe." Her gray eyes blinked quickly. "He shortened your second toes. You know, so they wouldn't look quite so . . ."

My jaw dropped and I stared down to where my toes, painted Chik Flik Cherry, nestled in my ribbon-tie wedges. It was true—and a sign of intelligence, I'd read somewhere—that my "index" toes extended longer than my big toes. Always had. Or did, until this appalling poster where I'd been—

"I've been *digitally enhanced*?" I growled, my eyes narrowing and my cheeks starting to burn.

"Uh-huh. Toe job." Marie grinned as she lit her cigar.

"That sonofabitch," I seethed. "It's bad enough that someone's using my feet without my permission, but this is insulting!" I traced my fingertip down the bottom of the poster to read the ad logo and see who was responsible.

"But we signed those waivers, Darcy."

I looked back over at Marie. "No, that's what I've been trying to tell you. This isn't one of the pictures from aboard ship. I didn't even bring my ankle bracelet with me this trip." My voice was rising and my rash was starting to prickle beneath my white off-the-shoulder top. "The whole point is that someone got hold of this photo from somewhere else."

Marie did a double take. "So, like the staple maniac is the photographer, or . . ."

Her brows wrinkled with confusion.

"Not necessarily," I explained. I wasn't totally sure myself but I'd definitely lost some sleep last night thinking it all over. "Could be a coincidence. The stapler guy could have simply recognized my feet on the poster. Same as Sam did."

"Ahhh . . . because you tiptoed around half naked through the firehouse." Marie did her Yoda nod.

I shot her a look. "Or he could have seen them on the beach or at the hospital softball game. Firefighters leave the firehouse, you know."

"Of course." Marie's eye crinkles were back. "And the Dale Worley leaves the car dealership. Like if he takes some barefoot nurse out for drinks, or—*ouch!*" She dodged my second finger jab. "Okay, but what are you going to do about this?"

I frowned and then glanced away for a moment as I caught sight of Ryan Galloway standing at the rail with Kyle a dozen yards down from us. Our groom was shaking his head and then put his hands on his hips, his jaw looking tense. I remembered the near altercation between these two at the bachelor party last night. What was going on there?

"I'm going to ask Kirsty about the ship's photographer again," I said as Patti Ann arrived and whisked Kyle away. "She said she has the information somewhere on how the spa shoot was set up, and I'll see if she knows how they got all the other photos for these Personal Training posters." I studied the bottom of the glossy ad one more time. "What's that wording down there anyway?"

Marie fanned her cigar smoke away, and then squinted. "BF, or a P maybe." She shrugged. "A business logo, I guess. Never heard of 'em."

I jutted my chin. "Well, they're sure as hell going to hear from me. I'll use this photographer for target practice before I gun down the Staple Nazi. But first . . ." I sighed and peered out over the rail at the incredible skyline arising from the shore beyond. My anger diffused as the sun broke through the clouds and splashed onto Elliott Bay in eddies of gold. I patted the pocket of my cropped twills to be certain I had my ship ID card. "Let's go taste this fabulous city." I inhaled deeply and then moaned, smiling back at Marie. "I swear Seattle air smells like Starbucks."

* * *

And fish. Seattle smelled a lot like fish, too, especially when you're nearly hit by one flying fifty miles an hour over your head. The infamous fish-tossers of Pike Place Market—I couldn't believe how loud I'd just squealed. Completely humiliating for a woman who could beat both her brothers arm wrestling. And, of course, Sam was still laughing. Yes, the big firefighter had managed to find me, and that was a whole other kettle of fish. I wasn't sure what to do about it yet.

"Oh, man. You should have seen the look on your face!" he said, clutching at his belly and nearly backing into the battalion of crabs squatting on a bed of crushed ice. His dark eyes danced. "It was priceless, it—"

"It had teeth," I said in my own defense and tossed a tight smile to a grade-schooler who was pointing at me like I was The Screaming Woman Sideshow. Where were the knuckle-whacking nuns when you needed them? "I'd like to see how you would feel about a monkfish wrapped around your head," I said, inspecting my collarbone for slime. "I could have gone downtown with Marie to do that underground tour and to find the Fremont Troll."

"Troll?"

"Yep," I said. "An eighteen-foot sculpture under some bridge around here." I shook my head remembering how excited Marie had been. "It's supposed to have a hubcap for an eye and an old Volkswagen Bug clutched in one claw." I saw the look on Sam's face and decided not to mention that there was a time capsule of Elvis figured in there somewhere, too. Not everyone fully appreciated Marie's unique interests.

"Anyway," I said, glancing warily down at a mound of congealed octopus, "it still beats getting bludgeoned by fish. I should've gone with her."

"No," Sam said quickly, his face suddenly as serious as a small boy watching his birthday balloon disappear into a rainy sky. "You wouldn't have gotten to see . . ." he stretched his denim clad arm to gesture around us, "all of this."

There was more than a little in his dark eyes that also whispered, "*And then I wouldn't have seen you here.*" But he was pointing down the cracked, cobbled aisles of the nine-acre, century-old farmers' market known as the "Soul of Seattle," Pike Place Market. A group of sidewalk musicians began again in earnest. And, despite the near miss with the monkfish, Sam was right. No way did I want to be in a dank, underground tunnel or snapping photos of a troll, when I could be experiencing this incredible place. I'd never seen anything quite like it.

The late afternoon sun turned everything sort of peachy gold, making the Market's kaleidoscope of color even more boggling—open-air stalls stuffed to bursting with fat bunches of flowers: tall and graceful delphiniums as blue as butterfly wings, golden sunflowers, clouds of baby's breath, pastel sweet peas like ballerina skirts, paprika red poppies, and more layers-of-velvet roses than I ever knew existed. Farther down, an endless row of bins held vegetables of every color and texture—green, yellow, and red peppers, purple eggplant, cabbages as big as my head, speckled tomatoes, bouquets of herbs tied with ribbon, and mismatched jars of spices lined up like magic potions. On shelves above were jellies and salsas as translucent and colorful as stained glass, boxes of exotic teas, and huge waxy wheels of cheese.

The salty breeze set hangers of tie-dyed and beaded cotton tunics fluttering and left an array of wind chimes and shiny metal whirligigs tinkling and twirling. Crowds of people meandered down the aisles, carrying ice cream and little cups of Dungeness crab or paper trays of crispy fries, stopping to inspect the wares or to listen to the flutes, guitars, mandolins, the chink-chinking of tambourines and—hey, was that Kirsty Pelham?

I tilted my head to see past a waist-high stack of silvery salmon, and caught another glimpse. It was the wedding planner, no doubt about it, dressed in what I'd bet was DKNY and walking our way holding hands with Mitch De Palma, that ship security guy. It took me a half-second to recognize him since he was in street clothes—black jeans and a tobacco brown sweater—and because his rugged face was, well, totally sappy with full-blown infatuation. His lips were softly parted, his dark eyes not leaving Kirsty's face for an instant. The wedding planner had better monitor her mail for poems. Which reminded me that I wanted to talk with her about some of that. Hell, maybe I should talk to both of them. Perfect opportunity.

Kirsty recognized me even before I could call out. Then Sam's wave caught her eye and a series of expressions crossed her face, surprise at first followed by something more. For a moment I thought she was in pain or that maybe her blood sugar was bottoming out again. Her beautiful face went fish-belly pale and she dropped Mitch's hand quickly before striding toward us.

Thirty minutes later, the four of us were sitting at one of the outdoor cafes off the waterfront side of the Market, a rough planked table covered in butcher paper and overlooking Elliott Bay. Our cruise ship gleamed white in the distance. The breeze smelled of sea brine and fried onions, and the sun played peek-a-boo through the clouds, teasing my bare shoulders with warmth one moment and then goose bumps the next. I'd piled my hair up high with a clip and was sipping a pretty decent Washington State chardonnay while waiting for my cup of chowder to cool. All the while trying to convince myself that every sailboat dipping in the distance didn't make me miss a certain federal agent like crazy. I wasn't having much luck.

I was glad, though, to see that the color had come back into Kirsty's cheeks. There was even a faint blush as she talked with Sam and then reached up to brush a strand of her corn-silk hair away from where the breeze had whisked it across her rosy lips. I'd been wrong about her diabetes causing the problem. It was obvious from the point she was making of avoiding skin contact with Mitch, that she'd simply been mortified when we'd seen them holding hands earlier. The woman had a bug about decorum. It made me hope that Marie didn't show up in some tacky Troll tee shirt at the bride's cocktail party tonight. But meanwhile, I intended to use this opportunity to pick the wedding planner's brain about that damned photographer. Sam beat me to the punch by a split second.

"So how did Darcy's feet end up on all those posters?" Sam asked, chasing his question with a swig of his bottled Canadian beer. He sneaked a sidelong glance at me and grinned like he was schmoozing Red Riding Hood. "Not that they don't look pretty hot up there."

I rolled my eyes.

Kirsty cleared her throat and fiddled with the lime in her soda water for a moment. When she looked back up, her frosty blues settled on me. "I did go back and check my records on the Spa Day," she said without a blink. "It was a stroke of luck, really, that we were able to coordinate our needs with a promotion that the Personal Training Team was planning."

"I understand that," I said, watching as Mitch draped his arm not quite casually across the back of the bench behind Kirsty—poor schmuck. "But the waivers we signed were for new photos and the ads I'm questioning have been here since we set sail. No way I gave permission to use that one. I didn't even know it existed. How did the ship's photographer get hold of it?"

"I'm not sure," Kirsty said, squirming a bit like she thought I was blaming her or something. "I only know that the new ad campaign was spearheaded by a doctor who's giving a series of lectures aboard ship."

"A doctor?" I asked, realizing that I knew absolutely zip when it came to the ship activities; I hadn't read the newsletter or anything. Hell, I didn't even know if that whole deal about a Hairy Chest Contest was true or just something Marie had made up to distract me. I should at least check into that one. But a medical lecture?

"Well," Sam said, chuckling into the mouth of his beer bottle. "If he's a surgeon, maybe he can remove that shitload of staples stuck to Darcy's big toe."

Mitch tore his eyes away from Kirsty's earlobe and jerked to attention, staring hard at me across the table. "What?"

"On the poster," I explained quickly, before he could overreact and call 911 on his cell phone. "Someone stapled the poster's toes— a photo of my toes, apparently—about a zillion times." I spooned a clam from my chowder and blew on it.

Mitch's jaw tensed. "Dammit," he said, looking back at the wedding planner. "I know you don't want me to make a big deal about this, Kirsty, but it's obvious these dumb-ass firemen aren't going to—" He bit off his words and his face colored as he looked across the table at Sam. "Hey man, I'm sorry. I didn't mean that the way it sounded."

"No problem," Sam said, raising a big palm. "I like a good joke same as anybody, but I wouldn't be involved in something that got someone hurt or—" Sam's eyes widened and he reached across to grab for Kirsty's drink glass as it upended onto the table, ice cubes skidding in all directions. "Whoa, let me get that for you."

We all reached for our napkins and Kirsty apologized several times as we maneuvered our plates away from the spill. I picked up an ice cube and the wayward lime wedge and then hesitated for a moment, studying Kirsty's face. She was watching silently, almost mesmerized, as Sam mopped at the paper tablecloth. And she'd gone pale again, just like before. Damn. This was my fault, for reminding her about all the pranks that had been affecting her plans for Patti Ann. I should have known better. There was no way this wedding planner wouldn't believe she was responsible for everything that happened on the cruise. This was no time to bring up the fact that I thought I'd heard poetry in the spa earphones, either, or to admit being the target of all that FedEx weirdness. I was anxious to ask her the name of the doctor who was lecturing, but I'd just have to find that out for myself when I got back onboard the ship.

"Well," Kirsty said, glancing down at her watch after we'd all chipped in for the bill. "I'm going to have to get back to the ship." She inserted a quick smile and I was glad to see that she looked less anxious despite the fact that she was marching to that rigid timetable again.

"I've got a few things to check on for Patti Ann's party tonight," Kirsty continued, glancing across at Sam and then into my face. She bit into her lower lip. The worried look hovered. "You'll both be back in time for that, right?"

"Absolutely," I said, probably nodding a few times too many, but then nurses are notorious fixers. "I'm going to be like five minutes behind you, Kirsty. Don't worry. I want to pick up a gift for my grandma and then I'll be heading up the gangway."

Of course, I had no idea that Firefighter Sam had other plans.

I should have known something was up when I'd finished paying for the sailboat wind chimes and then turned to find Sam holding a bouquet of sweet pea blossoms. Sam Jamieson, though sexy as hell, had always been about as romantic as a swat on the butt. But now I had to wonder if he'd been studying up, especially when he started saying things about "the perfect place for a sunset and a great view of Puget Sound." He took me by the hand and headed for the Elliott Bay Water Taxi. It had to be pre-planned. And even though I wanted to get back to the ship and check out that whole doctor and foot poster connection, it was clear that I needed to go along and move forward with a plan of my own. To finally set this firefighter straight.

*   *   *

Swat on the butt this wasn't. Sam had done his research all right— "Salty's" on Alki Beach was absolutely wonderful, all glass and sky and indigo sea. We sat on a wrap-around weathered deck jutting out over the ferry-dotted expanse of the Sound, offering a 360-degree view of Seattle's skyline from Smith Tower to the Space Needle. The sun was dipping low on the horizon, staining the sky crimson and purple and gold, and a jazz piano rendition of Steely Dan drifted out from the doorway as our waitress arrived with drinks and happy hour appetizers. I tried not to moan, I swear, but I'm a fool for cumin-spiced calamari. I figured that I could sample a little bit of everything—coconut prawns, Tilamook cheddar and cold planked salmon—and then move on to the setting-Sam-straight agenda.

"I'm glad we finally have a chance to be alone," Sam said, inspecting the label on his amber ale and then looking up at me with the puppy dog eyes that got me into trouble in the first place. "I still want to explain some things . . . about what happened with us."

"Mmm . . . not really neces-thessary," I lisped around a crispy tangle of calamari legs. I patted my lips with my napkin and blushed. "Sorry. I mean that you don't need to explain anything, Sam. It's all water under the bridge now." Or more like a troll under a bridge. And dammit, speaking of trolls, why hadn't I just gone with Marie? I could have been safely underground somewhere right now.

"Yes, I do," he said, then took a breath and exhaled softly. "I was a fool to lie to you about Chloe and—"

"Actually," I interrupted, surprised by my sudden and ridiculous need to get this right, "you didn't lie to me *about* her." I set my fork down. "You completely failed to mention that you had a wife at all. Right?"

Sam's squirmed like the nuns had caught him. "Right. You're right, Darcy. And, even considering your attitude toward relationships, I should have been honest."

Even considering my attitude toward . . . ? I decided not to pursue that cryptic comment further. I needed to steer this conversation firmly back to the present once and for all, finish my appetizers and head back to the ship. "So you and Chloe are okay now?"

Sam shrugged. "She's willing to give it a try, she says. But I don't know."

I wanted to hit him with the sweet peas. "You *don't know*?"

"I'm not sure I'm cut out for marriage. You, of all people, can understand that."

Me of all people? Okay, this was pissing me off and the calamari was beginning to look like so much squid.

"What, Sam?" I asked, jutting my chin. "Why would I understand what? What are you getting at here?"

"Easy there," he said, smiling gently and reaching across the table to brush a fingertip across the top of my hand. "I just meant that you were always so great about keeping our relationship simple; like you wanted to avoid anything serious." He shook his head. "I look at Kyle jumping into this wedding with Patti Ann so fast and it reminds me of myself a few years ago. I mean Chloe and I were barely out of college for crissake, and the next thing I know she's got a stack of bride magazines and her mom's inviting my folks over for dinner." His dark eyes speared me like a salmon gaff. "You never questioned anything, Darcy. You never asked why I didn't take you to my home or why I didn't tell you much about myself. You were okay with keeping things disconnected. I think anything more was too much of a risk for you." He plunged the gaff deeper. "I think that's still the way you are."

I swallowed a sip of beer and feigned interest in the wilting sweet peas. Damn him. Damn that Jamieson. I'd come here to set him straight about his misguided attentions, to let him know in no uncertain terms what I thought of someone who had such a low opinion of my scruples. But now I didn't know. Was this hulking firefighter smarter about me than I was? Apparently I'd dodged a stinking monkfish only to be hit square in the head by something that smelled way too much like the truth. I didn't want to think about it.

All I knew was that my rash was starting to itch again and a staple hunt sounded like as great a diversion as the Hairy Chest Contest. Regardless of whether or not Sam was right about me, I had a wedding to protect for Patti Ann and for Kirsty, too. And I still needed to avenge that humiliating toe job.

ELEVEN

Marie had a dozen digital photos of the Fremont Troll, a fringed batik sundress for Carol—and a disturbing revelation about the doctor who was giving the Wellness Lectures.

"Oh my God," I said, stopping halfway through pulling up my kiwi satin capris. They dropped to the cabin floor and I stumbled backward to the twin bed in my panties, beaded green cami, and with my mouth hanging wide open. "Are you absolutely sure about this?"

"Yup. Phillip Foote. That geeky podiatrist with the monster arch support mounted to the top of his Range Rover, and the very guy who tried like hell to get you to work for him."

"He's onboard?" My mind wouldn't wrap around other possibilities even as I glanced from the mysterious manila envelopes on my bedside table and then back to Marie. "You're not thinking that he could have something to do with all of this? With the FedEx poems and the photos and," my stomach lurched, "the chocolate pudding?" I pictured the paunchy, fifty-something podiatrist, bearded and balding, and tried to imagine him penning something like, ". . . *the grass is worn with the feet of shameless lovers* . . ." or orchestrating whipped cream and mink and snake anklets. "Is it possible?"

Marie fastened her fanny pack around the waist of her mocha satin big-shirt and sat cross-legged on the bed opposite mine. Her dark brows lifted as she nodded with a scary combination of Yoda and Animal Behavior Specialist certainty. "Feet? Jilted lover syndrome?"

"Jilted lover?" My mouth dropped open again and I stared at Marie like she was as crazy as she sounded. "First of all, Phillip Foote was not jilted, and secondly—*ugh*—he was never a lover for godsake! Not even close. How can you say that?" I narrowed my eyes. "If this is because I admitted to having one stupid little drink with Worley or—"

"Hey, quit that!" Marie lobbed a pair of balled-up glitter socks at me. "You're jumping to conclusions again. I wasn't saying you slept with the podiatrist. I'm just saying that it's highly probable that Dr. Foote has a thing for you. That maybe in his own ten-toed mind, he *is* your lover. Think about it."

"What do you mean?" I stood again, zipped my capris and looked around for my shrug jacket and flowered sandals. We were supposed to be at Patti Ann's cocktail party in half an hour and for some damned reason I was still troubled by that too-close-to-home conversation with Sam Jamieson. He thought that I was *afraid* to risk commitment? Could it be true? And was that my problem with Luke and the velvet jewelry box and . . . *no, I'm not going there.* A couple of tropical martinis would put things back into perspective pronto.

"I mean," Marie explained with a sigh, "that Phillip Foote tried for months to get you to take the orthotic rep position. And," she raised her brows again, "he didn't even have that particular position available until you needed a job. A little suspicious?"

I tried to think back. It was more than six months ago—after Sam and before Luke—when I'd been in such a frenzy about wanting to leave the ER. "But I don't remember Phillip being anything other than professional, Marie. Seriously. He spent a lot of time teaching me about his practice and about the—"

"Velveteen Arch Support?" Marie's nose wrinkled like Yoda sniffing the Dark Side.

"Huh?"

"That time you went over to his office after hours and he showed you how he molded that 'special' German orthotic?" She tried to bite back a grimace but I saw it anyway. "Remember? It gave me the willies when you told me about it. How he made such a ceremony of helping you take off your shoes and socks?"

"Right. And then he lowered my foot in that warm gel and I was worried that it might gum up the links in my ankle bracelet and—*Oh God!*" My hands flew to my mouth.

"What?" Marie asked, and then her eyes widened like it was dawning on her, too.

"He took pictures, Marie."

* * *

I've always hated that "waiting for the other shoe to drop," sensation. It's like the feeling I get when a radio call comes into the ER about some horrific case that's arriving by ambulance, maybe a strung out gang-banger who's punching out cops and paramedics despite the rusty pickaxe protruding from his chest. Anyway, my adrenaline's pumped until I'm almost twitching when at the last minute—poof—the rig's rerouted to another hospital and we never see that guy. There's a strange kind of letdown because, while it's not like I wanted to spend my Sunday dodging spit and double gloving against very risky blood, the point was that I was ready for it, right? That's the way I felt when Marie and I found out that, according to the Activities Director, Dr. Phillip Foote was still on shore in Seattle and might not be back onboard for hours. Maybe not even until we set sail for Vancouver. She had no way to reach him. The chief photographer had been equally unhelpful, not admitting anything about the foot posters or the "custom" props used in my spa shoot. He suggested that I ask the AWOL Dr. Foote. So, yes, I was frustrated, primed for confrontation—and Dale Worley was a damned good substitute. He was pissing me off royally.

"Isn't there some dolphin you could go terrorize, Dale?" I asked, glancing from my perch at the Spinnaker Bar and searching the crowd for a table I could join. Hell, at this point I was almost thinking that Paul Putnam's lap wasn't too bad an idea. Dale smelled like he'd swum in aftershave and he was wearing another stupid-ass tie, something with green fringe that lit up with pinpoints of light like a Ronco Christmas tree. It was making me dizzy.

"You're pretty sassy, aren't you, Cavanaugh?" Dale chuckled and leaned closer, straddling the barstool next to mine until his green slacks stretched shiny-tight across his thighs. He fondled the dubious tie as his tongue swept along the border of his handlebar moustache. His eyelids lowered to half-mast. "Yeah. A spunky redhead. I like that."

"*Don't*," I said quickly, squinting against the tie's twin red blinking lights and lowering my voice to warning level. "Don't start liking anything about me, and don't you dare come any closer." I ignored his sleazy laugh and swiveled the stool to get another look around the room.

Patti Ann's toasts were long complete, but the guests—except for Marie who'd abandoned me in favor of swapping stories with a medic in the cigar lounge—were in no hurry to leave the cozy, teak and brass bar. A band was set up in the corner beneath a mock-up of a fully rigged ship's mast, with a middle-aged blonde singer whose roots were in critical need of peroxide resuscitation. She crooned a medley of songs that reminded me of the endless Vegas Live tapes Mom used to play in the mini-van on our rare family vacations; Streisand, Cher, Ronstadt, Whitney Houston, and—

"Dance?"

I turned back to the Worley and showed him the hostile whites of my eyes.

"Well," he said nodding toward Mitch De Palma and Kirsty on the darkened dance floor, "looks like that security prick is putting the moves on the wedding planner." Dale snorted and reached for his Scotch. "Good luck, she's one cold piece of ass." A grotesque smile twisted his lips, "But then, she hasn't experienced the Worley heat—yet. Hell, I'm willing to bet I could even make your room-mate think about switching teams. You don't know what you're missing, sweetheart."

Ugh! I reached for my tropical martini, swallowing too much way too fast in an attempt to stop myself from grabbing Dale by his Ronco tie and shaking him to death. It was so tempting. If that toe-defacing podiatrist didn't show up pretty quick I was headed to the brig for sure. I took another swig of amaretto and coconut rum, then turned my attention to the dance floor. Kirsty and Mitch were there all right, and I had to wonder how many shifts the poor guy was giving away for the chance to have that blonde in his arms. But one look and you knew it was worth it for him. His eyes were closed, arms wrapped low across the ice-pink silk of Kirsty's dress as he held her close and moved to the music. He looked darned handsome in his linen blazer, too, and only an FBI girlfriend would guess that somewhere beneath it was the ominous bulk of a service revolver.

Dancing next to them was Sam, who'd been dragged unwillingly to the floor by one of the few non-hospital, non–fire department wedding guests. I think she was the bride's second cousin maybe, with raven hair slicked into a clip and dressed in a too-tight snakeskin jumpsuit that seemed appropriate considering the python grip she had on the hulking firefighter. It was probably the effect of the rum, but I could swear I'd seen her tongue flick out a couple of times near Jamieson's ear. Served him right. One of her hands slithered to his butt and he shot me a pleading look. I smiled and raised my martini. *Right. Let Chloe rescue you, big boy.*

"So what's with that wimp, Galloway?" Dale asked, making me realize—even in my martini haze—that I was still sitting beside him and that I was nowhere nearer to my goal of confronting the pervert podiatrist. The car dealer fiddled with his tie again and I decided that maybe the design was a palm tree not a Christmas tree. Yeah, with a couple of pink plastic half-round coconuts and blinking red lights.

"See him?" Dale asked, nodding toward where Ryan stood alone in the middle of the darkened dance floor, very near the blissfully entwined bride and groom.

"Yes," I answered, tilting my head to get a better look. I had to admit it was pretty strange. And there was something not good about the expression on Ryan's face. "Looks like maybe he's trying to get Kyle's attention."

"Looks like he's drunk off his ass," Worley said, obviously enjoying it. "This could be great. Ever seen Kyle toss a calf?"

As a matter of fact, I'd suddenly stopped thinking about Ryan, Kyle, Sam, the Snake Woman, and even about the blinking coconuts on Worley's tie. Because now my eyes were riveted on the Spinnaker Bar's doorway and on the paunchy and balding man who'd just arrived. The memory of chocolate pudding made my toes curl. I studied him; striped seersucker blazer, bow tie, beltless waistband a critical millimeter too high, salt and pepper beard neatly trimmed . . . Doctor Phillip Foote.

He moved smoothly toward the near end of the bar, a man built to waddle like a duck and yet somehow accomplishing the kind of Patrick Swayze saunter that could only be attributed to, well, a miraculous pair of German Velveteen Arch Supports. Otherwise, Phillip Foote looked much the same as he had the last time I'd seen him, when he'd taken me out for lunch to that interesting little Japanese restaurant where . . . *Oh, jeez.* Oh hell. How stupid was I? The restaurant where we'd taken our shoes off, for godsake! I'd been apologizing around my chopsticks for declining his job offer and all that time the twisted pervert had been ogling my toes? I squeezed my eyes shut for a moment's humiliation and my face flushed hot. Uh huh. Absolutely. I'd been driven by Range Rover to a friggin' foot farewell. Okay, I could accept that. What mattered now was that I was on to him. And I had a few more questions. About poetry and a poster full of staples.

I slid from the barstool, smoothed my satin capris and stretched as tall as I could, trying to catch Phillip's eye over a crowd that was getting louder by the second. I raised my hand, waggled my fingers and then our eyes met. He nodded. I gritted my teeth and forced a smile. I'd waited patiently for it, and now that other shoe had finally dropped. It was time to act.

Only I hadn't figured on the barroom brawl.

The next five minutes were ugly and surreal and so much like a bad rerun of *Gunsmoke* that my poor, demented grandma would have stood up, dumped her walker and squealed like a teenager. Rosaleen Cavanaugh had the hots for Marshall Matt Dillon for as long as I could remember, but this time it was Ryan Galloway's pale fist against Kyle's rugged jaw; followed by an incomprehensible male shout, a sickening skin-bone-skin thwack and Patti Ann's scream. Then, finally, there was an ear-jolting reverberation as our lounge singer flung her microphone—thud, bounce, screech—to the dance floor and bolted toward safety behind a potted palm.

"Oh shit," I said to no one, due to the fact that Dale Worley had abandoned his barstool to sprint toward the fray, shiny butt hustling, stupid tie flapping, and whooping like the whole thing was better than sex on the hood of a Humvee. I followed him, God knows why, arriving just in time to see Kirsty pull Patti Ann behind the faux ship's mast. Then Kyle staggered forward, lip bleeding, regained his balance, and fought back like the bulldogging cowboy he was. Ryan hit the floor and skidded on his butt, landing under Sam's feet and knocking the Snake Woman off balance. At which point, Mitch De Palma grabbed Kyle's arm and Paul Putnam appeared out of nowhere, waving his arms like a drunk and foul-mouthed referee. Mitch shouted a warning, the overhead PA sounded an ominous series of blasts, and I decided, STAT, that the space behind the mast was roomy enough for three. I moved out of the way just as Dale Worley, yowling like a cat in heat, launched himself at Mitch. Stupid, stupid idea. And, too late, Sam lumbered forward to intervene.

"Good Ga-awd!" Patti Ann gasped, eyes wide and her nails digging into my arm. "How can we stop this?"

"Well, mmm . . . uh," I stammered, flinching as Dale ducked a second punch and Mitch's fist slammed into Sam's beautiful cheek with the sound of a meat mallet hitting a flank steak. Sam stumbled backward into a wooden stage post. Stupidly I turned to Kirsty, like our wedding planner might solve this madness with a "bibbity bobbity boo" and a wave of her Palm Pilot. No such luck and—hell—was she smiling? Nah, I had to be imagining that.

"Herd mentality," Kirsty said, her voice icy calm and blue eyes unblinking. "Pack behavior. When there's no prey, they'll turn on themselves. It's just a matter of time." Her eyes followed the skirmish on the dance floor and I wondered for a moment if she was including her lovestruck Mitch as part of that generic herd, too. Then she shrugged and sighed before turning to Patti Ann with what I was certain was a smile this time. "But thank heaven," Kirsty said, giving the bride's arm a reassuring pat, "reinforcements have arrived."

It was true; Mitch's uniformed security cohorts were moving quietly and efficiently onto the dance floor, and the music had started up again. Ryan Galloway was nowhere to be seen and Dale had sauntered our way, sweating and sneaking sidelong glances at Kirsty now that Mitch was otherwise involved. And, finally, the band singer emerged from the palm fronds, found her microphone, and began a halfhearted rendition of Cher's "If I Could Turn Back Time." Could that be any more appropriate? At this moment there was nothing that I wanted more than to do exactly that: go back to a time when I wasn't worried sick about my grandma, scratching a miserable rash, running from a little velvet jewelry box and now, thanks to lunch with Sam Jamieson, maybe doubting my own heart. *"I think anything more was too much of a risk for you, Darcy."* Why did his words still feel so much like a sucker punch?

But I was spared the slide into pathetic soul-searching by the realization of two irritating new realities. The first—I glanced away from the leer on Worley's face—was that I had guessed wrong about his idiotic green fringe and red-lighted tie; it wasn't a Christmas tree and it wasn't a palm tree, either. And the pink plastic balls weren't coconuts. Dammit, I'd just gotten a close-up look. Grass skirt, hand-painted torso, twin peaks of flashing red: it was a hula girl. A disgusting battery-operated Tit Tie, for godsake. And secondly—I glanced once more around the Spinnaker Bar—Dr. Phillip Foote had conveniently disappeared.

* * *

Why am I out here alone with Sam?

"Just hold still, would you?" I said as Sam moaned under the makeshift icepack that I was holding to his face. I'd finally managed to get him to sit down somewhere out on the ship's deserted fantail. I'm guessing that an eye swollen completely shut was far more macho than being seen in public holding an icepack.

"It's dripping down my shirt," he said, his big shoulders shifting a little but basically obeying nurse's orders. "What is that thing anyway?"

"Plastic cup with the dregs of tropical martini that I couldn't lick off the ice cubes. And believe me, I tried," I answered truthfully.

"Well, that explains why I'm starting to smell like a coconut," he said, mouth curving into a slow, sexy smile.

"Actually, according to our wedding planner you should smell like a wildebeest."

"Huh?" Sam leaned away and an ice cube dropped into his lap. If he thought I was going to pick it up for him, he was crazy. I set the cup down on a table and returned to my perch on the edge of his chaise lounge.

"Yes," I said, nodding. "Kirsty thinks that what happened back there in the bar is a prime example of 'herd mentality' and 'pack behavior.'" I watched Sam's brows furrow and saw him wince at even that small movement. His left eye was as purple as a ripe plum. "What do you think caused that brawl?"

"I think," Sam lobbed the ice cube over the deck rail and scowled, "that Ryan Galloway has finally grown some balls and must have one hell of a beef with Kyle."

"About what?" I asked, realizing once again that it was true. Ryan's behavior on this cruise was completely out of character.

"How would I know?" Sam sat up on the lounge chair and swung his long legs over its side and suddenly we were sitting face-to-face and way too close. "I don't work there anymore. Not since you and I . . ." his dark eyes found mine and his voice lowered toward a whisper. "Is that why we're out here, Darcy? To talk about Ryan?"

"Sam, I . . ." *Oh shit. Good question.* I started to move away and he stopped me, his big fingers closing gently around my forearm. I didn't know what to say because, face it, I could have handed him an icepack in the bar and walked away. I could have handed one to the Snake Woman who looked more than willing to undertake whatever comfort measures were necessary for this big fireman. I could have done a lot of other things that wouldn't have put me out here under a star-strewn sky alone with my incredibly good-looking ex-lover. So why was I here? Because I was a masochist who couldn't stop thinking about that damned conversation that we'd had in the Seattle restaurant?

"You never answered that question that I asked you our first night aboard," Sam said, dark lashes blinking over his swollen eye. His chambray shirt was open at the throat and the fabric over his chest was damp from my martini icepack. Beneath our feet the deck began to thrum, the ship's engines starting for the sail on to Vancouver. It must have been approaching midnight. In the distance there was the sound of music from the sail-away party. He did smell like coconut.

"What question?" I asked.

"About that lawyer."

Luke. My throat squeezed and my pulse kicked up a notch. I had so many questions about that myself. I stared at Sam mutely, not even sure what I wanted to say. But maybe I wasn't out here to say anything myself; maybe I did need to hear more of what Sam had to say.

"I mean," Sam's fingers brushed my skin, "is it serious?"

Is it serious with Luke? My skin began to itch and it started a crazy war inside of me—tears springing to my eyes against a surge of strange, new anger that forbade them to spill over. The anger won.

"'Serious?'" I said, sliding my hand away and crossing my arms. "You can ask that after what you said today at lunch about my 'attitude toward relationships'?" I narrowed my eyes just a little, feeling more comfortable with this emotion. "And after implying that I'm afraid to risk commitment?" I waited for him to do the usual

Sam thing and back off. Very safe, since I knew that this man did not do emotion. And I kept waiting.

"Did I imply that?" Sam asked, leaning a little closer to me again. His voice dropped to a whisper and his eyes caught mine and held. His right eye anyway. His left was a goner. "Or is that what you think about yourself?"

What? Damn him. Damn that Jamieson. What had happened to him this past year? Where was the guy who could ask, "Do you want to have sex?" in six different languages—seven if you counted Klingon—whispered Forty-Niner football stats like they were fore-play but never, ever talked about love? What made him Dr. Phil all of a sudden? I glared at him.

"Does he love you?" Sam asked.

I sprang to my feet, stumbled on my flowered sandals and pointed a finger at him like it was a weapon. "Why in the hell are you asking me all of this?" My finger shook and when I pulled it back to scratch at my chest it worsened to palsy proportions. "Never mind," I said quickly clenching my fist, "I don't want to know and I'm leaving now. Keep some ice on that eye."

I started to back away and Sam stood, catching my arm.

"Because . . . maybe I do," he whispered.

I forced myself to look up into the face of a one-eyed alien. "What?"

The deck swayed. Sam was silent for a moment. "Maybe I love you, Darcy."

TWELVE

Okay, it was a huge mistake to think that there was something Sam might say that I needed to hear. I admit that. But, in my wildest imagination I couldn't have come up with this. Foot poetry paled in comparison. My voice emerged in a half-croak. "Wha-at did you just say?"

Sam did that slow smile again, but I could swear that his face turned a little pink around the deepening bruises. He cleared his throat. "I said that I might be in love with you."

"Hmmm." If ever there was a moment that called for full-out Klingon this was it, but suddenly I was struggling with simple English. "Well, then . . ." I think I might have shrugged.

"Darcy, could we please sit for minute?" Sam asked, his face growing pale. "And where's that ice?" He winced again and touched the bruise. "I'm dizzy and I think I just saw two of you."

Huh? Oh, thank God! I really shouldn't have smiled, but the panic was whooshing out of me like a pin-poked balloon. Sam didn't love me; Sam was brain injured. *Yes!* And—hallelujah—I was totally fluent in Nurse.

"Jeez. Here, Sam," I said, slipping my arm around his waist and easing him back toward the padded chaise, "sit down and let me have a look at you again."

He lay back on the lounge and I sat on the edge of it, prodding his swollen cheekbone with my fingertips.

"Ouch," he said, his face so close that I could feel the warmth of his breath. "This is not what I had in mind. I was supposed to be kissing you by now."

"Nobody's kissing anybody," I told him in my best Nurse Ratched tone. "Are you still feeling dizzy?"

"Only when I remember your tattoo," he murmured and then groaned as I pried open his swollen lids. His pupil looked fine, the faker. "Okay, okay," he said quickly, "I'm only dizzy when I move my head. Must have hit it pretty hard on that damned post."

"Post?" I hesitated for a moment and then remembered the awful bar fight images. "Right, Mitch hit you and then you backed into that wooden pillar at the edge of the stage. Is there a lump?" I leaned across him and buried my fingers in the back of his hair, searching through the silky and way-too-familiar curls until I found it—a soft swelling the size of a golf ball. "Damn," I said, angry with myself for not noticing it earlier. "I don't like this, Sam. We need to get you down to the infirmary." I reached for the cup of melting ice and he grabbed my wrist.

"Wait," he said. "I'm okay. Really." The suspended cup dripped onto his chest and he first shivered and then chuckled. "Unless I drown." He stopped me again as I tried to move away. "What I said before, it's true, Darcy. I need you to know that." Sam's eyes, both open somehow, watched mine. "Maybe I've been in love with you all along."

"Don't, Sam," I heard my voice beg, "don't say things like that. You've got a concussion and you don't know—"

"I do know," he interrupted, frowning. "And don't pull that nurse stuff on me. If you were standing in front of a burning house and telling me that you loved me, would I say you were full of shit because of smoke inhalation or . . . ?" he gave it up and smiled sheepishly.

"It's not the same thing." I lifted the ice toward his face again.

"I know," Sam said, watching my eyes. "But it was the best I could come up with to make you cut me a little slack here." He sighed. "I'm only saying that I've been thinking about this a lot lately. Way before I got whacked in the head. How do I know that the reason I can't get back with Chloe isn't because of something I feel for you?"

I shook my head. "We haven't seen each other in a year."

"Right," he said, closing his eyes as I held the makeshift compress against his cheek. The deck moved and for a moment it felt as if our lounge chair was drifting like a life raft. "But when I got those e-mails over these past few weeks, it made me start wondering."

"I didn't send those, Sam," I said, my jaw tensing. "I keep telling you that. And if you're here because you think that I invited you, then you're obviously the butt of another stupid joke. That's the MO of your buddies; can't you see that? Glue in Gordy's shorts, squirting cameras . . . phony e-mail?"

Sam opened his eyes and melted ice trickled down the rough stubble of his cheek, pooling into a hollow beneath his open shirt collar. I could tell from the look in his eyes that he hadn't felt it or heard a thing that I was saying, either. He moved closer and I wondered if the band had taken a break, because the distant music was gone and all I could hear was the slap of the sea against the side of the ship. And Sam breathing.

"You don't love me," I said softly, watching his eyes, seeing the bruise and feeling this strong sense of déjà vu. The first time I'd met Sam he'd had an injured eye. And those incredible eyes had drawn me in, almost like now. I was holding the cup of ice and thinking about all that and other ridiculous things, like if it were possible that eyes were actually an unmapped erogenous zone or—when suddenly Sam kissed me.

His mouth covered mine and I was stunned for a moment, confused by the heat of the contact, the familiar texture of his lips, the scent of his skin and the way his big hands moved to first cradle my face and then to pull me closer. It was a sequence that I remembered only too well, and I knew where it could lead. But then, because it *was* all so familiar, I started to think that if I kissed him back that it might be only natural and . . . Sam's fingers spread along my jaw and his kiss deepened and—*no, this can't happen!* I stiffened, dropped the plastic cup and began to lean away, my face way too hot and my lap full of ice, but Sam slid his palm to the back of my head and—a man's voice boomed beyond us and my teeth collided with Sam's as we both jumped.

"Well, we-ell . . . now what did I walk in on he-ere?" Paul Putnam's words were slurry-thick with alcohol. He ran a palm over his silver hair and then screwed his mouth into a knowing leer as he staggered forward, patting at his pockets. He produced a pack of cigarettes and laughed. "Just came out for a smoke. Didn't know there was a floor show, too."

My face flamed. *Oh for godsake, what was I thinking?*

"It's a ten-story ship, Putnam," Sam grumbled, struggling to sit upright, "with a shitload of decks. Maybe you can go find someplace else, huh?" He rested his hand protectively on the small of my back and then sighed when I stood up. My lapful of ice cubes plinked onto the deck.

"No big deal, Paul," I said as casually as I could. "And this wasn't what it looked—" Putnam laughed before I could finish.

"Sure," he said, flicking his lighter, "you're the nurse. Probably just doing CPR. I'm not going to question your skills. Hell, you saved me."

I stopped myself before I could say how very much I regretted that right now.

"But no skin off my nose if you folks want me outta here," Paul continued after taking a drag of his cigarette, "I don't care where I smoke." He shook his head. "I just wanted to get away from the dog and pony show that damned security dick is putting on back there."

"Mitch?" I asked, wondering what he could mean since the last time I'd seen Mitch things were back to normal in the bar. "Did something else happen?"

Paul gave a sharp laugh. "Not as big a deal as he's making out of it." He pointed his cigarette at Sam and grinned. "You'll love this, Jamieson. Someone got into Kirsty Pelham's cabin and vandalized stuff. Really pissed her off." Putnam laughed again, "Yeah, I'd say the wedding planner's got her panties in a bunch, but what they really are is stapled together."

*   *   *

Marie watched as I chased my gingko biloba pills with double-shot latte. I'd skipped so many doses, blast it. And I knew I shouldn't be drinking coffee at—I glanced down at my Fossil watch—one AM, but my brain was fuzzy. Obviously. And I was still hoping to catch that elusive podiatrist.

Marie shook her head, a smile tugging at the corners of her mouth. "Gingko stops memory loss, Darc', not bad judgment. Or are you thinking it will make you remember *not* to kiss Sam Jamieson?"

"Ah, jeez." I pressed my fingers against my eyes and groaned. I'd left two "just saying hi," messages on Luke's machine, gag-level perky, totally uncharacteristic and, I'll admit, completely guilt-ridden. He didn't check voicemail when he was working undercover—I knew that—but I was already composing another one anyway. "Please don't remind me." I peered through my spread fingers. "And I was the kiss-ee not the kisser."

"Right. Huge distinction. Like the difference between," she glanced around the dwindling crowd in the Crow's Nest Bar, "having your undies glued or stapled?" A burst of drunken laughter erupted from the vicinity of the bar and she rolled her eyes.

"Oh, right," I said, "Kirsty's lingerie. What happened with that, anyway?" I raised my latte again and peered over the edge of my cup toward where Sam sat a few tables away, alone, nursing his own coffee. The doctor had cut him loose from the infirmary, saying that he saw no signs of concussion. Sure. Just because the man could count the doc's fingers and rattle off the names of a dozen U.S. presidents didn't mean he was coherent. He thought he was in love with me, for crying out loud.

"Kirsty threw a fit and Mitch ripped into the groom's guest list like a rabid rottweiler," Marie explained. "Two of his guys had to hold him back. Kind of scary, considering that the guy carries a gun." Marie's breath hissed inward between her teeth.

"Yes." I raised my brows. "And it was just underwear for godsake."

Marie lifted a chocolate-dipped macaroon to her lips and hesitated. "Well, I'm thinking Mitch might have a vested interest in that particular underwear?"

"Oh. Good point." I nodded toward where our security man sat talking with a bar steward. His glum expression was only too apparent. "So where is Kirsty, anyway? Not sticking by her hero's side?"

"Nah, she took off right afterward. I think the whole business embarrassed her. You know how she is." Marie rolled her eyes. "I've never seen anyone eat antacid tablets so fast. She probably found a staple remover and went back to her cabin. From what I heard, it's going to take awhile."

"Yeah. Tough to get lingerie separated without snagging it all up," I said, wincing with sympathy. If the wedding planner's underpinnings were anything like her wardrobe, I was betting she had some serious money tied—um—stapled up there.

"And off the walls." Marie said, nodding.

"Wha-aat?"

"Yep, about a dozen bras and panties stapled up like hunting trophies along a stretch of corridor on C-Deck ."

"You're serious?" I asked, my eyes wide.

"Yeah. Someone really wanted to embarrass her."

Now I wanted to borrow Mitch's mace myself. How much more could that poor woman take? I narrowed my eyes and surveyed the

142

bar again. Almost everyone was still there, Patti Ann and Kyle sharing a dessert, the Snake Woman seated at the bar, flicking her lighter and eyeballing Sam, Putnam trying to pull a staggering Worley onto a barstool . . . "Where's Ryan?" I asked, turning back to Marie.

Marie squinted toward the bar. "Dunno. He was here maybe half an hour ago, pretending to apologize to our bridegroom, it looked like."

"Did anyone ever say what that fight was about?" I asked, remembering the ugly look on Ryan's face minutes before he hurled the first punch at the groom.

"No. But Worley was teasing the hell out of him about being calf-tossed by Cowboy Kyle and—" Marie jerked her head upright and grimaced. "Speak of the devil. Head's up, Darc'!'"

Too late. I clutched the edge of the table to keep from toppling over as Worley grabbed my chair from behind, tipping it backward onto two legs. I screeched as the latte streamed down the front of my camisole. "Dammit, what the—" I struggled to right myself and inhaled a lungful of Dale's Scotch-sodden breath. Sam shouted from across the room and Marie leaped to her feet.

"C'mon, Darcy, how 'bout a little kiss?" Dale asked and then suddenly let go of the chair and jerked upright. My elbows bounced on the tabletop as the chair righted itself.

"Hey there," Marie said, after grabbing Dale's arm and pressing herself against his blinking Tit Tie. He stumbled backward and then regained his balance, holding onto Marie's arms to steady himself. She grinned up into his face, fluttering her dark lashes in a way I never knew she could. Her lips curved into a delicious smirk. "Is that a stapler in your pocket, Worley, or are you just real happy to see me?"

My jaw dropped. *Go Marie!*

I stood and crossed my arms over my coffee-soaked breasts. Out of the corner of my eye, I saw Sam crossing the barroom floor, with Mitch and Kyle close behind. Who needed them? Superman had nothing on Marie Whitley.

Dale's face turned crimson and his handlebar moustache trembled. His eyes narrowed as he gave Marie's arms what had to be a painful squeeze.

She lifted her chin, unblinking, and continued to smile. "Well?"

"Sure, Whitley," Dale said with a sharp laugh. "I'd take you on. If I didn't know that the only reason you're standing here is 'cause you're hot for the chance to kiss Cavanaugh yourself." His tongue snaked across his moustache. "Hell, I might even want to watch that. Then maybe the three of us . . ." His grip tightened and this time I saw Marie wince.

"Get your hands off her, Worley!" I growled, lurching forward to grab a fistful of his shirtsleeve. I glared up at him, pissed beyond belief. Maybe it was because my shirt was soaked with coffee so soon after my capris has been doused with ice cubes, or the fact that there was another gigantic poster of my bare feet staring down from the wall beside us. I don't know, but right now Dale Worley was the bull's-eye in an endless concentric circle of disgusting bastards.

"Easy, baby," he said, turning toward me. "I'm a lover, not a fighter. All I wanted was a little kiss. You're a friendly gal, right? What do you say . . ." He let go of Marie's arms and took a step toward me, grinning like the fool that he was.

I felt Sam's arm on my elbow and heard the low rumble of Mitch's voice, but neither of them was going to stop me.

144

"Kiss?" I said shaking my head and feeling my teeth grate together. "Are you insane? I wouldn't touch your lips if my frigging life depended on it. And for damned sure not if your life depended on it! If you think you're going to stand there in that disgusting Tit Tie and—" I broke off as Sam shoved his big body in front of me.

"Back away, Worley," Sam said, his voice as low and as calm as if he were giving instructions for an elementary-school fire drill. "Or you'll have to deal with me."

Dale's mouth twisted into a sneer. "What? And then leave her to you? Maybe you didn't get it when she dumped your ass the first time, Jamieson. And maybe your wife needs to know that you're still sniffing around your old girlfriend, huh? Maybe I'll give her a call."

Sam tensed and took a step forward, his control slipping. "You prick . . ."

I'd taken hold of Sam's sleeve and opened my mouth to remind him that I could handle things by myself, when Mitch's voice barked orders and there was a sudden intrusion of security uniforms. A lot of them. Marie tugged at the back of my jacket.

"Let's get out here," she whispered hoarsely, handing me my purse.

I couldn't argue. Besides, I'd just seen the podiatrist pay for a drink and glide smoothly away on his Velveteen Arch Supports.

*   *   *

At two thirty AM the decks were deserted and the view from the stern railing was inky black over the deep churning of the wake several stories below. The lights of Seattle were long behind us, but we were still hours from Vancouver, a very adrift and disconnected feeling—matching my mood exactly.

"I'm getting nowhere, Marie," I said, resting my elbows on the sea-damp railing and cupping my chin in my hands. The air smelled of brine, diesel oil—and coffee, from my dry but latte-stained camisole. We'd made the rounds of all the clubs and bars, hunting the podiatrist without success.

Marie glanced at her Kermit watch and yawned. "So, I'm guessing that Phillip Foote's drink was a nightcap. Smart man." The tip of her cherry cheroot glowed orange in the dark.

I sighed and then scrunched my brows, glancing away from the rail and back toward the shadowy storerooms behind us. I could swear I'd heard giggling from that area several times now. "Yes," I agreed, "but I still think it was lousy that the Purser's Office refused to give me his cabin number."

"So you could con your way in and catch him penning poetry?" Marie shook her head. "Face it, you're going to have to solve this one head on, kiddo. By simply asking the man. About the posters and the poems. At least the Purser gave you a copy of his lecture schedule."

"Right," I said with another sigh. "I'll just pop in between 'Everything You Wanted to Know About Bunions' and 'Acupressure for the Foot Lover's Sole.'" I grimaced. "Something about that last one reeks of chocolate pudding." I turned back toward the deck at the sound of more muffled giggling. "Do you hear that? I swear it's coming from one of those storerooms."

"Fifteen-oh-five," Marie said with a quick nod followed by a wicked smile.

"Huh?"

Marie took a drag from her cheroot, puckered her lips and formed one of her maddeningly slow smoke rings. She watched it hover for a moment before answering. "The number."

"What number?" I was too tired for this.

"To that storeroom back there. 1505." She chuckled. "'The Love Shack,' or at least that's what the medic's steward called it."

"What?" My eyes widened. "You're not saying that—"

"Yup. Nothing but a cot in there. It's a long time at sea for most of these folks." She pointed her cigar at one of the huge lifeboats suspended several feet below the deck rail. "I heard they used to hook up in the lifeboats, but now those get checked by security, so . . ."

I glanced down, thinking that it probably would work—a secret rendezvous in a lifeboat—considering that these boats were enclosed and not at all like those old rowboats. But you'd have to be damned desperate and—I looked up as the newest murmur arose from storeroom 1505. My face flushed. "Jeez. But don't they get caught? I mean aren't there rules against crew fraternization?"

"Hey, don't look at me. I've never seen the inside of a Love Shack on any of my cruise gigs. All I know is that there's a long waiting list for storeroom 1505."

"C'mon," I said, shaking my head. "Let's head back to the cabin. It's been a long-ass day. After dodging a monkfish, two bar fights, and a kiss, tracking a podiatrist, and"—I grimaced at another chorus of moans—"discovering the Love Shack, I'm burnt out." I groaned, remembering something. "And, blast it, I was supposed to check for that fax I was expecting from Grandma's attorney."

"Oh, crap. Sorry." Marie pinched her cigar between her lips, freeing her hands to fumble with her fanny pack. "This note came to the cabin for you earlier. I forgot all about it." She held out an envelope and then smiled as I hesitated. "Lighten up. It's not a poem. The steward said it was a notice of a fax."

I opened the envelope, read the brief message and looked up. "It must be that release form they needed me to sign. I'd better go pick it up."

Marie nodded. "I'll go with you and, hey, I'm really sorry I forgot. I know how much you want to straighten out that mess for your grandmother."

"No problem," I said, "but you go on back to the cabin. I'm going to sign the thing and then fax it back—there won't exactly be a crowd in the Business Berth at this hour."

Marie chuckled and stubbed her cheroot. "Nope, not as popular as our storeroom 1505."

⋆   ⋆   ⋆

I tucked the folder under one arm and leaned my butt against the Business Berth door as I dug around in my purse for my key card. The corridor was deserted, just as I'd guessed, and one of the overhead lights flickered, making it harder to find the card. If I'd just put it in my wallet like any organized person would. Lipstick, toe ring—I needed to toss that stupid thing; it pinched—cocktail napkin sticky with dried latte, cell phone. Ah, there it was: key card.

I inserted it into the slot and waited for the whir and click, thinking that I'd fax the paper off for the lawyer, and then leave one more message for Luke before I crawled into bed. And tomorrow we'd be in Vancouver, where I'd signed up for that bus tour to Capilano Park—fresh air and hiking sounded like a really good change. I'd just finish this up and—I pushed the door open into the darkened room and then yelped with surprise . . . *Who?*

"Oh," I said quickly, backing out of the doorway after seeing the man. The flickering bulb from the hallway lit his form in stingy little glimpses since the only illumination inside was the glow of a computer monitor. I frowned. Jeez, was this the annex to the Love Shack or something? "Sorry, I didn't think anyone—" I stopped and stared, squinting harder into the darkness. Then I stepped into the room, warily. What was wrong here? The guy wasn't moving and why was he . . .?

"Um," I said, starting to feel very uneasy, "are you okay? May I turn this light on?" Why in the hell was this guy leaning over the copy machine in the dark? Green slacks, white shirt, whole body draped over the copy machine. No, it wasn't the copy machine; it was that shredder that Marie and I had seen before. The huge, commercial one, bolted to the floor.

But . . . my fingers trembled as I reached for the light switch. The room flooded with light and I blinked, dropping my folder of fax sheets. My heart lodged into my throat and my stomach tried like holy hell to shove it out. *Oh my God!*

Dale Worley's face was flattened against the top surface of the shredder, the Tit Tie sucked as taut as a hangman's noose into the stainless steel feeder slot. His skin was purple-gray and his tongue protruded. His eyes were wide open. Glazed and lifeless.

THIRTEEN

GET HIM DOWN. START him breathing. Cut the tie . . . Oh, God, how?
My mind raced, my hands shook and my breath came in small gasps as I gave up the futile attempt to pull Dale's tie from the feeder slot and began to frantically scan the room. *Something sharp . . . there, scissors!* I grabbed them from atop a heap of papers, cursing as I scattered a box of paper clips across the carpeted floor.

I fought a gag and slid the scissors into the pool of blood-tinged saliva beneath Dale's chin, then began sawing the blades against the tight silk knot. I forced myself to focus on the blades, the fraying fabric, the alarming sound of my heart pounding in my ears—anything but the dusky dark color of Dale's skin and the currant-jelly hemorrhages staining the whites of his eyes. *Asphyxiation.* Oh God, how long had he been hanging . . . ? *Don't think. Cut!* I gripped the scissors harder, my fingers going numb with the effort, until his body slid, dead-weight heavy and face up, onto the floor. In a wild swipe, I knocked the phone off its receiver and punched "0," yelling for help as I sank down beside the car dealer. Then, with my heart pounding, I tucked two fingers under Dale Worley's chin and lifted his jaw before covering his mouth with my own.

*   *   *

The morning light filtered through wisps of chilling fog and I hugged the plaid deck blanket closer, my face toward the endless dark stretch of North Pacific Ocean. I wasn't seeing anything but a continuous grim replay in my head. Dale's gray face and sightless eyes and the feel of his breastbone bowing again and again under the pressure of my palms. Only complete exhaustion let me sleep for a few hours, but even then, it was fitful. Marie sat up on the chaise lounge next to me. Bless her butt. She'd been such a mother hen that I'd half-expected to find feathers when I shampooed my hair.

"You're shivering again,'" she said, handing me the mug of brandy-laced coffee. "Here, take another swallow. And then in a couple of hours we'll be in port. You can take that hike in Capilano Park and, you know, get your mind off . . ." Her gray eyes were clouded with worry. "Darc'?"

"You know what I can't stop thinking about?" I said, grateful for the steam rising from the mug to warm my face. I gave a short, ironic laugh. "The last thing I said to Worley was something like, 'I wouldn't touch your lips if your life depended on it.'" I looked straight into Marie's eyes. "I said that horrible, bitchy thing. And now he's dead."

Marie was silent for a moment as she pulled a cigar from her fanny pack and then flicked the wheels on her VW bug lighter. The cheroot tip flamed and she took a drag and then exhaled, shaking her head. "But the point is that you *did*," she said, scrunching her brows. "Face it, Darcy, you did mouth-to-mouth on a guy whose face was purple and slimy with spit, and whose trousers were soaked with . . ."

I groaned, grateful that I'd showered twice.

"Sorry," Marie said, "but that's the truth, kid. You did CPR on Dale Worley until the infirmary staff forcibly pulled you off. And then they pronounced him dead. You gave Worley the only chance he had. A lot of people wouldn't have."

I sighed. "I know that, I guess. But still, it feels a little weird since I gave him such a hard time—"

"About being a complete jerk who sexually harassed countless women? And was cruel to helpless animals, made lewd jokes and—"

"And eventually choked to death on his frigging Tit Tie."

Marie smiled and a sigh escaped her lips. "Now there's my tough girl."

"Seriously," I said after taking a sip of the spiked coffee, "how did they think that happened? What did security say?"

"The last thing I heard was . . ." Marie, glanced up and then over my head. "Wait, here come Kirsty and Mitch. They'll know the latest."

I turned and watched as the couple approached along the freshly hosed deck and, even in the pale morning light, it was obvious that the wedding planner was already well into damage control mode. Kirsty held a cell phone tucked between her shoulder and chin, the PDA in her other hand, and her blonde hair, perfectly groomed as usual, swung in Swiss-clock precision with each step she took. She snapped the phone closed and smiled briskly as she spotted us. Mitch nodded and sneaked a glance at his watch.

"So much to handle," Kirsty murmured as they stopped beside us. "So little time." Her eyes met mine and her smile faltered. "I'm sorry, Darcy. How can I say that after all that you did back there in the Business Berth? You're the hero here."

I grimaced. "I wouldn't say that. It was a group effort, and . . . well, I'm just sorry we were too late to save Dale."

Marie sat forward in her lounge chair. "Mitch, have you figured out how he managed to get himself into that situation?"

I watched Mitch open his mouth to speak and then saw him frown when Kirsty beat him to it.

"Drunk," she said with a barely perceptible cluck of her tongue. "How could anyone be surprised by that? And careless." She reached up to adjust the frame on her dark-rimmed lenses. "I'm sure everyone remembers how he almost fell from the rail our first evening aboard."

I think my brows rose because, actually, I had forgotten that. Why did all that seem so long ago? Before Paul's near-miss with the peanuts, Gordy's up-close encounter with the Super Glue, my stapled foot poster, Kirsty's tacked-up lingerie, a barroom brawl, and now Dale . . . what kind of a wedding celebration was this? I took a quick sip of my coffee and peered up at the wedding planner.

"How's Patti Ann taking all this?" I asked. Even as a woman recently dodging an engagement ring, I could easily imagine how a soon to-be bride might feel about a dead body in her entourage. Tomorrow was Patti Ann's wedding day and right now the crew was trying to find a walk-in cooler with accommodations for one of her guests.

"She'll cope," Kirsty said without a blink. "Accidents happen."

I saw Mitch's forehead wrinkle and then his mouth opened and closed without saying anything. He looked down at his watch before finally speaking. "I need to get back to the security office. We're going to start interviewing some of the passengers."

Kirsty crossed her arms, her eyes fixed on his face. "I can't believe this, Mitch. You're interrogating people because of an accident?"

Mitch's mouth twitched on one side and he drummed his fingers on his uniform slacks.

"Interviewing. And it's standard procedure, Kirsty. There are still questions about how much he'd had to drink and where, who saw him last, why he was in the Business Berth at that late hour—"

"Oh?" Kirsty said, interrupting. "People have to adhere to banker's hours for business? I hate to think how much I'd get accomplished that way." She blinked quickly, stopping just short of rolling her eyes. "Okay then, why not ask Darcy the same thing? She was there, too. Go ahead, Mitch, ask her."

"I, uh . . ." I stammered, staring at the tight line of Kirsty's lips. What the hell was I supposed to say to that? I glanced sideways at Marie.

Mitch squirmed. "I'm not saying that I want to interview anyone. Some things are out of my hands. Especially now with—" he stopped short, like he'd said too much. He spread his palms in a helpless gesture. "Look, I have to get back to the office. I'm sorry."

Kirsty closed her eyes for a moment, inhaled and then exhaled softly, the same way I'd seen her do during that Yoga pose in the gym. When she reopened her eyes, she smiled first at me and then at Mitch. "No, wait. I'm the one who's sorry. Really. I'm being too sensitive I guess, because I'm thinking of poor Patti Ann and Kyle. And how they'll feel if Dale's accident takes the focus away from their plans. They've already had so many other distractions. Time is getting short here, Mitch."

I was tempted to say something about the fact that Dale Worley's time had run completely out, that death could hardly be called a distraction, and that maybe somebody should be sensitive to that, but frankly, I didn't think it was wise. Best not to irritate a woman who'd recently picked metal out of her underwear. Besides, I'd just remembered another couple of things that had been bothering me about that whole Business Berth deal. And I wasn't ready to share them with these folks.

"So what did you think about all that?" I asked as Marie and I watched Mitch and Kirsty walk in different directions down the deck.

Marie blew on her coffee. "First, I think that if you looked up the word 'intense,' in the dictionary, that Kirsty Pelham's picture would be next to it. And second, I think Mitch knows more than he's saying." She took a sip and swallowed, shaking her head.

"Like?"

"Like maybe he's thinking that Dale's death wasn't exactly accidental."

God. A splash of brandy wasn't enough and now I was even wondering if my hiking plans were going to keep my mind from heading the way it was. I pulled the plaid blanket up to my chin and fought another shiver. I nearly bit my tongue as I spoke. "Um . . . I just remembered something."

"What?"

I wiped my hand across my mouth as the awful scene tried to replay in my head again. "Maybe nothing. But weird. Something I found when I was starting mouth-to-mouth."

Marie's gray eyes were glued to mine. "What, Darc'? What'd you find?"

"Staples. There were staples on Worley's lips."

Marie's jaw dropped. "What do you mean?"

"Just a few, really, stuck in the"—I grimaced—"saliva. On his face and around his mouth. I kind of wiped them away, but . . ." I shuddered again.

Marie nodded. "But what?"

"I ended up spitting some out of my mouth. Afterward." I shook my head, wanting to make this something other than what I was thinking. Wanting like hell for Dale's death to have been accidental. "But it could have been because I knocked over some things on the desk, when I was trying to phone the operator." I squinted, remembering. "Paper clips, some pens, and—"

"A box of staples?"

"No," I said with a shuddering sigh. "I didn't see staples or a stapler anywhere. And there was one other thing. I forgot to tell security about it."

Marie raised her brows.

I groaned softly. "The lights were *off* when I opened the door to the Business Berth. Why would Dale be working in the dark?"

*   *   *

Six hours later, I found myself on the hike that made my attempted resuscitation of a car salesman look like a walk in the park. Especially since hiking this particular Canadian park now had me close to panic in the middle of the suspended foot bridge from hell. *Oh jeez.* I closed my eyes to keep from looking down some two-hundred-plus feet to the river below. Why on earth was I here? There'd been so many other choices . . .

Vancouver, from the ship's rail earlier, had looked like it was all about glass skyscrapers and incredible expanses of ocean framed by snow-capped mountains. With the addition of more grimacing totem poles than you could shake a Squamish raven feather at. But no, I'd passed on Stanley Park, Gas Town, Chinatown, and even the Vancouver Aquarium's beluga whales and poison arrow tree frogs in order to take what was supposed to be a relaxing hike—stupid damned choice. Because now I was frozen, motionless, and in a wimpy sweat, on the swaying planks of the Capilano Suspension Bridge, a 450-foot stretch of cedar and cable footbridge strung like a spider web above a roaring river. What in God's name had I been thinking?

I tried to swallow and my tongue stuck to the roof of my mouth. My head spun with another humiliating wave of dizziness. Dammit, what was wrong with me? The cable enclosure was shoulder-high, so it wasn't like it would be easy to fall off, and I'd never been afraid of heights. But maybe after slipping on that lighthouse cliff last cruise, or because I'd hardly slept since that horrific scene with Dale . . . now was not the time to analyze. I needed off this bridge.

I moaned and opened one eye, squinting down at miniature kayaks shooting the rapids on the river floor below. *God.* The bridge swayed as several more people stepped on behind me and began to make their way forward. My fingers snaked into the support cables like a monkey at the zoo. Someone growled about "moving it along there, sister," and I would have turned to glare but my eyes were stuck on the river and my knees were trembling. The roar from the rapids filled my ears and a chill breeze swept through the surrounding forest of ancient Douglas firs. The jerk behind me shouted again.

Maybe if I got down on all fours, very discreetly, and sort of crab-crawled—

"Darcy!"

Who?

I kept my death grip on the cables and tore my gaze away from the water to peer toward the far side of the bridge. Patti Ann, in hiking boots and a BAMA Elephants sweatshirt, marched toward me like she was practicing for her upcoming aisle walk.

"Got yourself a teeny bit stuck there, gal?" She called out, cupping both her hands around her mouth. Apparently she felt no primal need to hang onto anything.

"No, I was just—"

"Aw for crissake," the jerk behind me shouted, "get the redhead off the bridge before she wets her pants!"

This time I managed to turn and glare and—swear—if I'd had a hand free, I'd have shown the guy a bird he wouldn't see on any local totem pole.

"Pay no attention to him, darlin'," Patti Ann said, her ample thighs propelling her down the narrow span. "Think about this: the brochure said Marilyn Monroe crossed this bridge. Walter Cronkite, too. And Margaret Thatcher, the Rolling Stones . . ."

This was no time to tell our bride that I was pretty certain that Jagger hadn't always made rational decisions. And that I was, for damned sure, no Margaret Thatcher. Besides, all I could think of was that Patti Ann's rescue march was shaking the whole frigging bridge.

She stopped in front of me, a smile dimpling her round face and her brown eyes cocker-spaniel warm. "You're the bravest woman I know, Darcy Cavanaugh. I'm not lyin' one little bit about that."

She gave a quick nod and her silver earrings swung with the movement. "You just have to trust yourself here. Trust that you can do it. Okay?"

I nodded and managed to uncurl my fingers. The planks swayed beneath me again and I moaned.

"Here," Patti Ann said, turning away from me. "Slip your hand into my back pocket, darlin', and we'll do one classy little Conga right on outta here."

I reached my fingers into the embroidered rear pocket of the bride's cargo pants and started to walk. I wasn't entirely sure if it was a matter of trusting myself as much as I was just damned grateful the girl had a butt as substantial as a Southern buffet.

*   *   *

A blessed thirty minutes later we were settling back with grilled salmon burgers and a couple of Moosehead lagers at a table in the park's outdoor cafe. The air smelled of pine and wood smoke and shafts of sun slanted through the trees, warming my skin beneath the black fleece jacket I'd snagged weeks ago from Luke's closet. I played with the zipper pull, thinking of him and trying to ignore the ache that came as I wondered if he'd want to pack this jacket for his move to the East Coast. I'd tried to call him again around dawn, but no luck. I should get used to that. Like I'd have to get used to not seeing Luke. The ache squeezed again somewhere deep under the zipper pull. *He's going.*

Across from me, Patti Ann swirled her French fry in a blob of ketchup and raised her spa-waxed brows. "So Marie didn't want to learn how to carve a totem pole?"

"No," I answered, and then smiled sheepishly. "She's afraid of heights." I laughed into the mouth of my bottle. "I'm the gutsy one." I took a swallow of my beer, yeasty and bittersweet. "But speaking of missing persons, where's our bridegroom?"

Patti Ann opened her mouth and then hesitated, setting the French fry down. She sighed. "I needed a little time to myself today."

I wasn't sure, but I thought I saw very uncharacteristic tears forming in her eyes before she summoned a laugh and explained.

"I mean, shi-it, girl, this cruise is turning into a real 'B' movie, you know? Tomorrow's my wedding day. How am I supposed to toss a bouquet and do the Chicken Dance when one of our guests fooled around and got himself killed?"

I crossed my arms, rubbing my fingers across the elbows of Luke's sweatshirt and forced myself not to think about staples. And the possibility that Dale Worley didn't do anything to get himself killed. That maybe someone else did that for him.

Patti Ann sighed. "I thought that all my plans were so perfect, Darcy, and that it was going to be like I'd always dreamed it would." She giggled softly. "My best girlfriend, from Alabama, is flying out for the wedding. She's probably already there in Victoria. I know it sounds silly, but I keep thinkin' about how we used to play Barbie together—all those cute little plastic high heels and tiny purses— and how the wedding dress was best of all . . . well, you know."

I did my best to smile like I knew exactly what she meant. The truth was that I'd spent my childhood playing five-card stud with my mom and G.I. Joe with my two brothers. Barbie could have come along, but only if she'd shaved her head, pulled on her little plastic combat boots and promised never to draw to an inside straight. Maybe that was the root of my whole marriage phobia thing. Barbie deficit.

"And," Patti Ann's eyes were starting to mist again, "I figured that a West Coast wedding with some great Southern touches, would be a compromise for both families. But now . . ." Her breasts rose and fell in another heavy sigh.

Dammit. I shook my head, remembering the way she'd popped in on Marie and me that first night aboard, in her purple skirt, dotted Swiss veil, and "I AM THE BRIDE" glitter shirt, all excited about fried pickles and Mardi Gras. It had been ludicrous but somehow kind of great at the same time. There was none of that excitement in her eyes now and it just wasn't fair.

"Kirsty's getting things under control, Patti Ann," I said, reaching out to touch her hand. "If anyone can, she can. I think we need to be optimistic." It sounded lame even to my own ears.

I wasn't going to fool another ER nurse. Dead bodies are awkward.

"I know," she said, reaching for her beer. "Tomorrow will come, no matter what. I keep telling myself that." Her engagement ring flashed in the sunlight, and I stared at it, as transfixed as when I'd been watching the river from the dizzying height of that bridge.

"And I keep telling myself that a 'perfect wedding' isn't the important thing," Patti Ann continued. "A marriage is more than a ceremony. And, Lord knows, I want to marry Kyle more than anything I've wanted in my whole life and—"

"How did you know that?" I heard myself suddenly blurt. My gaze shifted from the diamond to her eyes and I was surprised by how urgently I wanted her answer. "How did you know that you wanted to marry Kyle?"

Patti Ann looked at me as incredulously as if I'd asked her how she breathes. She smiled and I saw warmth flood into her eyes. "Because I love him, of course."

"I know that," I said, leaning forward on the wooden bench. "But having, well . . . feelings for someone and wanting to be married aren't always the same." My fingers had found the zipper on the jacket again. "Marriage is a huge deal. God knows my parents couldn't get it right. Can't even get their divorce right, for that matter." I groaned. "Never mind about that. What I mean is that you really haven't known Luke all that long and—"

"Kyle," Patti Ann, said quickly, her brows scrunching.

"Huh?"

"You said Luke. I was correcting you."

"I did?" *Jeez.* I casually picked up the remains of my salmon burger, knowing my face was giving me away. "Well that's weird. I don't know why I'd say that when I meant Kyle and . . ." I babbled and brushed crumbs from the table, then glanced down at my watch. "Hey, I don't know about you, but I'm ready to head back."

"Trust," Patti Ann said suddenly and with a decisive nod of her head. Her earrings, which I now realized were pairs of little silver hearts, swung wildly.

"What?"

She smiled. "How I knew that I wanted to marry Kyle. I loved him, but it was mostly because I trusted myself—my heart—to know what's right for me. Kyle's right for me. I still want my dream wedding, but the truth is that I'd marry that man square in the middle of some dusty, damned rodeo or—" she broke off, squinting toward a stand of trees. "Hey," she said, nodding her head, "look."

"What?" I asked, trying to see what she was seeing.

"Over there." She started to raise her hand and then frowned. "No, wait. Well, that was sort of weird."

"Who?" I asked, totally confused now. "What was weird?"

"Ryan Galloway," she said, shaking her head. "I could have sworn he was watching us. But then he ran off before I could wave."

FOURTEEN

It didn't take a Margaret Thatcher to figure out that something was seriously wrong. And that Patti Ann's wedding party was headed into troubled waters. The first clue was the fact that the remaining shore tours had all been cancelled. The gangway was now, without exception, entirely one-way: bringing passengers back onboard. And then there was the matter of the crime scene tape.

"Where exactly was that crime tape?" I asked Marie, noticing that Paul Putnam was gesturing broadly to a group of wedding guests on the far side of the party room. He'd been the first to report its discovery and, from the way it looked, was milking the retelling for all it was worth.

"The Business Berth," Marie said, pulling up a chair next to mine at a table beside the groom's photo wall. I squinted up at the glossy pictures for a moment, wondering if was the lighting or if there were actually more staples up there. Jeez. Just the idea of staples was starting to make me cringe.

"And, from what Paul was saying," Marie continued, "Dale's cabin door has big swags of the yellow plastic, too." She rolled her eyes. "You want to take bets on whether it clashes with our wedding planner's color scheme?"

I groaned, remembering how I'd tried to convince Patti Ann that Kirsty could handle anything. I hoped to hell the wedding planner had brought a case of her ever-present antacids, because I had a good idea that this latest drama—whatever it was—was going to be more of a challenge than she'd signed on for. I kept remembering the look on Patti Ann's face when, as we'd climbed the gangway an hour ago, a minimum of six security staff compared our ID's to some new master list. There were pencil checks, lots of covert nods, and several mentions of "the wedding party" like it was a terrorist cell group. And now we were practically being held captive in this room. I groaned again through my clenched teeth.

Marie shook her head. "Chill, Darcy. There's nothing we can do about this."

"But I'd like to hear something official, you know?" I shifted in my chair, tugging at the hem of my printed orange halter dress. "It's spooky the way we're suddenly getting free drinks and appetizers as long as we stay put in this room. The ship is crawling with security. I swear I thought that one of them was going to hand me a towel when I got out of the shower."

"Nah, they're too busy finishing things up on the helipad."

"What?"

Marie glanced around the party room for a moment and lowered her voice. "I heard that there was a helicopter on the top deck around noon." She smiled. "Probably about the time you were on that bridge. Too bad they couldn't have dropped you a ladder."

I rolled my eyes. "Thanks for reminding me. But, seriously, why a helicopter?"

Marie shrugged. "I'm guessing to take Dale away."

Gordy and now Dale.

"Damn," I swore softly, gazing toward the photo wall and the firehouse shot with Putnam, Gordy, Worley, and Sam. And the girl with the dalmatian. "This is such bad juju. I don't think Barbie has an outfit for helicopters."

"Huh?" Marie looked at me like I was crazy. I was starting to feel that way myself.

"Never mind," I said, noticing that Sam had just come in through the door, followed by Ryan Galloway. Which reminded me. I turned back to Marie. "Ryan was spying on us today."

"What do you mean?"

"Up at Capilano Bridge," I said. "Patti Ann said he was watching us and then took off when he realized she'd noticed."

Marie frowned. "Why am I not surprised? Face it, Kyle's got strange friends. Every last one of them. And to tell you the truth, I'll be glad when we've marched our damned polka dots down the aisle tomorrow and I can catch that first flight back home."

"Me too," I admitted, feeling guilty but completely truthful. "But I know how much this all means to Patti Ann. And I still think that if there's something that can be done . . ." I stopped as I saw Mitch De Palma moving toward the little stage at the front of the room. Kirsty took a seat nearby, her expression tense.

"Looks like we're going to get an update, finally," I said, scanning the room. Everyone was here: Sam, Ryan, Paul, Kyle, Patti Ann. And—over by the bar—Snake Woman and the other remaining wedding guests who hadn't been glued, stapled, or choked. Shit. This wasn't Barbie.

"Thank you all for coming," Mitch began, spreading his stance and tucking his hands behind his butt, the way I'd seen him do that first night when he'd warned us all to behave. But I got the feeling that fart machines were way down on his list now. He cleared his throat and glanced very quickly toward Kirsty before he spoke. "I'm sure that you've heard rumors and I wanted to take this opportunity to clear things up." He nodded toward the doorway where there were now several of his uniformed security staff. "You may have noticed that we've called in some extra help—and an outside agency for the interviewing process."

Paul Putnam grumbled and Mitch leveled a look in his direction. "Yes. You will all be asked questions regarding the events surrounding Dale Worley's death." He raised his hand to silence some murmurs across the party room. "All of you. Without exception." He glanced once again at Kirsty and a muscle on his jaw twitched. "I want you to know that we are doing everything we can to wrap things up before the ship docks in Victoria tomorrow morning. It is not our intention to delay the wedding."

Delay? *Oh Lord.* I watched as Patti Ann's hand flew to her mouth and a wail escaped.

The Snake Woman waved her hand from her seat at the bar. "Do you mean my cousin's wedding could be," her voice rose, "postponed?"

I couldn't be sure, because he was holding a beer to his mouth, but I think that Ryan Galloway was grinning like a Squamish totem pole.

Mitch shifted his stance and his voice remained calm. "We will do everything we can to avoid that outcome."

Paul Putnam stood, his eyes narrowing, bulky frame posed like he was about to axe the door of a burning building. "Well that's mighty big of you, De Palma. Hell, I can do better than that. Victoria's only a couple of hours away. Maybe we should just take this party onboard a ferryboat. Skip the scenic cruise up the coast and your damned 'interviews.'" He whirled around, raising his palms toward the gathered guests. "What do you say, guys? How long will it take you to pack?"

"No." Mitch cut in before anyone could respond. "That is not an option, Mr. Putnam. We're continuing the itinerary. And no one leaves this ship."

Marie raised her brows in perfect unison with mine.

Sam stood and I noticed that the bruising around his eye was green as well as purple now. I was doing my best to forget the trouble I'd gotten myself into nursing that injury.

"You're saying that we'd be held onboard?" he asked.

"Detained, technically," Mitch answered, the twitch in his jaw returning. "Until the investigation is completed."

Sam nodded, brows furrowing. "So Dale's death wasn't an accident?"

Mitch could do nothing to stop the murmurs in the party room and I saw Kirsty pop an antacid. Followed by a second one.

"That's a possibility," Mitch said.

*　*　*

It was no use trying to avoid Jamieson. People were clustered everywhere in nervous little groups. It was like that old horror movie where everyone checks everyone else's eyeballs to see who is a body snatcher and who is a pod person. Only this time, someone could be a murderer. We wouldn't know more until our "interviews." But Mitch had assured us that we could move freely around the ship until then. When they were ready for us they'd page overhead.

"Great," I told Sam as I took a sip of my chocolate martini and gazed over the railing at the eighty-foot Teflon sails that were a landmark of Vancouver's pier. "What will they say over the heads of two thousand passengers? Something discreet like, 'Will the next murder suspect please report for a strip search?'"

Sam chuckled that familiar chuckle, low in his throat. From the look simmering in his eyes I knew I'd been stupid again. Apparently you don't mention nakedness to a man who's seen your shamrock tattoo. Especially after he's confessed that he might be in love with you. If I'd played Barbie I probably would have known these things.

He reached for his tie as the breeze caught it again, and I noticed that a hint of sunburn was competing with his bruises now. He'd opted for the Granville Island kayaking tour today, and had been openly disappointed when I'd declined to join him. Sam inched down the ship rail until he was close enough that I could smell his aftershave.

"So," he said, "do you really think that you're a suspect?"

I surprised myself by stammering a little. "I, uh . . . well," *Am I a suspect?* Sam spoke again before I could unstick my tongue and come up with an answer.

"I've been thinking about what they might ask me," Sam said. "At least about my relationship with Worley." He frowned. "I'd be lying if I denied the fact that I thought he was a complete waste of oxygen." He squeezed his eyes shut for a moment. "And then, of course, I threatened him." Sam opened his eyes and exhaled softly and then, before I'd realized it, he reached out to trace his fingers along my jaw. He smiled. "Over you."

I'd opened my mouth to say something—anything—when a movement caught my eye at a ship entryway, just yards away. Just a glimpse really, of a man with close-cropped blonde hair, muscular shoulders, gray tweed sport coat and . . . *no way.* My stomach did a strange little flip-flop and I think I might have gasped. Sam dropped his hand to take hold of my elbow, and I blinked into the distance but there was nothing left to see. *It couldn't have been.*

"What's the matter, Darcy?"

"Nothing," I said, feeling like an ass. What was the matter with me? "I'm just tired," I said honestly. "And a little edgy, I guess." I took a step backward, pulling my melon-colored shawl around my shoulders, and then looked over at the doorway again. I sighed. "This waiting around is driving me crazy."

"Then let's eat," Sam suggested. "We're on a cruise ship. I'm pretty sure we could find something to," he did that low chuckle again, "nibble on."

I'm sure that what Sam had in mind was something more like me feeding him peeled grapes in his cabin, our clothes in a heap, the porthole steaming up, and all to some romantic background ambience like—well, it was Sam after all—reruns of *South Park* maybe? Anyway, what he got was guacamole, chorizo, red peppers stuffed with goat cheese, skewered tiger prawns, roasted potatoes, and stuffed olives. Tapas. All washed down with Sangria. Lots of it. And there was plenty of company to drink it with, too. Our infamous rogues' gallery of murder suspects, the wedding party itself, was all hunkered down in the Lido Deck's Barcelona Tapas Bar.

And bitching about the fact that Dale Worley had died, subjecting them to the friggin' indignity of Mitch De Palma's interviews.

We'd arrived just after Marie received her page to report below decks.

Paul Putnam belched and wiped his mouth on a ship logo napkin. "Well, what did we ex-sh-pect, any-w-way," he slurred, "that our good buddy Dale's death would be treated with the dignity that it deserves?" He thumped his beefy fist on the table, shaking the oranges in a pitcher of wine. "No. Instead we get cross-examined by a bunch of damned attorneys!" He shook his head. "This cruise line's covering its ass, that's all. That's the bottom line here."

I looked over at Kirsty, who'd paused in her earnest conversation with Patti Ann.

"Is that true, Kirsty?" I asked. "The cruise line attorneys are doing the interviews?" My heart tugged as I saw the mascara streaks on our bride's face. Her bridge bravado was ebbing.

Kirsty pushed what looked like an untouched appetizer plate away and inhaled softly. Her voice was calm and surprisingly strong for a woman who never seemed to eat anything. "I believe that the legal department is involved. I would expect as much since the cruise line has an image to maintain. But I'm sure Mitch is heading up the interviews himself." She nodded and her perfect hair swung across the shoulders of her fawn gabardine suit. "And he's promised to fill me in, personally, on every detail of the process." She wrapped an arm around Patti Ann's shoulders. "Nothing is going to interfere with this wedding."

Patti Ann snuffled and then there was a strange sort of pantomime as Ryan tried to hand her a tissue and Kyle snatched it out of his hand. I raised my brows at Sam and he shrugged like he didn't know what the hell was with these guys, either. Maybe the pod-people explanation wasn't such a stretch.

"And," Kirsty said, glancing down at her watch, "on a positive note, I understand that the ship will raise anchor early. Around six PM instead of midnight. So we'll all be able to enjoy a beautiful daylight view of the Canadian coastline."

"What's that mean exactly?" Sam asked, with his glass of wine halfway to his lips. "We'll be arriving in Victoria earlier then?"

"No," Kirsty explained quickly, "the arrival time is still the same. It's just that we'll be sailing a more leisurely course up the coast toward—"

"Alaska?" Patti Ann yelped. Her mascara-smeared eyes bugged like a startled raccoon. "Oh my God! My wedding's in Victoria and we're going to Alaska?" Her sob was muffled against Kyle's Western shirt as he pulled her close. Beside them, Ryan quietly poured himself a hefty glass of sangria.

"No, no," Kirsty said, reaching for her briefcase, "I've got a map. I'll show you. We're simply taking a circular route, around the—"

"Bullshit!" Putnam roared. "All they're doing is getting us away from shore as fast as they can."

"That's real genius, Putnam," Ryan said with a sneer. He tried to stand, wobbled, and sank back onto his chair. "And did you also figure out it's because you were the fool who told security you were going to ferry us out of here? Huh, Putnam? Are you that frickin' smart?"

Paul growled and rose from his seat and Ryan grabbed the tabletop to steady himself as he struggled to get to his feet. Sam leaped up and wedged himself in front of Putnam. I heard Ryan curse as Kyle reached out to hold him back and—there was a sudden crackle from the PA system overhead and a crisp, British voice. Everyone froze and looked up.

"Passenger Ryan Galloway, please phone two-two-seven-one," the voice said. "Mr. Galloway, please."

Saved by Ryan's page.

Putnam sat, Sam sat, and Kyle slipped his arm back around Patti Ann. Kirsty picked open the end of a roll of antacids with her only unchewed fingernail.

Ryan took a last swig of his drink.

I didn't want to even think about how the newest interviewee was going to make it down six decks, or how intelligible he'd be after three or four sangrias. That was Mitch De Palma's problem. And besides—my eyes scanned the miserable, huddled group at the table—I was already too bummed by what had just happened here. And my continuing, helpless feeling that I could do nothing to fix any of this. For godsake, the bride was crying, the wedding planner was living on antacids, and the groom and groomsmen were just short of going for each other's throats. How was it possible that in just a few short days we'd moved from Mardi Gras and limbo, wedding photos, white tulle, mimosas and Spa Day pedicures—*wait*. That reminded me. What time was it? I checked my watch and stood.

"Sam," I said, grabbing my shawl and my purse, "when Marie gets back, tell her I've gone down to the Java Café lecture room."

"Why?" Sam scrunched his brows. "For what?"

I smiled, feeling maybe there was something that I could fix after all. "I'm going to catch the last of that seminar," I told him, "'Acupressure for the Foot Lover's Sole.'"

* * *

173

I'd forgotten all about my strappy wedge sandals until I arrived at the door of the conference room. I glanced down. Cute shoes—substantial chunk of paycheck shoes—mango leather, beaded and perfect with my dress. But bare toes. And after that scene I'd just endured in the Tapas Bar, the last thing my psyche needed was to witness Doctor Phillip Foote fully inflamed by toe cleavage. Of course, then, maybe that was an unfair assumption. After all, I didn't know for certain that Phillip was behind the gigantic foot posters all over the ship, or that he'd ordered the chocolate pudding for my pedicure. And the poetry . . . well, the poetry was just a guess. No proof at all there. I shouldn't go off half-cocked. I was here to ask him questions. I grabbed a class brochure and slid through the door, hobbling as nonchalantly as I could with my toes sucked back into my sandals. No point in taking chances.

I slid into the back row of the dim-lit room just as Phillip apparently made some very funny reference to plantar warts or maybe it was heel spurs since he had graphics illustrating both in his Power-Point presentation. There was a good buzz of laughter and I could see that the podiatrist was eating it up the same way that he'd slurped up those udon noodles at our lunch meeting that time. At that Japanese restaurant where we'd sat, disgustingly, wantonly barefoot, and . . . *no!* I wasn't going to do this. I was going to give this man the benefit of the doubt; just simply ask a few pertinent questions. I was a nurse, a professional with cool, clinical objectivity. I could do it. Phillip Foote would not lower my standards. Although my standards could never be as high as that man's pants, for godsake. *Eew.*

I slid my feet protectively under the chair in front of me as I tipped a little sideways and peered between two elderly women to get a better view. He was wearing his standard, elasticized, no-belt slacks at about rib level, with a striped polo shirt buttoned up to the collar under a mauve linen blazer. Its lapels were studded with what looked like . . . professional logo pins, maybe? He rocked back and forth when he talked, one hand behind his flabby butt and the other holding a pointer that he used to stroke the images on the screen. The screen that just went black. Perfect timing—I already knew more about orthotics than I cared to.

The lights came on and I waited while the attendees gathered their belongings and several came forward to shake Phillip's hand and to get a closer look at the custom orthotics he'd assembled on the table at the front of the room. I was proud that—although I shuddered a little—I managed to maintain my cool even when some innocent woman picked up the German Velveteen Arch Support. I bit my lip, bided my time and waited until, slowly, the room cleared and Phillip spotted me. It was scary how fast the guy could glide forward. Especially since I was pretty sure he was looking down at my feet.

"Darcy, great to see you!" Phillip took one of my hands between both of his, and I caught a whiff of cologne that smelled strangely like shoe polish. "I was so surprised when I saw you in the bar the other night."

Yeah, right. I forced a smile and reminded myself that I had no proof that Phillip had been stalking me. I was on a fact-finding mission, pure and simple. And, most importantly, I was a cool, objective professional.

I slipped my hand away and lifted the glossy color brochure, trying to think of something neutral to say. Something to start the conversation rolling and keep his eyes off my toes.

"Yes, it surprised me to find you aboard, too, Phillip," I said as I ran a fingertip down the front of his brochure, "lecturing about—"

and that's exactly when I spotted the curious logo at the bottom of his list of credentials.

I blinked a couple of times, thinking maybe it was the effects of sangria, but it was really there: the familiar winged foot. Yes. Hermes or Mercury or whatever Carol's lesbian poet group had concluded it was when they were reading the poetry from the FedEx envelopes and—my mouth dropped open, blood rushed to my face and I jabbed my finger at the brochure, incredulously and then again viciously.

"What is this thing?" I finally sputtered, lifting my chin and closing in on him. But before Phillip could answer, I spied the little initials below the emblem, the "PF." The same ones that Marie had noticed on the foot posters. PF. Phillip Foote. His initials . . . *oh my God!* My face on fire, my red hair flying, I whirled around to get a better look at the huge foot poster just yards away on the classroom wall. The winged logo was on that one, too. Along with my ankle bracelet, my feet, my ten toes, digitally enhanced, and—*bastard!*

"Dammit, Phillip!" I exploded, whirling back toward him and screeching way more like a banshee than a cool professional. "You gave me a *toe job*?"

"I, uh." Dr. Foote attempted to glide backward. His orthotics failed.

Somehow my fist was over the front of his blazer and I was poking my finger at the matching winged foot pin on his lapel and glaring up into his very red face, the whole pent-up litany just rolling off my tongue: "Nasty poems, chocolate pudding, teddy bears, and snakes." I narrowed my eyes dangerously. "And how about staples, Phillip? You don't want to get me started with staples, do you?"

"*Staples?*" Phillip squeaked the word, his eyes dilated and his face blanching. When suddenly my own name buzzed in my ears. Huh? Deeply ingrained guilt made me think at first that it was my conscience—good Catholic girls do not pummel podiatrists. Then I realized it was coming from overhead. I was being paged.

"Passenger Darcy Cavanaugh," the British voice said, "please dial . . ."

I stopped my assault on Dr. Foote's jacket.

It was time for my murder interview.

*   *   *

"Okay, there's my signature, right below Marie's," I said, handing the pen back to Mitch in the hallway outside a security office door. I wasn't sure if my stomach was bouncing around because I'd realized, in the elevator on my way down here, that I'd just attacked a man. Or because I was about to recount that awful scene when I'd done CPR on Dale Worley. "Hey," I said, going for the grim joke to settle my nerves. "Just don't fingerprint me afterward, okay?"

Mitch smiled. "Deal. Go on in. And then afterward I'll take you to the interview room."

I wrinkled my brows. "This isn't—then why am I going in here?"

Mitch gave an exhausted sigh. "This attorney wants to explain something about a conflict with your interview. I'm not sure what it's about. But go on in. I'm right behind you."

Great. This new complication did nothing for my stomach. Apparently everyone had conflicts. Ryan, Kyle, Kirsty, Dr. Foote, and now—I opened the door and my heart wedged into my throat.

Luke?

FIFTEEN

I closed my mouth before a girly squeal could launch me shamelessly into Luke Skyler's arms. Because, dammit, Mitch was right behind me. And because I'm a quick study. Six months in FBI Girlfriend School taught me to recognize that almost imperceptible shake of Luke's head and the Morse Code in his sexy blue eyes. Right now those eyes—so very capable of conveying, "I can't wait to get you under the covers. Hell, the floor will do"—unfortunately read: *Undercover. I don't know you.*

So now Luke was standing only a few yards away, his eyes on my face, sun-shot blonde hair a bit mussed from the helicopter ride, the cuffs on his oxford shirt—always a little snug over those amazing shoulders—rolled back over his tanned forearms, and his tie loosened. He shifted his weight and his khaki slacks stretched over his muscular thighs and a butt made world-class fabulous by jogging the San Francisco hills. Damn, this was so like someone holding a bowl of Häagen-Dazs just inches—and yet cosmic miles—out of reach. The feds owed me big time.

"Darcy," Mitch said, nudging me into the room and then stepping past me. "This is Mr. Skyler, from the cruise line's legal department." He nodded at Luke and tapped his clipboard nervously. The poor guy was clearly stressed. I knew the feeling. My body was tingling with stress right this second.

Mitch cleared his throat. "This is Miss Cavanaugh, sir. She's, uh, the one who did that mouth-to-mouth."

"Oh?" A truly naughty look flickered in Luke's eyes. "Yes. She looks quite capable of mouth-to-mouth." Then his eyes softened with genuine concern. "But it must have been an awful experience, Miss Cavanaugh. I'm sorry."

"Yes, well," I said, suddenly aching like crazy for this man's hug, "I'm a nurse. That's pretty much what I do."

My eyes wouldn't leave Luke's no matter how hard I tried. He didn't blink. And the stretch of silence was killing me.

Mitch turned at a sound outside in the corridor. Then he looked back toward Luke. "That could be the other interview, sir. Should I . . . ?"

I think I may have whimpered, but that was far more acceptable than screaming, "*Yes! Get your ass out of here, for godsake!*" Which was what I wanted to do. But didn't have to—because Luke did. Or at least something mercifully close.

"Yes, De Palma, check on that. Then wait outside. I'll bring Miss Cavanaugh out in a few minutes. After I advise her."

The door had barely closed when we slammed together like opposing freight trains.

There was quick laughter, rapid-fire taunts of "advise me quick, sir" and "mouth-to-mouth," and then somehow I was off the floor with my dress hiked up like a hussy and my legs wound around

Luke's waist. A mango sandal clattered to the floor. And then the laughing stopped.

I breathed in the soap and leather scent of Luke's skin and felt the brush of his beard stubble just before his big hand grasped the back of my hair, fingers sinking deep to my scalp. His open mouth covered mine and . . . was so worth the hellish waiting. He took a few steps, carrying me easily astride him and kissing me over and over, hardly pausing to breathe until my spine met the cabin wall and stopped our forward momentum.

The man was a world-class kisser, and I'd started to think of practical things like floor versus tabletop and speculating on the privacy factor of how well Mitch De Palma could be trusted to follow orders when—dammit. Luke's cell phone buzzed, his mouth pulled away from mine and I found myself sliding not so gracefully back down onto the carpeted floor. I stumbled over my remaining wedge sandal, pulled my dress down and pouted like someone had just washed my Häagen-Dazs down the sink.

"Sorry," Luke mouthed as he turned away and spoke in soft monosyllables into the phone. I used the few minutes to pull my clothes back together and limp in search of my other shoe, chiding myself for my stupidity in being so surprised that Luke was here. The FBI did cruise ship investigations in international waters; that's how I'd met him last year, for heaven's sake. On that New England Fall Foliage cruise. Had I forgotten that? Yeah right. *Not ever.*

I smiled and glanced over at his great butt, remembering him forced to do the cha cha and merengue, even dress up as Captain Hook for the ship's Halloween party, all undercover as a dance host. It had been crazy and scary and weak-knees romantic. But that time it began as jewel theft and this time it was malicious attacks and . . . murder? Was Dale Worley really murdered? And—goose bumps rose on my arms—did the FBI think I had something to do with it?

Luke set the phone down and turned to face me, running his fingers through his hair. He glanced down at his watch and then stepped closer, sighing. I was pretty sure the love scene was over.

"Look, Darcy," he said, voice gentle. "This is going to be awkward as hell. I'm not going to promise you anything different. And we've got like five minutes before one of the other agents arrives to interview you."

"Not you?" I asked, knowing that was foolish even as the words left my lips.

Luke shook his head. "Can't. You know that." He laughed and glanced toward the wall he'd just pinned me against, like he expected to see a scorch mark. "I'm only here until they can find someone else. It doesn't take a law degree to know that our relationship makes for some conflict."

He was serious, but I couldn't help myself. I don't cool down as efficiently as he does. "I didn't see any conflict back there, Skyler," I said softly, reaching up to slide the knot on his tie. "I'm thinking it was pretty cooperative. And I'm thinking that I could prove it if—"

He laughed and grabbed one of my hands, pressing his lips quickly to my fingers. "I know you could. And there's nothing I'd rather take you up on—*that* is the conflict."

No ice cream, obviously.

"So?" I asked, squaring my shoulders. "What's next?"

He sighed and then smiled, and the look in his eyes made my throat catch. "Thanks. You're the best. And okay then, by the book: you interview with Scott. He knows about us, but he won't make concessions. Can't. No one else—De Palma and his security staff included—knows about you and me or about the fact that I'm not a cruise line attorney. Except the captain. And a few key crewmembers."

"And Marie," I said quickly.

"And Marie." Luke's eyes lit and he smiled broadly. I should be jealous of how he felt about my cigar-smoking, smart-ass girl-friend. "By the way," he said, "she's hoping we postpone this wedding. Something about polka dots and Ethel Mertz? Anyway, I'll be doing interviews and then moving around the ship, talking with people candidly. As a lawyer, not as a federal agent. I can't talk with you. Or . . . be with you."

I think I pouted again. By the look on Luke's face, I must have.

"It's sixteen hours, that's all, Darcy. Until we dock in Victoria."

"You counted?" I asked, genuinely touched by the idea. "You counted how many hours until you can be with me?"

Luke smiled. "And, as I was saying, we're going to work our asses off to have this case settled before that. So that you can be a brides-maid and I can finish up my other case and . . ." Luke hesitated and my chest got that familiar, painful ache.

And then you can pack up and move away to the East Coast.

"And," Luke continued, "I can't let you tell me anything directly about Dale Worley's death, and I can't question you about it. We can't be seen alone together." He smiled. "For sixteen hours. Deal?"

"How many agents are on board?"

"Lawyers. And I can't tell you that."

"Was Dale really murdered?" I asked, realizing that I'd started to shiver a little.

Luke pulled his shoulder holster and gun from the desk drawer and secured it in place under his arm. "We're technically investigating a 'death under suspicious circumstances,'" he said, reaching for a gray tweed sport coat. "That's all I can say."

For some reason, Luke's coat caught my eye and I stared at it as he slid his arms into the sleeves. And then the sound of voices outside the door interrupted my thoughts.

Luke squeezed my arm gently. "That's probably Scott, ready for you." His brows scrunched. "Are you okay?"

"Sure," I lied, fighting a sudden uncomfortable confusion. It was stupid, but something about Luke's coat was really bugging me. Reminding me of something. It was strange because I was pretty sure I'd never even seen that one, but . . .

"Good, then." Luke started toward the door, and then stopped.

He turned back and a look flickered across his face that I couldn't read. "I do have one question I'd like to ask you, though. Not about Worley."

I raised my brows. "Okay."

Why was the pit of my stomach starting to feel funny all of a sudden? What was wrong?

Luke watched my eyes very intently as he spoke. "Why didn't you tell me that Sam Jamieson was coming on this cruise?"

I opened my mouth and then closed it as I remembered what was bothering me about that coat. It was that tweed sport coat I'd seen earlier, the one on the man watching me from the ship's corridor. When I was with Sam. *Oh hell.* That man was Luke.

"I didn't know he was coming," I said, knowing how lame that must sound.

"Oh."

"I mean I knew he was an old friend of Kyle's, of course, but I didn't know he'd be coming. At all, not a clue and—" Blast it, I was babbling like an idiot. I took a breath and smiled as casually as I could. "Basically, it's just a weird coincidence."

What was that in Luke's eyes? Doubt? Oh please, not doubt.

"Yeah. Sure is." Luke's eyes had gone cloudy gray and completely unreadable.

The door opened from the outside and he moved toward it.

I touched Luke's arm, feeling uncharacteristically desperate. I needed to make him believe me. "Luke, really, it's—"

"Time for your interview," he said.

* * *

In less than two hours, I was topside again, zipped into my one-shoulder copper gown and, frankly, very surprised to see full attendance at our assigned dinner table. Because, after an initial round of interviews, Patti Ann's little wedding party was obviously shell-shocked. If I hadn't already figured that out, my first clue would have been when Snake Woman—whose name I now knew was Sissy Rose—made that big mistake on her grilled seafood order. She asked our waiter for "alibi" instead of albacore. Apparently, it was a subject on everyone's mind. Mine, too, except for the huge portion of my brain that was still numb with shock about Luke's arrival.

"I still can't believe Luke's here and that all this is happening," I whispered to Marie, after glancing down the table. Patti Ann, dark eyes stressed, was huddled close to Kyle. Beside her was Kirsty in a lilac satin gown. Ryan, Putnam, Sam . . . everyone accounted for.

"Believe it," Marie said with a sigh. "I actually had to dig bar receipts out of my fanny pack to prove my whereabouts last night.

The guy who questioned me must have started out with the IRS. In my opinion, these guys are going to have a hard time finding someone who didn't want to kill Worley."

"We still don't know that he was murdered," I said, remembering how I'd asked Agent Scott just that and had been met with tight-lipped silence.

"Did you mention your," Marie lowered her voice, "staple theory?"

"No. I started to and then it felt stupid." I frowned. "Especially since I haven't managed to put two and two together with that weirdness myself."

Marie shook her head. "I'm pretty sure that's what *they're* here for, Darc." Marie glanced over her shoulder quickly, and then mouthed *F-B-I*. "It's their job to solve this, not yours. You need to remember that."

"Yeah, well, I'd be a fool not to try to prove that I'm not a murderer." *Or a cheat.* I squeezed my eyes shut against the memory of that awful, doubting look on Luke's face when he'd asked about Sam. "And besides," I said, tilting my head to get a better look at the bridal couple, "I'll do anything to make sure that wedding happens tomorrow." I looked up as a voice boomed across the table, thick with drink. Putnam.

"Back off, Kirsty, would you?" Paul growled, after signaling to the waiter for a refill of his drink. "I've got every right, and you're not going to stop me." He tugged at the collar of his tuxedo and I could tell by the bleary shine in his eyes that he'd been at the bar before dinner. Which had, no doubt, prompted his morbid insistence that a place be set in Worley's usual spot. I tried not to notice the glitter-eyed armadillo bolo tie he'd coiled on the plate. Or the cardboard llama standing like a pallbearer at the end of the table.

"I'm doing my own little inter-r-r-view here." Paul half-rose from his dining chair, eyes bulging like Perry Mason. "I'm not some goddamned lawyer, folks. I'm Dale Worley's best friend. Ten years." He reached down and picked up the hammered tin armadillo and dangled it like a noose. "Just where in the hell was everyone when my good buddy choked to death?"

God. I glanced sideways and saw Marie grimace.

"Paul, please," Patti Ann begged. "Don't do this."

Kyle started to stand and Kirsty took hold of his arm, stopping him.

"No," she said calmly. "The last thing we need is another fight. And maybe Paul's right. If we clear up some of our own questions, we can be more supportive of each other. We've already given this information to the interviewers, so it's no secret." She smiled at Patti Ann. "I'll start."

Kirsty took one of her Yoga breaths and straightened her shoulders. "At one o'clock this morning—that's apparently when Dale had his accident—I was in my cabin." A faint flush rose to her cheeks. "Repairing my lingerie."

She gave a nod as Putnam sank back into his chair, and then she turned to Kyle. "Kyle?"

Kyle's jaw tensed as he glanced toward Putnam. "I was with Patti Ann."

"In the Java Café," Patti Ann added, "going over our vows." Her brows scrunched and I saw her chin tremble. "So we'll be ready for tomorrow."

Ryan hunched his shoulders and stared down at his plate, silent.

The Snake Woman spoke up, taking Ryan's turn. "I was in the Piano Bar. I gave my receipt to one of the lawyers, Mr. Scott. It has the time marked right on it." Her tongue flicked across her lips. "But, like I told the lawyer, I barely knew Mr. Worley and—"

"Dammit, Galloway," Putnam interrupted. "No holding out. Where were you?"

Ryan glared and it was a long time before he answered. "In my cabin," he finally said. "Which is exactly where I'm going now because I don't owe anyone here any damned explanations." He threw his napkin onto the table and strode off, flattening Worley's llama on his way.

"Uh . . ." Kirsty closed her mouth and was silent.

"Crow's Nest Bar," Marie said quickly and then shrugged. "I had a receipt, too, and the bartender would remember me. I've sailed with him before."

Shit. My turn.

"On deck," I said, fighting the heat creeping to my face, "back at the fantail. Sam was hurt and I was . . ." I looked up and saw Kirsty watching my face as intently as a parochial school nun. I could almost feel a knuckle-rap coming.

"She fixed me an ice-pack," Sam said, nodding way too many times in that boyish, telltale way of his. He reached up to touch his cheek. "After Mitch slugged me." He scowled. "Which turned out to be a dumb-ass thing to tell that lawyer. The sonofabitch grilled me like I was a street punk."

"Which lawyer?" Putnam asked.

My stomach sank. I could guess which one.

"Skyler," Sam said, shaking his head. "The man has an attitude."

Putnam, who had somehow fastened Dale's bolo over his own bow tie, took a swig from his drink and laughed sharply. "Don't worry about Skyler," he said. "Your alibi's tight. Yours too, Darcy." He laughed again and waggled his finger back and forth between Sam and me. "Hell, we've all got each others' backs. The three of us. All for one, one for all."

The three of us? Excuse me, but there's no way I could see this man as D'Artagnan.

Marie murmured sympathetically beside me as my stomach started to do scary things. I didn't like where Putnam was going with this. And it didn't help that Kirsty was staring me down.

"What do you mean, Putnam?" Sam asked, eyes darting toward me for a split second.

"I mean that I told that lawyer the plain ass truth," Putnam sputtered over another mouthful of booze. He wiped his mouth and then his smile turned into a full-blown leer. "I told Mr. Lucas Skyler that I was out there watching while you two were busy sucking face."

Oh shit! There was nothing I wanted more than to grab the silver-tipped ends of that armadillo tie and yank it until Paul Putnam's eyes popped out and rolled across the tablecloth; but then that would probably look suspicious. MO and all. Besides, the PA was crackling overhead. I was being paged back down to the interview room.

* * *

I must have done something very, very wrong in a former life. It was the only possible explanation for the fact that I was spending the final night of a luxurious cruise in the humid, windowless bowels of a ship with a sweating Mitch De Palma, two FBI agents—now camouflaged in tuxedoes to blend with the passenger crowd—along with one other targeted person. I didn't know which was more hellish, that the second federal agent was a very terse-looking Luke Skyler—or the fact that my fellow interviewee was Doctor Phillip Foote. Why on earth was the podiatrist here?

"Miss Cavanaugh," Agent Scott continued. "I appreciate your helping us out with a string of confusing facts that have come up during the course of our interviews with the wedding party and with ship personnel."

I stole a glance at Luke, who was showing as much expression as a granite slab. Phillip, on the other hand, was sort of smugly beaming, his gaze flitting alarmingly foot-ward now and then. I crossed my ankles and turned back to Scott. "No problem, but I can't imagine what I could know that would help you." I summoned an uneasy smile.

Agent Scott folded his arms and I heard a shoulder holster creak under his jacket in a very unlawyer-like way. "It has to do with staples, Miss Cavanaugh."

I was pretty sure that he heard me choke. "Staples?"

For some crazy reason Phillip Foote put his hands on his hips—or somewhere below the waist of those chin-high slacks—and began to nod knowingly.

"Yes," Scott said. "What can you tell me about that?"

SIXTEEN

THE WEASLY LITTLE PODIATRIST had provided the FBI with—*oh jeez*—footage. Video proof of my rant at the Foot Lover's Sole lecture. How was I supposed to know that those things were taped? Who in the hell would want one of those tapes? But, regardless, it wasn't looking good for me.

"There," Phillip said, pointing to the wall-mounted TV screen like a witch hunter. "Rewind it and play that last part again. Turn up the volume this time. So Darcy can hear all the words."

Mitch hit the button on the VCR and I groaned as my image filled the screen once more: polite smile and batting lashes, really cute dress . . . green eyes beginning to dart, smile twitching, shoulders whirling . . . then red hair flying wild and my finger poking relentlessly into Dr. Foote's lapel. Jab, jab, jab. While, way worse, my voice—the reason I played tambourine for the Holy Spirit choir—snarled in perfect Exorcist pitch, "*And how about staples, Phillip? You don't want to get me started with staples, do you?*" The button clicked, my image lurched backward and forward again like a Stepford wife on crack: *". . . You don't want to get me started with staples, do you?"* The button clicked again, my image moon-walked backward in slow-mo and—

"Okay!" I blurted, a shade louder than I'd intended, "could we stop this now?" My voice softened as I tried to make out Luke's silhouette in the semi-darkness. "Please?"

The room lights came on and I sighed. "I can explain that," I said glancing again at Luke and vowing to get him alone somehow, somewhere, to explain so damned many other things. "But first," I narrowed my eyes at the podiatrist. "Maybe the doctor has some things he needs to explain. Don't you now, Phillip?"

I could have murdered Foote when he shrugged. Luke looked worried that I might.

"I have no explanation for your behavior there, Darcy," the podiatrist said, his voice as calm as a man laying out bunion options. "Unless this threat had something to do with my decision not to hire you for that orthotic rep position last year."

"Wha-at? *Your* decision?" *What the*—was I hearing this right? I jutted my chin, took a step toward Phillip and felt Mitch move in close beside me.

Phillip sighed and tossed an almost embarrassed look at Scott. "A gentleman can't go into details, of course, but I simply wasn't comfortable with the relationship being anything other than professional. I was flattered, certainly, but nevertheless it wasn't something I wanted to pursue. I explained that as gently as I could to Darcy, but . . ."

Omigod. My jaw dropped and then clamped shut over sputtering noises as my face flamed. Fists clenched, I finally found my voice. "Dammit. No. Wait. I won't let you get away with this!" I took another step toward Phillip and Mitch grasped my elbow.

I shook him off and turned helplessly to Scott and Luke. "I didn't threaten that man, for godsake! It's just the opposite. Make him explain the foot poems and FedEx and"—my jabbing finger rose with a will of its own—"all the horrible little feet with wings. Huh? How about those feet, Foote? See, he's got a matching pin." I pointed to Phillip's coat lapel. "Right there and—"

He didn't, of course.

I coughed. "Okay. Well, make him tell you about the snake in the spa and the teddy bear and the whipped cream"—I gulped for breath, my stomach sinking as I saw the look forming in Agent Scott's eye.

"Miss Cavanaugh . . ." he said gently.

"No," I insisted, holding up my palm. "There's more. Let me finish. Ask Phillip about the chocolate pudding and the mink and the posters and that godawful toe job and . . ." My voice faded and I think maybe my eyes filled with tears, because suddenly Luke looked all blurry as he stepped forward to intervene. I blinked and, sure enough, a tear slid down my face. Great, now the crazy finger-jabbing woman was crying. I swiped at my face and groaned.

"That's all then, Dr. Foote," Luke said briskly. "If we need any-thing else from you we'll let you know."

"But I still have some questions for him," I said, in something that sounded a lot like a pitiful whine.

"Goodbye, Doctor," Luke said, ignoring me and opening the door.

I could have sworn that Phillip glanced at my feet before he glided smugly out on his Velveteen Arch Supports.

"I swear I wasn't threatening him with staples," I said after a ten-minute break and enough swigs of bottled water to bring my heart rate down to a reasonable level. I looked across the interview room table, first at Scott, then Mitch, and then finally catching Luke's eyes in a covert plea. "You have to believe me. I was only trying to find out if he was the one who stapled that unauthorized poster of my feet." I rolled my eyes and reached for my water again. "And now you're telling me that those posters are all gone?"

Mitch nodded. "Can't find any of the ones you described. We checked the whole ship." He leafed through his notebook for a moment. "Right after Sam Jamieson mentioned them."

Luke frowned. "Jamieson's not a reliable source of information."

I raised my brows. "What's that supposed to mean?"

Luke pinned me with a look and tapped his pen on the table. "Only that he may have other motives for helping you, Miss Cavanaugh."

It was all I could do not to scream.

Scott glanced quickly between us and cleared his throat. "So what's the sequence again, De Palma?"

Mitch raked his fingers through his dark hair and I noticed once again how exhausted the poor man looked. It was probably killing him not to be able to be with Kirsty. I looked at Luke. I knew that feeling only too well.

"Miss Pelham's pink stapler was missing. We investigated it initially as part of a series of practical jokes. The bride's picture collection had accumulated a lot of extra staples. Then there was the incident with that groomsman, Gordy Simons." He grimaced. "In addition to the glue injury, there were some staples stuck in his leg, sir." He flipped a few pages in the notebook. "And," he glanced quickly at me, "the alleged staples in the allegedly unauthorized foot poster." Mitch cleared his throat. "And then Miss Pelham's . . . um, clothing incident."

"Her underwear?" Scott asked.

"Yes, sir." Mitch's jaw tensed. "Stapled."

I raised my water bottle and took another sip, thinking about Mitch's staple sequence. He wasn't completely accurate, of course; he'd missed at least one mysterious stapling. The very first one, in fact. Paul Putnam's peanut-spiked Buffalo wings. But something warned me not to bring that up. Not yet. Besides—

"What's all this about, anyway?" I asked abruptly, setting my water bottle down. For godsake, it was time to cut to the chase here. "Why are the staples so important all of a sudden?" I twisted a thick strand of my hair between my fingers and frowned at the three men opposite me. "And when the hell are you going to tell us—was Dale Worley murdered or not?"

There was silence for a moment, disturbed only by the faint leather squeak from beneath Scott's jacket as he shifted in his chair. And then I realized that Mitch De Palma was looking as curious as I was. Obviously I wasn't the only one in the dark.

Once again, Luke mouthed a hurried dismissal, thanking Mitch and escorting him to the door. After advising him, gently, that it would be a good thing if he grabbed a few hours' sleep.

When Luke sat back down, he pulled a thick manila envelope from his briefcase.

I tipped my head a little to see: it was stamped with the words, "*Office of the Medical Examiner. Federal Bureau of Investigation. Quantico.*"

He pulled what looked like a sheaf of photographs from the envelope and laid them face down on the table. Luke turned to Scott and raised his brows and for some reason my legs started to tremble.

Scott leaned forward, watching my eyes. "You performed rescue breathing on Dale Worley. That was your statement?"

I glanced at the stack of photos and fought a wave of queasiness. "Yes, I did. But you already knew that. Why . . . ?" I bit into my lower lip and shook my head.

Scott's forehead wrinkled. "Did you notice anything unusual during that act?"

Oh God, is he talking about . . . ? I looked helplessly at Luke and then down at my hands before taking a shaky breath. "In the Business Berth, when I was trying to save Dale, I needed to use the phone. I knocked over some things—office supplies—so maybe that's where they came from or—" I cleared my throat. "Okay, there were some staples."

Luke exhaled. Scott nodded. "Where exactly?"

I brushed my fingers across my chin, remembering the moment too vividly. "Just a few, really. On his face, stuck to the saliva. And there was some blood." I looked down at my fingers, half expecting to see them wet, but seeing that they were trembling instead. "That's all. Why?"

Luke turned the stack of pictures over and handed the top one to me. My stomach lurched. Dale Worley's autopsy photos. The purple-gray face, lifeless eyes, and the handlebar moustache—darkly comic somehow in death. And there was something else. Lying beside his head on the Medical Examiner's sheet. *What is that?*

I looked up and saw that Scott was still watching me. "Mr. Worley's cause of death was asphyxiation," he said. "Choked by the tie after it became entangled in the shredder. But there was another injury that probably rendered him unconscious prior to that." He nodded. "A blow to the back of the head."

"You mean . . . ?" I swallowed the rest of my question.

"Someone knocked him out and then fed his tie into the shredder."

"Oh." It was a pointless thing to say, but I couldn't come up with anything better.

"And," Scott said, nodding as Luke handed me a second photo, "there was something else that was found." I glanced down, preparing myself for another grim view of Worley's face. But it wasn't. It was a close up of that thing that I'd seen on the sheet next to Dale's head. About an inch long, metallic with parallel grooves, sort of bridge-shaped . . . *a chunk of staples?*

I looked back up at Scott, my brows scrunching. "Staples?"

"Yes," the agent said as Luke handed me a third photo. This time it was a close-up of Dale's handlebar moustache and purple lips, his mouth being pried open by gloved fingers, to reveal . . . *omigod.* My hand flew to my own mouth.

Scott nodded. "Staples. Under his tongue. And wedged in the back of his throat."

*   *   *

"Thanks," I said, taking the frosty cosmopolitan from Marie's hand. Thank God she'd snagged us a tiny table in the cushy, mirrored and palm-dotted lounge outside the theatre doors. "Keep 'em coming. I need to drink enough to forget the murder I'm suspected of and then get too shit-faced to carry out the one I'm currently planning." I swallowed a cranberry-orange sip, and then nodded toward the row of windows looking out onto infinite dark ocean. "Do you think the two of us could chuck that porky little Foote over the rail?"

Marie peered up through her dark fringe of bangs in that non-judgmental, but very clearly what-were-you-thinking look she's perfected since meeting me. "Caught on tape?"

From the doorway of the theatre beyond there was an ill-timed roar of laughter.

I groaned. "I'm looking at the bright side—it was just some finger jabs and a little shrieking. I could have whipped off my wedge sandal and flogged him with it."

"Um," Marie's nose wrinkled. "Probably not a good idea. Unless you're looking for an Internet fan club. It's creepy enough that Foote has the pudding photos."

"Ugh." I groaned, holding the icy glass to my cheek. "Not that anyone believes me now that all the posters have conveniently disappeared. No, I'm just a crazy redhead lusting after a podiatrist who dumped her." I groaned again. "And the nurse too stupid to realize she was blowing staples into a man's lungs. Oh, God. How horrible is that?" I took a huge swallow of my drink. "I guess I should be grateful a dead guy can't sue when he starts to rust like the Tin Man."

"Hey," Marie flicked her finger with a ping against the rim of my drink, "stop that crap. How many cautions about office supplies have we read in the CPR guide? You blew out, the air went in. That's the drill. The staples were, well . . ."

"Crammed into Worley's mouth by the killer." I stared at Marie, my mind still trying to wrap around that one huge question mark. "Why? What in the hell is it with these staples?"

Marie raised her voice over a swell of music escaping from the theatre. "I don't know. But from what you're saying, I don't think the FBI believes that the staple incidents were random practical jokes. Not after Dale's autopsy."

"Did they mention them to you?" I asked.

Marie shook her head. "No, but they might have questioned me before the report came in. You've been in twice now."

"Don't remind me," I said, realizing that my glass was empty and not only because I could see the bottom of it. I had a definite little wooz going. Probably a good thing, considering . . . "Oh hell. What am I going to do about Luke?" I asked suddenly, a new, panicky feeling crowding my cosmo wooz. "He's got this whole thing in his mind about Sam and me, thanks to that jerk Putnam. And I can't get him alone to talk to him. Against damned federal regulations." I squeezed my eyes shut for an instant. "Do you think Paul actually said, 'sucking face,' to Luke? Do you think he would say it just like that?"

Marie hesitated, and then frowned. "You mean, do I think Dale Worley's best friend is capable of disgusting behavior?"

"Oh God."

"But," Marie said quickly, "I told you that Luke asked me about it and I told him the true story. About the phony e-mails that made Sam come aboard in the first place and then how he ambushed you with that kiss. That it was never your intention to—" Marie turned and looked back over her shoulder toward the theatre and I tugged at her sleeve, anxious for her to finish what she was saying.

"Do you think he believed you?" I asked, and then frowned when she sat there smiling without answering. I hate her I-know-something-you-don't-know smirk. It isn't the ordinary cat swallowing a canary deal; with Marie it's more like the smart-ass kitty just brought down a California condor—barbecued.

"Marie, c'mon, tell me," I said, losing the battle to control my jabbing finger. "Did Luke believe you about the kiss?"

Her smile broadened as she pointed to the man standing beside the parted velvet curtains at the doors of the darkened theatre. She winked. "Ask the big fed yourself, babe."

* * *

"Luke . . . believe me?"

"Yes."

"Swear?"

"Swear."

"Case over soon?"

Masculine sigh. "Don't ask."

"But, just . . ."

"Can't talk."

Finger jab. Pause. Teasing purr, "Want me?"

Deep masculine groan. "God."

It was about as intimate a conversation as could be managed. Considering that Luke and I were sitting in a theatre with a thousand early-seating passengers watching a Chinese human pyramid balance plates spinning on sticks. Jeez. And all standing on the stooped shoulders of a man too old to be riding a unicycle. I shielded my eyes with the program brochure, trying not to notice that the cycle guy was breathing funny. No way. The only mouth-to-mouth I was interested in right now was mine . . . on Luke's. Not that there was much hope of that. Damned FBI. You had to hate a job that puts a gun under a man's armpit and has him talking out of the side of his mouth to a woman he's pretending isn't there. Not that I was making it any easier with the way my hand was exploring his thigh. I can't resist this man in a tux.

I traced my fingertips along the silky crease of Luke's slacks and his muscles shivered beneath the fabric. I knew full well what other reaction I was getting. Then my fingers walked over the crease, toward the stitching at his inseam and I think I heard a low groan, but it was hard to be sure because of the sudden and horrific thunderclap of what were probably two hundred plates hitting the wooden stage. Terrific. The crowd gasped and some people stood and then everyone began to applaud and cheer with support.

I'd raised my chin enough to peer over the fuzzy-perm head of the woman in front of me, hoping that the geriatric cyclist hadn't actually bitten the dust when—*ooh.* Warm fingers crept beneath my arm and across the coppery fabric toward my left breast, one finger moving—with trigger-trained skill—under its seamed edging and onto my flesh. I smiled. Count on a Special Agent to take advantage of a diversion opportunity. *Whoa.* I raised my brochure and returned Skyler's wicked smile. If it weren't for the facts that I was wearing a gown that cost half a hospital paycheck, that this guy had a 9 mm Glock under his jacket and that we were in the throes of a floating murder investigation, this would be nothing short of a sweaty adolescent grope. I loved it.

Smug masculine chuckle. "Tattoo?"

"Wanna see?"

"Mmm." Maddening finger circles getting expected localized response.

Eyes smoldering behind brochure. "Case over?"

Masculine growl.

I wanted to laugh, but who was I kidding? I was no teenager. I wanted Luke somewhere alone, even if it was just to feel his arms around me for a few minutes. A simple damned hug. He was a great hugger. And, oh man, I needed that after the surreal episodes of the last several days. But—

"Meet somewhere?" My hand back on his thigh accompanied by Chinese theme music.

Silence. Furrowed brows and observable plotting.

"Your cabin?" My fingers back to the inseam.

Muffled curse. "Roommate. Scott."

"Then where?" Exit music. Applause.

Glancing at his watch. "No time. Damn case."

Emcee. Loud burst of Chinese theme music.

The crowd sprouted to its feet in a standing ovation and we stayed seated in the enveloping darkness, secluded like we were on the floor of some ridiculous towering forest. For a moment. And just long enough.

"Darcy. Here." Luke's hands cupped my face, his mouth covering mine, and he kissed me like he was starving and then—dammit—the house lights flicked on. Breathless, blind, and hopelessly horny we leaped to our feet.

Side of the mouth curse. Luke tapping watch. "Meet. Twenty minutes."

Behind my brochure, while jostled by fat woman. "Where?"

A thousand people pressed forward, filing up the aisles and toward the exits.

Blast it. Luke was nudged ahead and the crowd—now a virtual jungle of garish sequins, dinner jackets, and moth-scented furs—filled the space between us until I could barely see him. Only those wide shoulders in the dark tuxedo jacket, a glimpse of the cropped blonde hair. Then he paused and looked back, and I saw him smile and mouth something, but . . .

"Where?" I mouthed back trying, ridiculously, to rise on tiptoe to see better as the crowd swept me along. He said the words a second time—slowly like to a dense lip reader—and then I stumbled and lost sight of him.

I sighed and shook my head at the bizarre nature of my life. Then I tried to remember where the nearest ship schematic was. Because, unless I was mistaken, this particular murder suspect was headed for a quickie with an FBI agent. In a lifeboat.

SEVENTEEN

IF I WERE DATING a Coast Guard man, he'd have warned me about the degree of difficulty in boarding a huge enclosed lifeboat suspended in darkness over a moving cruise ship. Especially in three-inch heels. People love to tell those stories about ninety-pound grandmas summoning enough superhuman strength to heft a half-ton pickup off Grandpa's chest; well, I'm a testament to the fact that lust inspires things like that, too. It sure had me scuttling like a sailor. But I knew that some quality time with Luke would make up for all the confusion and chaos of the last few days. Thank God one of his "key people" had access to the plastic emergency cones to block an exit, a great flashlight, a working knowledge of ship mechanics . . . and a discreet sense of "Brotherhood." The man gave one last respectful boost to the tush of my satin gown and I was in.

I blinked, waiting for my eyes to adjust to the darkness and then my breath caught like a goosey virgin. Damn. It had to be criminal how good that man looked by the light of an emergency lantern.

I smiled slowly, while my heart did pathetic flip-flops. "Hey there, Skyler."

"Hey, yourself."

Luke sat a few yards away, tux jacket and shoulder holster shed, bow tie dangling against the snowy, pleated shirt unbuttoned to his navel. The lantern light flickered over faint golden stubble along the curve of his jaw and settled with glint and shadow over the tight muscles of his chest. He chuckled low in his throat and his blue eyes crinkled at the edges. "What took you so long?"

Sue me, but I couldn't resist it. "If I told you, I'd have to kill you."

"Very cute. Now, get over here."

I took a few coy steps and Luke sprang to his feet—rocking the lifeboat—to cross the distance and pull me against him. Two arms have never, ever felt so good. In an instant my own were twined around his back and I was laughing into the soft furry warmth of his chest. I breathed in the clean, woodsy scent of his skin and sighed. "I don't know what feels better," I murmured, "holding you or being able to finally speak in full sentences."

"Without Chinese music," he agreed, his hands grasping the curve of my behind. "But then talking is highly overrated."

Luke stepped away for a moment, lifting a long, wavy strand of my hair, rolling it between his fingertips and studying my eyes like there was something he needed to see there. Then he took hold of my chin and raised my face toward his, kissing me gently—in maddeningly slow progression—on my brow, then the tip of my nose, the tender curve of my neck, the corners of my mouth . . . lips so warm yet still way too far away to taste. For godsake, he had a hungry woman here. Couldn't he see that?

I took the initiative and snaked my arms around Luke again, taking hold of that very fine butt and snugging him tightly against me, my body leaving no doubt where this was going. My lips whispered urgently next to his. Not that I was impatient or anything but . . . "So exactly how much time do we—"

I loved it that his eager mouth made me completely forget what I was going to ask. And, after a minute or so, had me so stricken by amnesia that I wasn't even sure of my own name. Finally, I had to wonder if I would even remember to breathe as we sank to the floor and a continuing federal investigation uncovered my shamrock tattoo and a whole lot more.

"Ahh . . . Luke, wait, you'll get shark repellent on your slacks if you just throw them over there like that."

"Sharks can eat the damned pants," he said moving back over me. "Now where was I?"

"Ooh. Yes. Pretty much right . . . there. Watch out for the oar."

It's very possible that lifeboat ambience is the purest form of aphrodisiac. Creaking chains, cool, slick fiberglass, scratchy wool blanket and that strange, visceral maritime potpourri of dried sea brine, diesel fuel, and musty canvas. Along with the exquisite tingle of ocean mist seeping across bare skin and the pitch and yaw of floor panels as they strain to accommodate, well . . . the various inventive hip movements required in a limited space. I was born to sail.

And I should never have given Luke Skyler a watch with an alarm. You can bet your ass that 007 would never . . . "You had me on a *time schedule*?" I teased, lifting my head from where my tangled heap of hair was splayed like a sated mermaid across Luke's chest. "You cut that pretty close, Skyler. What if—"

An insistent thumping on the side of the lifeboat made me stop short and made Luke sit sharply upright. Not easy with one bare leg tucked under a bench and the other buried somewhere beneath a puffy pile of orange vests. The thump came again and Luke kissed me quickly.

"I have to go," he said, reaching for his pants and then standing to signal through the window. "My dinner break's over." A rascal twinkle lit his eyes—"My compliments to the chef, by the way." Then his expression turned businesslike. "I have another interview to do in about twenty minutes."

"Who?"

"Can't—" Luke frowned. "All right, Jamieson."

"Again?" I pulled the scratchy wool blanket over my breasts, wondering what Firefighter Sam could know about murder. And hating it that we were heading back into what had become, macabre as it was, business as usual.

Luke glanced at his watch and then looked back at me in the darkness, sighing. "We've got maybe six more hours to get a handle on this case, Darcy. We're getting some good information, but we need a lot more. Otherwise people will have to be detained by the local authorities in Victoria."

I watched as he finished dressing and reached for his gun and holster.

"And Patti Ann's wedding?" I asked, picturing the bride's eyes and dreading the answer.

"Don't know yet. But in all likelihood, I'll be gone before that decision's made."

"Gone?" For some reason I'd started to tremble and it didn't have anything to do with the night air. That familiar ache squeezed my chest.

Luke opened his mouth and hesitated for a moment. "The helicopter's coming for me at first light. Have to get back and wrap things up in Monterey. Not much time left before . . ."

Not much time until you move away.

I watched Luke snug the leather holster under his arm the way I'd seen him do dozens of times before, but this time I started to wonder if it were the last time I'd see him do that. And then I started wondering how many more times we'd make love and—"What?" I looked up at Luke, not understanding what he'd just said.

"Boston," he repeated, his eyes soft in the lantern light. "It's beautiful there, Darcy. The cherry blossoms are gone now, but summer's coming and my grandparents have that place out on the Vineyard, with clambakes on the sand and these great bonfires. There'll be fireworks on the Fourth and . . ." Luke swallowed softly.

Okay, he was killing me. He could stop now.

Luke smiled and shook his head. "It's funny really. You and I met in New England. Almost exactly six months—" his cell phone buzzed and he turned away to answer it. I told myself to breathe. Maybe that would chase the ache away.

By the time he was finished on the phone I'd dressed, my gown surprisingly none the worse for wear, considering. But I was. Worn out and cold, just like I'd been after that awful ordeal with Dale.

"You're shivering," Luke said, giving me one last hug. "Stupid boat—dumb idea. I'm sorry. I should've found some other place."

"No," I said summoning a smile and touching his arm. "Best time I've ever had in a lifeboat. Seriously. And it has to beat Love Shack 1505."

"Huh?"

"Room 1505." I shook my head. "A storeroom, back on the fantail. The local hot spot for hooking up."

Luke raised his brows.

"Or so I'm told," I said, giving his tux sleeve one of my infamous finger jabs. "Don't worry. You wouldn't catch me dead inside that place."

*　*　*

I showered—staring at the soap for a long moment and wondering how many times I'd share a shower with Luke before he left for Boston—then slipped into my tiered chiffon camisole, capris, and a pair of animal-print slides. I grabbed my jean jacket and glanced at my watch. It was nearly eleven and steadily ticking toward Patti Ann's wedding day. Doomed, if the FBI didn't snare Dale's murderer. But actually, after the lifeboat encounter and before my misty-eyed shower reverie, I'd begun to think that maybe there was something I could do about this whole wedding glitch after all. My stomach rumbled as I reached for the cabin door. I was hungry as a Serengeti lioness and I needed to run an idea by Marie. Something that had been making me more than a little edgy—a crazy hunch about staples. So I arranged to meet her in the Dolphin Bar. I could talk and eat at the same time. No problem.

Twenty minutes later, Marie reached toward the half-ravaged plate of appetizers, carefully, like she wasn't sure if I might mistake her finger for a jalapeño popper. A smile played on her lips. "Worked up an appetite, did we dear?"

I mumbled around a creamy mouthful of nacho cheese, as close to macaroni comfort food as I was getting tonight. "Hmmph— sorry. Here. There's plenty," I said, pushing the plate toward her and ignoring the obvious sleazy implication. My stomach was full and it was time to present my staple theory.

Marie wasn't about to let up. "I could have been here faster," she said, voice rising an octave and glancing toward the doors to the deck, "but since I had to avoid that area all blocked off by emergency cones and guarded by some muscle-bound guy with . . ." Her dark brows rose.

"Jeez!" I whipped around, my eyes darting toward the deck window. "He didn't take the cones down yet?"

"Busted," Marie said, laughing. "When I saw Luke head toward that lowered lifeboat and then . . ."

"It was an emergency," I said, reaching for my beer and then smiling as my face warmed with the memory.

"I'm sure it was. I know you two, remember?"

Marie lifted a nacho clump and glanced around the sparsely populated Dolphin Bar. Her eyes moved to where Kyle sat nursing a beer at a far table and then back toward me again. "But what did you mean by that message you left on my cell? About taking 'office supply inventory'?" She shook her head and scraped an onion chunk off a chip with her fingernail. "You're getting as irritatingly cryptic as your fed, by the way."

I leaned forward, lowering my voice. "I meant that I made a detailed list. An interesting chronological accounting of—" the overhead page interrupted me.

"Passenger Jamieson, call two-two-seven-one. Mr. Sam Jamieson, please."

I looked from the ceiling back to Marie. "Isn't that the third time they've done that?"

"Sure is," Marie said, then nodded toward the bar doorway. "Looks like maybe Firefighter Sam is ignoring our 'lawyers.'"

Sure enough, Sam was just walking in accompanied by Ryan Galloway. Both men had changed to casual clothes, and Ryan—true to his strange new habits—was noticeably unsteady on his feet. They grabbed a table not far from Kyle's and I hunched a little in my own chair, hoping Sam wouldn't spot me. I dug around inside my leopard-trimmed clutch and produced a folded piece of paper. My list. I think I inherited my compulsion for lists from my grandma. Of course nowadays she probably uses hers to organize the fish food dosing of her neighbors.

"Here," I said, seeing Putnam meander through the doorway, "check if I've got this sequence right." I flattened the paper on the tabletop and traced my finger down the column. "First night: Patti Ann tells us that Kirsty has the groomsmen stapling up crepe paper on the party room picture wall—Dale, Ryan, and Ed, I think. Then, later, we see that big pink stapler lying on the floor beside the photo wall." I nodded. "From that whole pink-handled set Kirsty has, with the hammer and the pliers and everything?"

"Right." Marie nodded. "And then Paul Putnam has anaphylactic shock from a Buffalo wing with a peanut inside. That I remember clearly."

"Exactly," I said, tapping my finger on the list. "A peanut stapled inside."

"Wait," Marie said after swallowing a swig of beer. "Are you saying that you think those guys did all this because they had access to the stapler? Because, hell, Ed flew back on the helicopter with Gordy, and Dale's the one who's dead so . . ." her brows rose and she looked back toward where Sam sat with Ryan Galloway. "Oh, shit, you're saying—"

"No!" I said quickly, fighting the still-disturbing image of Ryan peering from those bushes at Capilano bridge. "I'm not. I'm not pointing my finger at anyone . . . yet. I'm just trying to get this staple thing right." I traced my finger farther down my list. "And then the next morning Gordy Simons is glued."

"And there are staples in his thigh."

"Exactly," I said. "And then we stopped by the party room on the way to dinner and saw all those bunches of staples added to the photo wall."

"Then at the dinner we all met Mitch for the first time." Marie started to nod. "And he announced that Kirsty's big pink stapler was missing."

"Yep—oh crap," I said, looking back toward the bar, "Foote." I grimaced as Phillip Foote slid onto a barstool, tasseled loafers dangling from the heels of his argyle socks. "Which reminds me. The next incident was when Sam saw that poster of my feet. With staples in it."

"So maybe Foote . . . ?" Marie nodded faster, her fringe of bangs bobbing.

I shook my head. "He admits to nada, the dirty little pervert." I crossed my legs, jiggling my foot toward the bar like a fishing lure. "But as much as I'd like to see that podiatrist in Folsom Prison, I doubt he's got the cojones to actually kill someone. Unless you can do it by mail."

"So what's next?" Marie asked, tipping her head to peer at my list.

"Kirsty's lingerie," I said, realizing I hadn't seen the poor woman since dinner. I hope to goodness she was snuggled up somewhere with Mitch. Buck naked. They both needed that. The two of them were a double-lit candle burning toward the middle. "And then . . ."

Marie retrieved a cigar from her fanny pack. "And then Dale Worley buys the farm with a mouth full of staples."

"Yes," I said, looking down at my list and wondering how in the hell this had all happened in just a few short days. "But now I'm thinking that it might be easier to figure this all out a different way."

"What do you mean, Darc'?"

"I mean that we should go about it more backwards," I said, thinking. "Instead of wondering who did the stapling, maybe we should think about who got stapled. And why."

"You mean, start with all the practical jokes and . . . ?"

"No," I said, noticing out of the corner of my eye that Ryan was standing near Kyle's table now and that Sam was joining him. "I'm thinking that this was never about practical jokes in the first place. Squirting cameras and fart machines aside, of course. I think that everything that was marked with a staple was a malicious, intentional attempt to target an intended victim." My stomach tensed. "Paul, Gordy, Kirsty, Dale, and—"

"You?" Marie said with her eyes fixed on mine. "You're an intended victim?"

I hesitated, not wanting to believe it anymore than she did. "I'm not sure. But, still, I think there's a connection between all of us and the kill—" *What the hell?*

212

I whipped my head around at the same instant that Marie did, and just in time to hear Ryan shout again before taking a swing at Kyle. And then for some damned reason I was jogging over. The truth was that I was sick of this high-testosterone crap and I wasn't afraid to say so. After all, I was raised with two brothers. Boot camp. Marie was right behind me.

When I got to the table, Sam had hold of Ryan, Kyle was moving in fast and I couldn't tell if Paul Putnam was wedged in there to help or to instigate things further.

"Oh for godsake," I growled, stepping in front of Ryan with my hands on my hips. "Why don't you guys give this thing a rest, huh?" I scowled at Galloway. "Aren't we all in enough of a mess here already?" Marie started poking her finger into my back and I stepped forward, shrugging her off. She wasn't going to stop me. I was just getting started. I turned my head toward Kyle and narrowed my eyes.

"You think this kind of crap is going to ease Patti Ann's—" I stopped as a truly rabid-growl erupted from Ryan's lips. Sam struggled to hold him, but one of Galloway's fists broke free and grabbed hold of the front of my jean jacket.

"Ask him," Ryan screamed, reddening and speckling my face with spit. "Ask that sonofabitch Kyle how much he cares about Patti Ann's feelings. Go ahead, Darcy, ask him!"

"Hey," I said, as calmly as I could with Ryan mangling the front of my jacket and Marie poking the back of it like a crazed woodpecker. "Can't we all just . . ." I hesitated for a moment horrified that I was about to quote either Mr. Rogers or Big Bird. And then I realized that Marie had stopped poking. And that everyone, including Ryan, had suddenly shut up. Because now they were all looking at . . . Luke. Who was standing beside me.

"Let go of her," Luke said, his voice deep and deadly calm. "Now."

I held my breath and tried not to think about the fact that one of these guys could be a murderer. Maybe even the one who had his fist under my chin. Or that Luke had a gun and—Ryan let go. I was pretty sure I heard Marie moan. And then out of the corner of my eye I saw Phillip Foote sipping on an umbrella-topped drink and craning his neck to see.

There was silence for a moment and then Paul Putnam laughed, a sound equal parts nervousness and taunting bravado. His eyes swept over Luke quickly from bottom to top—calfskin loafers and slacks to black polo and pewter twill sport coat—clearly sizing him up. And getting it all wrong. "Well, looky, boys," he said, clapping Kyle on the shoulder. "The cruise line's fancy lawyer is here to read us the rules."

Luke blinked once and a muscle on his jaw tensed. Then he turned to me. "You're okay, Miss Cavanaugh?"

"Yes," I said, not much above a whisper, mostly because my tongue was stuck to the roof of my mouth. I glanced over at Marie, not at all comforted by her helpless shrug.

"I'll walk you out then," Luke said, after leveling a look at Putnam.

"No," Sam said stepping forward. "I'll take care of Darcy."

Luke's eyes narrowed. "Doesn't look like you're capable, Jamieson."

Shit. I should do something. Like now.

"Hey, really," I said, smoothing out the front of my jacket. "I'm fine. See? I don't need—"

"Right, Skyler," Putnam, said, with a sharp laugh and making no attempt to hide his sneer. "Maybe we should place a little bet on how lawyers compare to firefighters. Carry anyone off a burning . . . golf course lately?"

Sam smiled, but to his credit at least he kept his mouth shut.

There was a prolonged silence and I was torn between a dizzying mix of panic and the urge to laugh out loud at the complete ass Paul was making of himself by unwittingly taking on the FBI. But mostly I was blown away by the surge of respect I had for the calm, confident look on Luke's face. This was a man who trusted his instincts. And I was pretty damned sure that it sprang from the kind of man he was, not from the fact that he could turn Dirty Harry in the blink of an eye. Although I wouldn't have minded him blowing the umbrella out of Foote's piña colada.

"Nope. Not lately," Luke said, sliding his fingers under my elbow. His thumb made an imperceptible movement along my skin and I smiled. "And now I'm escorting Miss Cavanaugh out." Luke looked over at Sam. "I'll be waiting for you in my office below deck, Mr. Jamieson. Unless you'd rather respond to a warrant? I can arrange that."

Sam opened his mouth, but never got a chance to answer. Because Patti Ann came rushing in behind us, breathless.

I saw Ryan narrow his eyes at Kyle and then our groom cleared his throat and smiled as Patti Ann stopped in front of the group.

"Darcy, Marie," she said, gulping for air. "Oh thank God! I need you to come help me. Kirsty's pitchin' a fit and I don't know what to do anymore. We can't find Mitch and"—she shook her head—"dammit, someone vandalized the party room! It's a mess. And all those photos that she worked so hard on . . . ? Staples all over them."

EIGHTEEN

Patti Ann wasn't just whistling Dixie. The party room was trashed with such adolescent flair that I was surprised there weren't rolls of toilet paper looped over the light fixtures. It was bad enough that there were Magic Marker moustaches on every frigging photo of me.

"Gad," Marie said, peering over the rope barricade that security had installed, "you look like Dale's burly sister"—she coughed into her fist—"from the circus."

"Okay." I jabbed her. "Fine. I get it."

I peered around the room, checking to see who else had come for the viewing. Not many key members of the wedding party, actually; only Sissy the Snake Woman, Patti Ann, Kyle—who'd had a strange hangdog look since passing Ryan in the hallway outside— and Kirsty Pelham. Poor Kirsty. Martha Stewart looked happier in those news clips from prison.

"I'm cautioning everyone about touching anything," she said, poking the stylus at her PDA and stepping closer to me. Her voice lowered to a whisper. "Apparently you can lift fingerprints really easily from photos and I want whoever is responsible to pay." Her eyes narrowed. "Pay dearly." She squeezed her blue eyes shut behind her glasses. "This is really the final straw, Darcy."

I looked back at the shredded crepe paper, slashed and withered balloons, and even the incredible silver tracks of staples randomly puncturing the walls. Then I studied the misery on our wedding planner's face, thinking of the irony that she considered this act of vandalism the "last straw." In my opinion, murder weighs a lot heavier in the bad juju haystack. Which reminded me that I needed to get back to my Who and Why list. I was getting close now.

"Did Mitch say that someone would be taking fingerprints?" I asked, noticing with a tinge of alarm that Kirsty had two different shoes on. Same style—her classic linen slingbacks—but mismatched colors; one pistachio and one decidedly mauve. Somehow I doubted she was trying to make a fashion statement. Great. Now I had to wonder when this compulsive woman had last stopped to eat. She was clearly coming undone.

Kirsty swept a rare, errant strand of hair behind her ear and sighed. "No one's seen Mitch. I called down to the interview room several times but they said he wasn't there. And he's not in his cabin or answering my pages or . . ."

I patted the sleeve of her suit jacket and smiled, deciding not to say anything about seeing him at my interview earlier. It wouldn't help, and maybe he was simply bunking down somewhere else. God knows the man needed some sleep. But then again, there was the real possibility that Mitch De Palma had been rethinking the wisdom of a relationship with this intense woman. Right now, I couldn't blame him.

Kirsty raised her hand and waggled her fingers toward where Patti Ann stood huddled in what appeared to be a deep conversation with Kyle. Then the wedding planner excused herself, hustling—green shoe, pink shoe—over to join them. She fished her PDA from her purse the instant she got there and for the first time the word "elope" flitted across my mind. I'd turned to confess my evil thought to Marie—that maybe Patti Ann should pack up her "I AM THE BRIDE" tee shirt and bolt—when I realized Marie was no longer standing there. She was gesturing urgently to me from a bank of photos a few yards farther down the wall.

"Come here. You've got to see this," she hissed, beckoning again. "Holy shit."

I joined her in front of a collage including Kyle's engine company and rodeo friends and tried to see what was so damn intriguing. I grimaced at yet another shot of me, this one mustachioed and riding on the fire department's Burn Center charity float. That's when I saw the trail of staples. A spare sprinkle at first, like the trail of crumbs the witch left to lead Hansel and Gretel to the oven, then thicker and thicker with the nasty metal bits, all leading to one particular photo and . . . I tilted my head and blew a tattered piece of crepe paper aside. *Oh jeez!*

"That's pretty sick, don't you think?" Marie asked, grimacing.

All I could do was nod and stare at that firehouse photo of the four uniformed men and the chubby girl holding the dalmatian puppy. Or what was left of that photo, anyway. I leaned across the rope, remembering what Kirsty had said about fingerprints and kind of hoping, now, that there were some to lift. Cause I sure as hell wanted to know who had stapled the grotesque criss-cross of X's across the eyes of Paul, Gordy, Dale . . . and Sam.

There was a soft cry, followed by a wrenching wail and suddenly our bride ran from the party room. Then Kyle took off after her. Marie and I stared at each other, clueless.

* * *

Sam, on the other hand, seemed to know everything. And it looked like he might be using that knowledge to snag me for a midnight repeat of his "I think I love you" spiel. Time was limited and the man was as persistent as Smokey the Bear dousing a campfire. But what Sam didn't know was that I was equally as determined. To find out the truth about what had been going on within this nautical wedding party that had led it to murder. Not to mention spurring the ugly and puzzling staple assault on this man's gorgeous eyes.

"So that's why you were ignoring those interview pages?" I asked, noticing with amusement that Sam had chosen a booth in the darkest corner of the Crow's Nest Bar. Tucked behind a discreet grouping of potted palms. The candle of a hurricane lamp bathed our bamboo table in a warm glow and reflected in the darkened expanse of windows overlooking the bow. And flickered in Sam's dark eyes, which were fixed way too intently on mine. I raised my brows, not sure if he'd even heard me. "You say you were 'babysitting' Ryan Galloway?"

Sam lifted his beer and frowned. "Yeah, the guy was determined to start trouble with Kyle and I thought I could stop it so . . ." he sighed and his eyes did that puppy-dog thing again. "Darcy, I'm sorry Galloway grabbed you like that. I thought I had him covered and—"

"Hey, quit it," I said, my fingers moving instinctively to the front of my jean jacket. I met his gaze and knew Sam was recalling Luke's critical assessment of his White Knight skills. "Since when do I need someone to fight my battles for me?" I took a sip of my chardonnay, determined to get Sam back on track. "So what gives with Ryan anyway? He's acting like some pod-person invaded his brain."

Sam smiled. "I'm not sure it's his brain that's involved at all."

"Meaning?" Of course I knew what he meant. But I was still confused. There are some people who are easy to peg, who can be counted on to be easygoing and benign. Ryan Galloway was like that. Until this cruise.

Sam's fingertips inched slowly across the table toward where my hand rested at the base of my crystal glass. "Meaning that sometimes love makes people act crazy."

"Love?" I lifted my glass and peered over the rim at Sam. "Ryan?" I raised my brows. "Wait—do you mean with Patti Ann?" My mind whirled, remembering the series of skirmishes between Ryan and Kyle, the way he'd always been there in the background, watching. Like today at the bridge. Was it possible? "He told you that he has a thing for Patti Ann?"

Sam shrugged. "Not exactly. I'm only guessing. But the guy's doing everything he can to screw up this wedding, Darcy. I'm sure you noticed that."

I fought an uneasy feeling deep in my stomach. "And how far would he take that?"

"I'm not sure. He did say that he 'has something' on Kyle. Something that would 'make Patti Ann reconsider.' And that he threatened to tell her if Kyle didn't."

"What was it?" I asked, remembering the intense conversation I'd witnessed between the couple in the party room an hour ago. Had Kyle been pressured into something?

"Don't know. But I do know that a lot of people have been questioned about Galloway in those interviews. I sure was."

"Oh?" I'd been purposefully avoiding the interview subject after that uncomfortable exchange between Luke and Sam in the bar. But now he'd brought it up. "How'd that whole thing go with the . . . lawyers?"

Sam drummed his fingers on the tabletop, glancing quickly around the bar. He laughed sharply, and then lowered his voice to a whisper. "You're not going to believe this." He looked over his shoulder again. "That guy, Skyler?"

I shifted in my chair and nodded.

He leaned across the table, staring into my eyes. "FBI—I'm serious."

I let my jaw drop in what I hoped looked like infinite surprise. "Whoa—jeez—how'd you know?"

Sam frowned. "The big-ass gun under his coat was a clue. That and the badge he tried to cram down my throat. I got the impression the guy doesn't like me."

"Really? Hmm." I hid a smile, wondering if Sam Jamieson had just destroyed my image of cool, confident Special Agent Lucas Skyler. But then again, there was something sort of primal-sexy about a territorial man.

"He asked some things about you, by the way," Sam said, shifting a little as our waiter set down a second beer. "About those e-mails." He raised his palm before I could protest. "I know, I know. You didn't send them. But Skyler made me pull them up on a laptop anyway. Not sure why."

I wasn't, either. But I was certain that after our lifeboat rendezvous, that Luke believed me when I told him I had no romantic interest in Firefighter Sam. He was being thorough, that's all, checking all the connections. Same way I was and—*oh jeez*—like Jamieson was trying to do right now, by connecting with me. He reached across the table and took hold of my hand.

"I meant what I said before, Darcy," Sam said, his smile gentle. "I think I'm in love with you."

Oh, hell. I looked up into Sam's eyes and struggled for words. What was I supposed to do with this? Sure, there was a time when . . . no, that wasn't true. If Sam had said this last year, I would have panicked and signed up for every friggin' overtime shift in the ER. I'd have switched the answering machine to first ring and pulled the covers over my head. The sex was great and the laughs were, too, but love was another matter. Sure I'd been furious about Chloe, but the fact was that I had been nowhere near ready for a commitment. Even now—*God*—even with Luke who . . . no, I wasn't going to let this conversation with Sam make me think about that. I blinked, realizing that he had just asked me something.

"What?" I asked, feeling Sam's fingers move against mine.

"Does he want to marry you?" Sam repeated. "That lawyer back home?"

Oh boy. *Does he?* I'd opened my mouth to say something vague and dismissive when I realized, with a little shock, that I hadn't thought about the mysterious black velvet jewelry box in days. Not even after the surprise of finding Luke aboard ship. The strange fact was, that I'd been so intent on being *with* Luke that I'd forgotten I was running away from an engagement ring. Hell, I'd even forgotten to itch.

Sam raised his brows, prompting me.

"We're from different worlds," I said, maybe needing to test this out loud finally. And not caring that it was weird to be doing that with Firefighter Sam. "They're fourth generation Southerners," I explained, shaking my head. "His folks have been married forever and I'm betting his mother wears her pearls when she irons the Judge's underwear." I laughed at the immediate scrunch of Jamieson's brows. "The lawyer's father is a judge. Grandfather, too. You tell them all apart by their Roman numerals." I groaned softly. "You remember my dad? Bill 'the Bug Man'?"

Sam nodded. "Sure do—can't miss the cockroach stencil on that van." And then he grinned, rubbing his thumb across the tip of mine. "But hell, Darcy, the way I look at it, being an exterminator just makes your old man . . . judge, jury, and executioner. Screw those Southerners and their starched boxers!"

I grinned back and if I hadn't thought it would complicate matters, I might have kissed Sam. I settled for a mouthed thank-you. Then I slid my fingers from his and picked up my chardonnay.

He tipped his head and frowned a little. "You're not thinking something crazy like you're not good enough for this guy, are you?"

"Hell no," I said in a flash and with enough fervor to slosh my wine. "No way. That's not it at all." *Okay, smart-ass, then what is it?* I took a sip of my wine, stalling, thinking . . . and really, really not wanting to be doing this at all. I sighed. "I guess I haven't seen too many uplifting examples of successful long-term relationships, you know?" I shook my head.

"Your folks still sneaking down the block and into each others' beds?" Sam winked over his beer.

I grimaced. "Yep. Failed at divorce, too. Not that there aren't still some fine examples of it in the family. Both sides. My big brother now, too. His divorce was final last month. That's what I mean—genetic relationship failure."

"So because of all that, because of them . . . you think you can't trust yourself?"

Aagh—the pod people had Sam, too. This was insane and I was a fool to have opened my mouth in the first place. I wasn't going to sit here and watch Sam do Dr. Phil.

"What I think," I said, wiping my mouth with a napkin and straightening my shoulders, "is that I'm all talked out, Sam. And, speaking of relationships in jeopardy, I'm going to go find Patti Ann and find out what upset her so much and then—" I stopped short as Sam reached across the table to grasp my wrist.

"Wait," Sam said. "Please, Darcy. I wasn't trying to pressure you." He groaned softly. "I only wanted to know if there was any small chance left for us. I mean, if it's not so serious with that lawyer then . . . well, then that's good." He nodded like he was trying to convince me. "And maybe if I came back to Morgan Valley and got an apartment . . . you know, so I could work some shifts at the engine company? You just say the word, Darcy, and I'll be there."

"No, Sam," I said, catching a glimpse of someone at a far table, "don't start that kind of thinking. There's no way I want—"

"Okay," Sam said quickly, cutting me off. "We'll talk about this later. Just whistle. I'll be around." He gave a short laugh. "Hell, it's not like anyone's going to be sleeping tonight." He glanced at his watch. "In fact I'm due back with that Government prick Skyler in ten minutes." Sam squeezed my wrist gently before he let go. "So we'll meet later then, okay?"

"Sure," I said, partly because it was obvious I'd have to try harder to make him understand, but mostly because I now recognized that the person in the distance was Kirsty Pelham. I needed to get rid of Sam. And get over there. It looked like she was crying.

And drinking. I didn't want to believe it, but the wedding planner was a little slurred in addition to teary-eyed, and I wouldn't have to poke her finger to diagnose the cause this time. Not low blood sugar—just high Jello. As in Jello shots, for godsake. And—by the smell of her breath when she did the goofy air-kiss beside my face—the last jiggly mouthful was watermelon with coconut rum. What had prompted this?

"Kirsty, with your diabetes, should you . . . ?" I tried to smile and resisted the urge to check her shoes under the table. But then mismatched shoes were the least of her problems tonight.

"Not to worry," she said, wiping at her mascara-streaked cheek. "I took an extra pill. And I'm eating peanut-sth." She reached into the beer nut bowl and placed one delicately on the tip of her tongue to prove it. It was the most I'd seen her eat during our three days at sea. She smiled and I noticed that her lenses were nearly opaque with oily smudges.

"Here. Give me your glasses and I'll clean them for you," I said. She handed them over and I rubbed at them with a napkin while she picked the skin off another nut and broke it into miniscule pieces. At least there were only two shot glasses on the table and I knew she'd eaten a little at dinner. My curiosity got the best of my tact. "Shouldn't you be somewhere trying to finalize some plans for Patti Ann and Kyle?" Obviously the wrong thing to say.

Her red-rimmed eyes blazed. "Right. Sure. You mean our dumb as a stump Southern belle and her lying, cheating bull rider?"

Whoa! I stopped rubbing the glasses before I put a finger through her lens. "What?"

She groaned low in her throat and the sound escalated to a mournful howl that made the hair rise on my arms. Kirsty stared into my eyes. "Kyle confessed that he cheated on her. Patti Ann locked herself in their cabin. Ryan Galloway is buying rounds in the Sports Bar. And Mitch won't return my calls."

Dear God.

"So . . ." What on earth could I say?

Kirsty was quiet for what seemed like forever and then she pushed the melting Jello shot aside with a frown. She spit on a napkin, dabbed it over her face and then brushed her hair away from her eyes, tucking it smoothly behind her ears. With a steady hand she flicked peanut bits from her lapel.

"I'm sorry, Darcy," Kirsty said, suddenly flashing me the confident smile that I remembered from that first evening aboard ship. Back when all she had to worry about was Dale Worley bumping and grinding into the sunset under a limbo pole. "There was no excuse for my behavior. And you're absolutely right. There's still plenty to be done."

She unzipped her purse and lifted out her PDA. Stuck to the back of it was what looked like an old photo. It fluttered to the tabletop and I picked it up. In the photo was a heavyset woman with short, dark hair and leaning on a quad-cane. She looked vaguely familiar. But then after a while everyone looks familiar to nurses.

"Oops," I said, this was stuck . . ." I heard Kirsty's breath catch as she took it from my fingers.

"Thank you," she said. "My mother."

I nodded, remembering how Kirsty had said she wanted to make her mother proud. And how important that had seemed to her. I hoped she knew that this wedding cruise wasn't a personal failure on her part. That there would be other opportunities to—

"She's dead," Kirsty said, tucking the photo into her purse. "And I'm sorry, but I need to leave now, Darcy. It's late and I've got so much left to take care of."

I watched her leave, a very steady gait in two matching sling-backs, and I felt better. Until I realized that I was still holding Kirsty's glasses. I lifted the dark frames to my eyes to see if I'd gotten the peanut smudges off. Weird, it was almost like looking through plain glass. Not much correction that I could see. Shoot, why even bother to wear them?

I tucked Kirsty's glasses into my purse and checked my watch. I had an interview date with Agent Scott. Maybe now was the time to show him that list I'd been working on.

* * *

It was somehow after five AM and we were somewhere off the coast of British Columbia. Nobody had any idea if today was a wedding day or not. But right this minute, all I could think of was what Federal Agent Scott had just told me. It couldn't be true.

"What do you mean that Luke's being sent to Boston 'immediately'? He was supposed to have two more weeks." I wrapped my arms around myself, rubbing my hands against the sleeves of my jean jacket. It was so freezing cold in the interview room that my breath was sticking in my chest.

Scott puffed his cheeks out and exhaled, clearly regretting the words he'd let slip. "I'm sorry, Darcy. I thought Luke already told you. We got the fax about an hour ago. An agent will be flying in this morning to replace Luke here. There was an unexpected break in the Monterey case, so he's off the hook there. The Bureau needs him in the Boston office . . . like yesterday." He clucked his tongue. "You know how it is with this job. I'm sorry."

"When?" I asked, thinking that, yes, I did know how it was. But I didn't know until right this minute that it could hurt so much. My mind was slogging through molasses—what was today anyway? Saturday? Yes, Saturday and I would fly home on Sunday and then we'd still have—"When will he leave for Boston?"

Scott sighed. "You'll have to ask Luke the exact flight time." He ran his fingers through his graying hair. "But he's leaving tomorrow, Darcy."

NINETEEN

No one was smiling anymore. Except Phillip Foote, and I was sure that that was because of my toe rings. Two of them. The damned things pinched and I swore I'd never wear them again, but I was desperate. The clock was ticking and I needed this twisted podiatrist's help.

"So you'll do it, Phillip?" I asked, my voice as sweet as . . . chocolate pudding.

Foote pursed his lips, looking at the small envelope I'd handed him. He glanced at the door to the interview room and then at my face via my toes. "Give this envelope to that lawyer in there?"

"Yes," I said, trying to keep my hands from clenching. "Mr. Skyler. That's who you're seeing—isn't that what you said?" Dammit, I couldn't figure out any other way to contact Luke. He and Scott had been squirreled away for the last two hours, and it wasn't that long until dawn. When the helicopter would come and . . . "Please, Phillip?"

Foote raised his brows. "How do I know this note doesn't contain some trumped up story about me?"

Because truth is stranger than fiction, you nasty little troll.

I smiled and—Lord forgive me—flipped my hair, wriggling just enough to drop a strap on my flirty camisole. I drew the line at flashing the shamrock; I wasn't going to hell for this guy. I stroked his tie. "It's not about you, silly," I purred. "So you'll do it?"

Phillip smiled slowly. "What's in it for me?"

I glanced at my watch: minutes until Phillip would be called in. There was no time for his stupid games. Or this coy approach. I stepped away and narrowed my eyes, my smile disappearing and voice dropping low. "How about if I don't pursue the snake and pudding deal?"

Phillip's smile never faltered. "You signed a release."

"Not for those posters."

Phillip glanced around and gave an innocent shrug. "What posters? Where?"

My teeth clenched. "Okay, Longfellow—how 'bout the poems?"

I could have sworn I saw a gleam of pride in his eyes, almost the same as when he first showed me the Velveteen Arch Support. I wiped that gleam away. "If I made a formal complaint, those poems could be traced." I crossed my arms. "Isn't harassment by mail considered a federal—"

"Okay," Phillip said quickly, his smug smile gone. "I'll give Mr. Skyler the envelope."

I had no idea if he would, of course. But I had to take the chance. Meeting Luke in storeroom 1505—probably the first time that place would be used for talking—was the only idea I could come up with on short notice. And at least I'd be able to say goodbye before the helicopter whisked him away.

I started off down the dim-lit corridor and headed for the elevators. It was time to work on the second half of my plan. To grab Marie, pull out that list I'd started, and do some furious brainstorming. I needed to do all I could to help the FBI solve this case and not only because of Patti Ann, Kyle, and Kirsty. Who knew if there was even going to be a wedding this afternoon? I wasn't thinking as a bridesmaid anymore. I only knew that I wanted Dale Worley's murder solved, so I could catch the first flight from Canada to San Francisco. To have one more day with Luke.

*   *   *

The smoke ring floated slowly upward, stretching into a wispy *Ghostbusters* apparition. Heading right for the cabin's smoke detector.

"Oh crap," Marie leaped onto her bed, fanning the air with a pair of Garfield boxers. "Guess that wasn't too swift." She sat back down on the bed opposite me. "So how's that list, Nancy Drew? Anything clicking yet?"

I glanced toward the window—still dark. Still time. I sighed and made a note on the second page before reaching for my coffee cup. "It's got to be here, somewhere. Some evidence of motive. Who hated Worley?"

"Everyone except his mother, and I'm not so sure about her. You think he wore Tit Ties to Thanksgiving dinner?"

"Hmm. I'm not going at this broadly enough," I said, still thinking as I picked at a Styrofoam cup full of congealed pasta. "I mean, making it all about hating Worley. He wasn't the only target." I frowned at a piece of rotini—what I wouldn't give for good old Kraft Macaroni and Cheese. Real brain food. I pointed my pencil at Marie. "Paul Putnam was deathly allergic to peanuts. Someone hated him, too."

"Easy to understand that," Marie agreed. "And then there was poor old Gordy Simons. Definitely hateful to glue a man's dick. Not that he wasn't capable of raunchy jokes himself. All of those guys were, really. Seems like the killer picked—" she raised her brows, blinking through a waft of cherry smoke.

I dropped the cup of pasta. "That's it! Oh my God, you're brilliant! This is all about revenge!" I grabbed another piece of paper, pulled it into my lap on top of my Neiman's catalog, and started to write. "What could these guys do to get someone pissed enough to want to kill them? And who'd they do it to? Think back. What do we remember?"

"Blue gum, squirting camera . . ."

"Not bad enough," I said, circling the word "malicious" on my paper.

"Fart machine," Marie said, "but I doubt that would provoke murder. Security found it in Worley's cabin, by the way. Hey, do you think they'd sell—"

"Dammit, Marie," I said, squinting at the window, "the sun's going to come up. Think. What could these guys do to piss someone off enough to want to kill them?"

Marie stubbed out her cigar and her eyes clouded with a rare look of discomfort. "Humiliation always worked for me," she said. She chased the look away with a quick laugh. "Face it, babe, those guys were your basic jackals when it came to picking on someone who was different."

Different? I don't know why I suddenly thought of Ryan, but I wasn't going to give voice to it in one of my infamous leaps to conclusions. Not enough time to sprint down a wrong road.

Marie shrugged. "I mean, remember those disgusting things that Worley and Putnam were saying at the bachelor party? Like that one about the firehouse volunteer? Asking Sam if he 'boinked Fatty'?"

"Yes," I said, the hairs lifting on my arms. "Yes, I do. And I never told you, but I asked Sam about that woman." I set my pencil down and twisted a chunk of my hair, remembering. "They played a horrible joke on her and took cruel advantage of the fact that she had this huge crush on Sam." I shook my head. "Got her to show up for a fake date, laughed at her, took pictures . . ." I grimaced. "Who knows how far they would have gone if they hadn't received a fire call?"

Marie frowned. "Shit. Sam would do that? I know the man can lie, but I don't think of him as that kind of evil pig."

"No," I said, thinking of how pained Sam had looked when he'd told me the story. "He says he wasn't even there. He was as upset as she was."

"I doubt that. Who was that woman anyway?"

"I can't . . ." I squeezed my eyes shut, trying to remember the name. Total blank. Dammit, memory was going. Maybe because I had forgotten to take the gingko and vitamins. Great. I was probably headed fast toward genetic fish-food craziness. "Can't remember. I don't think I saw her more than once or twice in the parking lot at the firehouse. But when Sam reminded me, the name sounded familiar. Almost like I'd heard it at the hospital, or . . ." Marie was looking at me funny. "What's wrong?"

"It wasn't the woman in the photo, was it? That one in the party room. You know, holding the dalmatian puppy?"

"Yeah," I said, remembering how Putnam had shown that same photo in his slide show. Marie had been in the pantry and hadn't seen it. "That's the woman."

Marie nodded. "The one who looked familiar to both of us. And you thought she could be Putnam's daughter. But I never saw Putnam's daughter, so it didn't make sense that she'd look familiar to me."

"Yes," I said, trying to follow her line of thought. "And . . . ?"

"And I need to see that photo again," Marie said, strapping on her fanny pack. "Let's go."

* * *

The decks were deserted. Every sane person was sleeping. Except for the wedding party, of course, who were either being grilled by the FBI, crying in their locked cabins, or punching frantic damage-control notes into their PDAs. Or missing, like Mitch De Palma. Because, while he wasn't technically a member of the wedding party, Kirsty had learned to lean on Mitch and that was impossible when the man couldn't be found.

No one was in the party room, either.

I followed Marie across the floor, shaking my head and remembering how just days ago I'd been surprised to find Sam Jamieson walk out of my past and into this very room and how, only minutes later, we'd knelt beside a choking and barely conscious Paul Putnam. It was the same night I'd first learned about the wedding planner's diabetes when her sugar bottomed out and she dropped her purse, scattering her medicines and her glasses—oops, I still had her glasses. I stopped beside Marie and looked up at the photo wall, a closer view now that the security had taken the barricades down. It was still a mess.

"There she is," Marie said, brushing her finger along the front paw of the dalmatian puppy. "I still think I know her. You can't remember her name?"

"No," I said, staring at the face in the photo. Double chin, thick dark bangs, unkempt brows over big, expressive eyes—beautiful, vulnerable blue eyes. Marie was right. Those guys were damned jackals, Putnam and Worley and—*oh no.* I looked over at Marie who was nodding at me.

"You see what I see?" She asked, running her fingers across one face to the next, touching the painstakingly placed overkill of staples. The metal X's placed over the eyes of . . .

"Our victims," I said, barely above a whisper. "And in order, too: Putnam, Gordy, Dale, and . . . Sam?" I reached out and touched Sam's staples myself. "But Sam wasn't harmed."

Marie was tapping the dalmatian again. "No, but he was connected to that cruel hoax and I'm willing to bet that the guys who planned it were"—she repeated the names at the same instant that I did.

"Putnam, Gordy, and Dale."

"I just remembered something else," I said. "Sam said this woman had a sick relative—maybe a hospitalized relative?"

"Which is why I'd know her, too," Marie said softly.

My brows scrunched, my brain sputtering even after the caffeine and pasta. "But what difference does all this make? She's not one of the wedding guests."

Marie nodded, watching my eyes. "Maybe not an invited guest, but it's a big boat, babe."

I glanced at my watch and my chest squeezed. "And it won't be long until dawn. Should we go downstairs and try to interrupt the interviews? Give this information to Scott?"

Marie shook her head. "We need a name to tell them, Darcy."

"Okay," I said, taking one last look at the photo, at the one face that wasn't stapled.

"Let's find Sam. He knows her name. You cover the front of the ship, I'll take the rear."

The problem was that Sam, like Mitch before him, seemed to have disappeared.

* * *

Ryan Galloway, nursing a Bloody Mary in a corner of the empty Sports Bar, was the only member of the wedding party I could find, and the very last person I felt like dealing with right then. What was bridesmaid etiquette for talking with the groomsman who'd sabotaged the whole damned wedding? Truth was I wanted to kick his scrawny butt down the deck or shake him until his teeth rattled. But when Ryan looked up at me, unshaven, hair rumpled, and with his gray eyes so full of pure misery, I couldn't do a thing. Behind him, the bank of TV screens droned in a blend of game scores, golf instruction, and Spanish soccer clips, along with the occasional tinkling of glass as a lone bartender restocked his inventory. I looked at Ryan, thinking that at long last here was the somber firefighter that I remembered, except now it looked like his heart had been dug out with a soupspoon.

"Hey, Darcy," Ryan said, his voice a soft monotone. He tried to smile and failed utterly. "I thought I was the last rat on this sinking ship." He groaned. "Wait, scratch that. I didn't mean you're a rat. I only meant—"

"No problem," I said quickly, seeing now that his eyes were red rimmed, his lashes damp. Jeez, he looked about twelve years old. I kept my voice as gentle as I could, but, dammit, he'd brought this on himself. And I needed to understand the reason. "Why did you do all this crap, Ryan?" My brows scrunched. "Why would you want to wreck—"

"I love her," Ryan said before I could finish. He ran an unsteady hand through his hair, his voice raw as skin sliding across pavement. "I have for a long time now. Before Kyle."

"So you and Patti Ann . . ." I tried to remember a time when they'd dated, but I was so out of the loop after breaking it off with Sam. I didn't remember Patti Ann saying anything about Ryan.

"Never," Ryan said and then gave a painful laugh. "Look at Kyle. Hell, the guy bench-presses two ninety-five and rides bulls. Who can compete with that?" He shrugged. "And then suddenly Patti's asking me to be part of their wedding. Telling me that I'd always been such a good friend. I thought I could do this, but . . ."

"Was that the truth about Kyle and some other girl?"

"Yes," Ryan said, frowning. "It was months ago and I don't know how far it went. Maybe it never went beyond a couple of kisses. Probably didn't. But when I saw Patti Ann in that wedding dress and I thought of how damned lucky a guy would be to have her . . . how much I'd wanted it to be me. You know what I'm saying? I guess I went kind of crazy. And now she's crying and . . . *shit*." He rested his head on his hands, moaning.

Oh hell. Part of me wanted to say something sort of sisterly while part of me still wanted to smack the bejeebers out of him, but when I glanced at my watch the selfish part of me took full control. Forget Ryan. It was nearly dawn. I grabbed hold of his shoulder and shook him.

"Ryan, I need to know where Sam is. It's important. Have you seen him?"

He looked up at me like I was a certifiable loon. "You're joking, right?"

I scrunched my brows. "Why would I—what are saying?"

Ryan sighed. "He's on his way to meet you, of course. Left twenty minutes ago, right after you called him. He was like a kid at Christmas." Ryan shot me a wary look, "Hey . . . first you send him all those e-mails to get him to come on this cruise and now you act like you didn't say you'd meet him. What is this? Are you playing some kind of sick joke on Jamieson? Getting even maybe?"

What the—I tried to make my tired brain understand. A sickening dread tried to strangle my voice. "Sam got a call? I don't understand. Where did he go?"

Ryan shook his head and tossed me a bitter smile. "Love Shack 1505. Like you don't know." He raised his Bloody Mary in a rueful toast. "And not very original, Darcy."

Five minutes later, I was taking the stairs, my slides clattering and the idiot toe rings pinching, clambering upward as fast as I could go. I jogged the steps, arms pumping, my jean jacket swishing against my body and my hair flying wild . . . one deck landing, next set of stairs, next landing . . . four flights of stairs to the top level fantail. To the ship's stern, a full seven stories above the cold Pacific. And then I was out the door and skidding onto the just-hosed decking in the chill dawn air. I was gasping and my heart thudded in my ears so loudly that I couldn't be certain if I heard the blades of a helicopter hovering overhead. But I couldn't think of that now. I had to get to storeroom 1505. Something was seriously wrong.

* * *

"Sam?" My voice echoed into the dim-lit interior of the storeroom and the metal door creaked on its hinges as I prodded it open wider. I blinked against the white-green glow of an emergency lantern as my eyes struggled to adjust. The air was damp and musky with the scent of wool blankets, canvas, stale alcohol, and . . . too much more. I shivered uneasily. "Are you there?"

I glanced over my shoulder, back toward the main bulk of the ship, searching for that house phone I'd seen mounted somewhere along there. Maybe it would be better if I called someone and—a voice pulled my attention back to the storeroom. Someone called my name.

"That you, Sam?" The overhead stutter of helicopter blades nearly obliterated my voice as I stepped one foot across the threshold, listening for Sam's answer and giving my eyes a moment to focus. They finally did and I exhaled in a whoosh of relief. Sam was there. Thank God.

He was silhouetted against the lantern glow on a cot against the wall, big shoulders leaning a little sideways almost like he was . . . dozing? I took another step, shaking my head and way too exhausted for some pre-dawn game.

"Sam, hey, if you're trying to scare—*aagh!*" I gasped as a hand closed painfully around my arm and yanked me, stumbling, into the darkness.

TWENTY

"Dammit, what—" I struggled out of the grasp, regaining my balance and then froze, completely confused as I stared at Kirsty Pelham. Why was she here? I rubbed my arm then whipped my head around to look at Sam's face—very still, eyes closed. And worse. A trickle of blood seeped from a discolored swelling at his hairline, drying in a dark trail in the stubble along his jaw. His breathing was slow, deep, and saliva pooled at one corner of his mouth. The lantern light glinted off something shiny on his cheek—embedded there—parallel bits of metal . . . my eyes widened.

"Oh my God, Kirsty," I said, taking a step toward the cot. "What happened to Sam?" I'd taken another step toward him when I noticed the purse upended on the floor beside the cot, its contents spilled onto the storeroom floor. Even in the lantern light I could see what I didn't want to believe was there: medication vials, syringes, the familiar pink hammer . . . and that huge missing stapler. *Oh shit.* My stomach lurched as I turned back—to see Kirsty holding a gun.

"Don't touch him, Darcy."

Kirsty squeezed her eyes shut for a fleeting second, but kept the gun shoulder high, steady in two hands—and aimed square at the center of my chest. Her voice was hollow and cold, like it was drifting up from the bottom of a well. She groaned. "Why did you have to come here? It was supposed to be only Sam."

"Uh, wait . . . Kirsty, don't—" *Oh God.* My mind raced and my voice failed as I stared at her in total disbelief. Finally, a single word escaped my lips. "Why?"

Kirsty shifted enough that I could see her better in the glow of the lantern, aided by the pale dawn spilling through the half-open door. She was barely recognizable now, the beautiful face devoid of makeup and hair pulled tightly into a ponytail. She was dressed in baggy sweats, old and worn and so many sizes too big that her neck and forearms emerged scarecrow thin. Her blue eyes, without the heavy lenses, were little-girl vulnerable and achingly sad. There was a faded screen print of a dalmatian puppy low across the front of the sweatshirt in a cuddled pose almost as if it were being held. Almost like the dalmatian puppy in that firehouse photo . . . *Oh, no.* I looked into the wedding planner's eyes, familiar eyes that had been hidden behind those plain-glass lenses but now . . . my hand rose to my mouth as the puzzle pieces finally fit. My throat squeezed tight.

"I'm Karen," she said softly, watching my face. "I changed my name legally. But it used to be Karen Pinkel. I guess it doesn't matter if you know that now. I used to see you at the hospital when I was there with my mother. You were kind to her."

"You're that firehouse group—" I said, biting off the unflattering word. "You're the volunteer?" I asked, still reeling with confusion. How could this possibly be the same woman in that photo? She

241

didn't look anything like that. What had she done to Sam? And—
please, God—how could I stop her from doing it to me? I tried to
remember something, anything, from the hospital workshops on
Managing Assaultive Behavior. All I could come up with was something about avoiding getting spit in your eyes. Great. From this angle
a loogie in the eye looked way better than a bullet in the chest.

Kirsty's face twisted into an ugly sneer. "Go ahead and say it:
Groupie. Go-fer. Toilet scrubber." She grasped the gun with one
hand and plucked at the front of her sweatshirt with the other.
"Fatty. That was Dale's favorite name for me." She looked back up
at the obvious confusion on my face and gave a tortured laugh.
"Size twenty-four. I guess I deserved that name. But then after a
little hair bleach, some brow waxing, and glasses . . . those were
the easy parts." She bit into her lower lip and her eyes narrowed.
"Want to see the hard part, Darcy? Can you handle it?"

I didn't want to see anything but the outside of this storeroom
and Sam's eyelids open again, but I watched, shocked, as the wedding planner lifted her tent-size, puppy-decal sweatshirt. *Holy crap.*

"You're a nurse," she said, watching my face. "Surgical compli-
cations, isn't that how you explain these things? To remind us ugly
ducklings that vanity comes with a risk?"

I stared at the mass of thickened scars across her abdomen—
purple-red, with deep, blackened crevices—the whole effect like
something out of a bad horror movie.

"Staples. The gastric stapling from hell," she said, dropping the
hem of her shirt, "complete with dumping syndrome and low blood
sugar attacks, infections, adhesions, and . . ." she groaned, "fistulas.
Nasty little holes from my guts to the outside world. You want to
know how it feels to ooze pus for six months? Let me tell you that it

doesn't attract men." She glanced over at Sam and her eyes clouded. "The funny thing was that at first I thought I was doing all that for Sam. To finally be the beautiful kind of woman he would want. Now I only want to make them all finally pay. Paul and Gordy and Dale and . . ." She waved the gun in Sam's direction. She gave a sharp laugh. "The staples were a nice touch, don't you think?"

"Um . . ." I didn't know what to say. I only knew that I had to keep this woman talking until I could find a way to get her to set that gun down. Where'd she get a gun anyway? I couldn't even get my nail file through the port's security scanner. I took a deep breath.

"I heard about how cruel they were to you that night behind the firehouse," I said as gently as I could. "I'm so sorry about that. But it wasn't Sam." I extended my palms in a sort of plea. "He told me that he wasn't even there that night, that—"

"Then he lied!" Kirsty growled, lunging forward and pointing the gun. "He sent me that note. He asked to meet me." Her lips twisted into a sneer. "Funny, how easily he fell for a lie himself. Those fake e-mails I sent to get him to come on this cruise? Easy to get him here tonight, too. All I had to do was dangle your pretty name." She shook her head. "You are so pretty, Darcy. But why would you have anything to do with him? He played you for a fool, too. Lying to you about his wife."

"That's right," I said, unsure of which direction to take this and noticing, with a stab of fear, that the firefighter in question had slumped lower onto the cot and that his staple-studded face was pale and glistening with sweat. "But that's over," I said, "for you and for me, too, Kirsty. We're strong women. Who gives a shit about those losers? We don't need to make anyone else pay for—" I jumped as Kirsty jerked forward again, shaking her head, eyes wild.

"Not pay for killing my mother?" Her voice rose to a strangled scream. "For making me leave her alone that night . . . so I could be the butt of a vicious joke?" Her eyes widened with the memory. "Letting her die in that fire?" She moaned. "I never left her at night before. Not with her diabetes and the stroke and the way she was so careless with those cigarettes . . ." tears slid down Kirsty's face.

Fire? Sam had said something about the joke date being interrupted by a fire call. A fire call to her mother's house?

"I'm so sorry," I said gently, "but I swear that Sam—"

"Sam's going to die, too!" Kirsty said with a growl. "If the insulin doesn't do it, then I'll . . ."

Insulin? I glanced down at the vial near the pink hammer. "Wait. You hit him with that hammer and then . . . you gave him insulin? Your mother's insulin?" A movement beyond the doorway caught my eye. A steward's uniform, maybe. Not sure. I breathed a silent prayer and kept talking so that Kirsty wouldn't notice, too. "How much insulin did you give him, Kirsty? How many units? What kind—regular or long-acting?"

Kirsty squeezed her eyes shut and groaned. "Mitch got most of Mama's sleeping pills in the wine, so all I had left was the insulin and—don't ask me so many questions! I'm getting confused."

Mitch? She did something to Mitch? Oh jeez, the gun. It was Mitch's gun.

The weapon trembled in Kirsty's hands. "I had it all planned out so carefully and now everything's screwed up." Another tear slid down her face and her eyes filled with desperation. "I never meant to hurt you, Darcy, but now I'm going to have to."

Whoa. "No, wait a minute, Kirsty, there has to be another way. I'll get some help for you. I'll—"

"Shut up!" She screamed, lunging forward and shoving me aside. "I promised to do this for Mama. It took all of her insurance money to get me here and I'm not going to fail her now. No matter what happens to me. What do I care what happens to me anymore?"

I watched in horror as she lowered the gun toward Sam's head.

"No! Don't!" I risked a step toward her, reaching for her arm—just as she whipped around toward a sound at the doorway. A voice—calling my name. My heart wedged into my throat as I recognized it. Oh God, no—I'd asked him to meet me here. *Luke.*

"Darcy?"

"No!" I shouted, "Luke, don't—"

There was an ear-deafening blast and the acrid scent of gunpowder, then a deep gasp and low groan. Luke stumbled backward a few steps and then crumpled to the deck.

"Luke!" I screamed, starting forward. Kirsty sprang past me through the doorway, wild-eyed. Then she aimed the gun again. This time at me. There was no time to think, only to react; and we both did it at the same instant—when the sound of running footsteps began thundering along the deck. The PA system shrieked overhead. I launched myself toward Luke a fraction of a second before Kirsty took off running. A crowd of security staff and probably half a dozen feds posing as lawyers started after her. And somewhere in the commotion, I swore I heard Marie calling my name.

"Oh, God, Luke," I cried, kneeling beside him and probing frantically through warm, sticky blood for the site of the bullet wound. He groaned and struggled to sit, trying, maddeningly, to brush me aside and reach for his holster. I caught his hand, torn between tears and frustration at his impossible stubbornness. "Stop it! You're shot, for godsake—act like it. Hold still. I've got to stop this bleeding." I pulled off my jean jacket and rolled it up.

"I'm . . . okay . . . ugh, easy there," Luke whispered as I pressed my makeshift compress against the blood welling from his shoulder. "Let me up, Darcy." His face was pale and his blue eyes dilated with pain but—*thank you, God*—Luke's breathing seemed fine. And if it was a shoulder wound, not his chest—*please not his chest*—then maybe . . .

"Not on your life, Skyler," I said, my throat choking against a rush of tears. "I'm giving the orders this time. You're allowed to say, 'Yes, ma'am.'" I pressed my palm harder against his wound and then rested my chin on top of his hair as he stopped struggling and leaned against me. I held him close as I scanned the uniforms milling around us. And then I saw Marie. Behind her were Kyle and Patti Ann—carrying a first aid pouch. Three faces were never a more welcome sight.

"Ryan's right behind us, bringing a stretcher, more supplies, and the infirmary staff," Marie said, dropping down beside me and resting her hand on Luke's forearm. Her fingers slid expertly to the pulse at his wrist and she nodded with observable relief. Patti Ann wedged in alongside us and began to gently question Luke about his symptoms as she tore open packages of gauze pads.

Marie leaned close, using Patti Ann's distraction to whisper in my ear, "The feds ID'd Kirsty from tracing the e-mails just minutes after Luke took off to meet you." She shook her head. "They found Mitch in her cabin, unconscious." She searched my eyes. "You okay, Darc'?"

"Yes," I said, turning my head toward the storeroom. "I'm fine. But Sam's still in there. She injected him with insulin . . . he's completely out. Check her purse. She always carries that injectable glucose and—" Marie bolted through the doorway before I could finish, shouting for Patti Ann and Kyle to follow.

I held Luke against me, closing my eyes and mouthing prayers for all I was worth. For Luke, Sam, Mitch, and then the page came overhead: "Man overboard!"

I looked up into the eyes of Agent Scott as he knelt down beside Luke. He answered the question before I could ask it.

"Kirsty Pelham went over the rail."

TWENTY-ONE

I CUPPED MY HANDS around my mouth and shouted toward the sailboat's wood-planked bow: "Heads up, Marie—you're luffing. Trim the jib!"

"Aye, aye, babe. Got it!" Marie pinched her lips around her cheroot and hauled on the rope with both hands. Then she grinned and shouted back through the wind, "You sound like a damned sailor!"

"Thank you." I smiled, my face warming from the sunshine . . . and so many memories. "Blame my sailing coach."

I pressed the tiller extension starboard, heading the *Shamrock Tattoo* into the salt-scented breeze and felt it respond; rising, dipping, and slapping gently against the motion of the sea. Behind us the San Francisco skyline gleamed silver, pink, and lavender in the late afternoon sun and in the distance the Golden Gate rose from its piers in the Bay, a majestic span of vermilion-orange and scalloped with cables like . . . frosting on a wedding cake.

"You're not complaining, are you?" I asked, glancing to where Marie, in a madras windbreaker and shorts, now lounged on the bow. "Do I need to remind you that just two weeks ago we were zipping each other into polka-dot bridesmaid dresses to the tune of a fart machine?"

Marie scooted on her butt along the decking, dangled her legs over the cabin's narrow entryway, and then hopped down to sit on the bench opposite me. She peered through her bangs and over the boom. "It still doesn't seem possible does it? But then I don't think I'll ever be able to use a stapler again, without . . ."

"I know," I said quickly, my hands moving to the front buttons of my old embroidered jean jacket. I didn't care if the bloodstains could be laundered out of the other one; I'd tossed it. Some things just don't Spray and Wash away. "But thank God we had angels on our shoulders; that the feds found Mitch in time and that you and Patti Ann got the sugar into Sam so fast." I grimaced. "And that he was still too confused to feel the Doc picking those staples out of his face." I let myself wonder for a moment how Chloe had reacted to all of that. But then I had to wonder if Sam really went home to her after all. Or if he'd show up in Morgan Valley one of these days.

Marie rolled her eyes. "Jamieson's a chick magnet, Darc'. A few little scars on that jaw will only draw more firehouse groupies like—" she stopped short, her gray eyes catching mine. "Still can't believe she survived a two-deck fall with only a broken leg."

I rubbed my palm along the crease of my pink capris, nodding. "Kirsty had no idea the lifeboat awning was there when she jumped; she intended to . . ." I sighed. "But maybe now she'll finally get some help." I scrunched my brows. "It was all such a sad, horrible waste."

Marie layered the jib rope across her palm and then smiled. "But Patti Ann and Kyle still ended up married. And even if it was two days late and not exactly what they'd planned, they still look pretty damned happy." She rolled her eyes. "If the hundred and seventy digital photos spamming my inbox prove anything. And, hey, Patti Ann even ended up with one Alabama girlfriend in polka dots. With Galloway escorting her down the aisle—go figure that one."

I shrugged. "They worked it out, I guess. Patti Ann told me that she trusted the way she feels about Kyle." I chuckled. "Said she'd marry him in the middle of a 'damned rodeo,' if she had to. Glad she got a zillion tulips in Victoria Gardens instead."

"Yeah," Marie agreed, turning her head toward sounds at the cabin doorway. She winked at me and then raised her voice, "But it still can't beat malingering around on the federal budget. Isn't that right?"

"Damned right," Luke said, sleep-rumpled and squinting as he climbed out into the sunlight. He was dressed in faded jeans, a rugby shirt, and his old leather flight jacket, its left sleeve dangling over the arm sling. But, thank God, today's sail chased away the pallor that had lingered since the shooting. His skin was sun-kissed and healthy and it looked like the nap had been good medicine, too—if that rascal gleam in his eye was any indication. I chuckled and Luke gave me one of those slow, lazy smiles that make my heart dissolve into girly little flutters. Then he glanced back and forth between Marie and me. "Now if one of you fine, sympathetic nurses could help an injured man open a bottle of champagne?"

I watched in surprise as Luke produced a gleaming green bottle from behind his back. *What the . . . ?*

Marie took the champagne from his hand, inspected the label and then raised her brows. "Whoa, baby. Hey, Darc', hope you have something better than mac and cheese in that hamper down below. The government's springing for the good stuff today." She watched as Luke checked the sails and as he slid onto the bench beside me. "So what's the occasion?" She asked him as he locked the tiller to hold our course.

Luke turned to me, the breeze lifting his hair in sandy rifts. His blue eyes were warm and something new in his expression made my heart stand completely still. He smiled, brushing aside a long strand of hair that had blown across my lips. "Special days," he explained softly while watching my eyes, "always call for champagne."

Special? *Oh God.*

Luke slid his right arm around me, pulling me closely enough against his chest that I could feel the deep drumming of his heart. I peered over his shoulder and saw Marie's eyes widen and her lips mouth, *"Special day?"* She cleared her throat loudly. "Probably ought to go get us some glasses. Suppose the feds sent those, too?"

"We think of everything," Luke said, chuckling against my hair. "Look in that cupboard over the galley sink."

She brought them out, opened the bottle and then—without making eye contact with me again—filled her glass and disappeared into the shadows of the cabin like a discreet . . . and totally traitorous little groundhog.

If you drink a lot of cheap champagne really fast the bubbles burn your nose and in the morning you feel so bad that nose bubbles seem like a blessing from the Pope. But I can tell you that the French stuff—vintage 1975 for the year I was born and worth more than I pay for groceries in a month—makes everything feel warm and wonderful and . . . very, very right. Especially the way it tastes on Luke Skyler's lips. And especially after nearly losing him. *Dear God, what if I'd lost him?*

Luke kissed me again and then leaned away, glancing toward the cabin door. "Is Marie hiding down there?"

"Probably. She knows about our lifeboat emergency, remember?"

Luke smiled down at me. "Oh yeah. I remember." He sighed and his face grew serious. "I got word from the Bureau. Looks like I'm leaving for Boston next week."

The champagne was failing and my breath stalled like a windless sail. "But you're in a sling. I need . . . I mean you need . . . more time."

"I'll be at a desk for a while. And if you . . ." he left the sentence unfinished as if he'd changed his mind about saying something. Then he pressed his lips to my forehead, his breath warming my skin as he whispered, "I love you."

I couldn't blame it on the wind because there wasn't any, but for some reason my eyes stung with tears. It wasn't the first time Luke had said those words, of course. He'd whispered them low in his throat at critical moments in our darkened bedrooms, joked about it once in front of one of the other agents, even shouted them one time to make some damned point in a ridiculous argument. But this was the first time Luke had said that he loved me after I knew how it would feel to lose him. And for some crazy reason, it made me think of the moment at Capilano Suspension Bridge, when I'd asked Patti Ann that very important question. Asked her how she knew she wanted to marry Kyle. She'd made it sound so simple—because she loved him she'd said, but mostly because she trusted her feelings. She made it sound like trust was some sort of key. It was the same thing she'd said about crossing that scary bridge—*"you've got to trust yourself, Darcy."*

Well, dammit, maybe I did. And maybe now I was ready to cross an even bigger bridge. I looked up into Luke's eyes and realized the champagne warmth was still there and that the breeze had started up again. And I knew, too, that there was no reason that I should be afraid to say . . .

"I love you, too, Luke."

He started to kiss me and then stopped, fumbling with one hand in the pocket of his leather jacket. "Wait, I've got something for you. Dammit, I can't—" Luke frowned and started to slip his injured arm from the sling.

"No," I whispered, my mouth going dry. "I'll get it." I reached into the pocket until my fingers touched velvet. *Bridge . . . trust . . . bridge . . . love . . . Oh God.*

"This is the other half of the champagne," Luke said, looking down at the jewelry box in my palm. "I almost gave you this a couple of times before. But I'm glad I waited for today."

I hesitated; squeezing my eyes shut for a moment against the image of a glittery "I AM THE BRIDE" tee shirt. Wait. I could be engaged long-distance for a while . . . and then maybe we'd think of some way to compromise and . . . *Oh jeez.*

"Go on. Open it," Luke said. "I hope you like it."

I couldn't stop myself from glancing toward the cabin to where Marie was frozen in the doorway like Wile E. Coyote stepping off a cliff. I smiled to reassure myself as much as for her. Then I took a deep breath and lifted the velvety lid open on its hinges to finally see the . . . *earrings?*

"Happy anniversary," Luke said, slipping his arm around me. "I had them made in that jewelry shop you liked in Carmel. Platinum, with the six diamonds . . . you know, one for each month we've been together." He prodded his fingertip against the delicate design. "See. They're little boats, because we met on a ship and because of this sailboat and, maybe that lifeboat now, too, and—" his brows drew together. "What's wrong? You don't like them?"

I opened my mouth and closed it. And for one weird minute I didn't know how I felt. I should have felt relieved, but . . . and then I heard Marie snort through her nose and scuttle back down the steps into the cabin.

I ran my fingertip over the tiny platinum sails sparkling with diamonds and then smiled up at Luke. "They're perfect," I said, honestly. "Thank you. And happy anniversary yourself, Skyler."

We talked Marie into coming back above deck to man the jib and to toast our anniversary; after all she'd been there from the beginning, too. Pretty much laughing like she was now, pretty much always lighting up a damned cigar and shooting me one of those wise-Yoda "told-you-so" looks.

And then we trimmed the sails and headed the *Shamrock Tattoo* back into the wind and toward the marina, discussing more pressing issues. For instance, my latest strategies concerning Grandma's fish food problem. And answers to probing questions, like why hadn't I guessed that gingko supplements could cause a rash? Every pill in the world causes rashes for godsake. And then there were the dilemmas like: where had Dale Worley's remote control fart machine ended up after it disappeared from the feds inventory? And, finally, what in the hell was I going to do if my feet—ankle deep in chocolate pudding and metal snakes—showed up on the frigging World Wide Web?

I snuggled against Luke as he steadied the tiller and headed into the setting sun while laughing at my best friend's attempt to blow one of her famous cherry smoke rings. I shook my head. This Special Agent wasn't fooling me. He'd figure out how to get reassigned back to California. The guy was nuts about me. And, secretly, I was still pretty sure he wanted to marry me someday. Meanwhile— hell—the man had access to helicopters, right? Trust me. He'd be back.

Photo by Nigel

ABOUT THE AUTHOR

Candy Calvert is a registered nurse who blames her quirky sense of humor on "survival tactics learned in the trenches of the ER." Born in Northern California and the mother of two, she now lives with her husband in the beautiful Hill Country of Texas. Grueling cruise research for the Darcy Cavanaugh Mystery Series has found Candy singing with a Newfoundland country band, roaming the ruins of Pompeii, doing the limbo atop a jet-powered catamaran, and swimming with stingrays. Visit her website at: www.candycalvert.com.